FALL OF THE DRAGON

The Phoenix's Ashes, Book Two
A Circus of Shifters Reverse Harem

By
Rebecca Ethington

Published by Imdalind Press

Production Management by Imdalind Press

ISBN (print) **978-1-949725-26-1**

ISBN (e-book) **978-1-949725-09-4**

Printed in USA

This Edition, October 2018

❀ Created with Vellum

CONTENTS

For My Kids

1

ELLIOT

EVERYTHING SMELLED LIKE SMOKE AND BLOOD. THE HOT summer air was drenched in it, the night sky burned with it.

Pools of scarlet fluid covered the ground, surrounded by the crumpled remains of scaffolding and circus equipment. Shards of the once massive circus tent circled in stripes of red and black, the color haunting against the blood, against the bonfires that glowed in odd shades of violet thanks to the dragon fire that had started them.

The blood, the fires, the crumpled remains of the last ten years of my life.

One little lovers quarrel and I had turned everything into a fucking end-of-the-world dystopia.

My current predicament with my three dragons wasn't helping to ease that notion either. Lover's quarrel my ass, this was the bloodiest lovers quarrel I had ever heard of. All of them were covered in ash, blood, or both. And thanks to both my current placement and the dragon destruction zone we were sitting in, so was I.

Jarron's arms held me on his lap, his blonde hair

streaked with Drake's blood as it dripped over my arm. Any other time I would be disturbed by the bright red drops, but not this time. Killian was drenched in the stuff too after using every article of clothing to close Drake's wounds, his once pristine suit was oozing over all of us as he leaned closer, his hand shaking against me.

And Drake? Drake sat as close to me as he could get with the bulk of his brothers pressing against me, his hand closed around mine. Even that was a miracle. I stared at him with eyes so wide I could feel the burn of the smoke.

But I couldn't close them, and I wasn't going to look away.

Drake was right there. He was human, not a trace of the battered creature in sight. I had somehow pushed his broken dragon back inside of him. I wasn't even going to get started on how high that registered on the what-the-fuck-just-happened scale.

I had performed magic. Magic that was now giving me the deer in the headlights look that was burning my eyeballs.

Okay, maybe I wasn't so much deer in the headlights, as a deer when he realizes he's actually a mother fucking unicorn.

Except I wasn't a deer, and I sure as hell wasn't a unicorn. Those don't exist.

"You are one of the Fae, my dear," Suvi said, as if that cleared it all up.

Yeah, because all of this was making so much sense.

I was sure they had also told me my father was a dragon. Oh, and then there is the whole 'I turn into a phoenix' thing. I am pretty sure that Fae don't do that.

"What are you on about, old woman," Killian said with a

growl, the burly man pressing his hand harder against my leg as if the weight would stop me from turning him into a cantaloupe, or whatever Fae do.

In fact, I should probably move, in case that was a possibility, but between Killian's hand, Jarron's arms, Drake's fingers that were now tracing my hand, and my absolute confusion; I wasn't going anywhere.

"A Fae?" I asked, very aware that my voice was shaking. "That's not a possible. I'm... I'm a phoenix."

My soul bristled with warmth at just saying it, but it wasn't that calm soothing heat that my phoenix usually brought when she was mentioned. No, this was a boiling 'let me out so I can prove how badass I am' heat. Competitive much?

Suvi looked at me with a grin so bizarrely twisted that I was genuinely worried she was going to explode with clown-filled joy. Her eyes glittered as a small chuckle broke past her lips, thankfully not sounding as though she was prepping for murder. If it wasn't for the sheer amount of multicolored fires we were surrounded by I would say she was glowing. Which, who knows, she might be. The old wrinkled woman was a witch, after all.

I had nothing to judge her power from, but if I had to guess I would say she was top of the line.

Except, you know, for a witch. And not a car.

"You said my father was a dragon, not a Fae." I continued, as if that somehow solved it.

It didn't. Judging by the looks of confusion that were smothering every dragon in the vicinity, I was clearly not the only person who was having trouble wrapping my head around this new piece of information.

Or bomb.

Because it felt more like a freakin' bomb.

"Elliot was banished..." Zoe began, her voice was so distant and far away, that when the sound of sirens picked up it was drowned out.

Well, crap.

I may not know who the hell I was right then, but I knew enough to know that poor little police officers walking in on the scene of a dragon battle was probably not the best thing that could happen right then.

"That's bad," I said more to myself than to anyone else.

"I will handle the mortals. A simple spell, a simple lie and none of them will know what happened here tonight," Suvi said, producing a pipe from who knows where and sticking the thing in her mouth like an old man on a porch swing. "The rest of you have bigger problems."

Like Fae, and Drake's dragon bleeding to death inside of him.

Except the look the old witch was now fixing us with had a bit more of a warning to it then the possibility of me turning people into cats. I seriously needed to figure out what a Fae was.

No time for that, it seemed. Suvi's scowl drifted to the sky as the three men jumped in alarm as a gentle buzzing filled the air. It took me a second to recognize that it was a cell phone. I had never had one, there had never been a need, I didn't know anyone outside of the circus. The way Killian was looking at the glowing surface made me glad I never had one. It was as if the devil himself was crawling out of the screen to attack him.

I had never seen Killian look scared. Hell, I didn't think Killian could look scared. With the way his look was turning my insides into the outsides and drenching me with ice, I never wanted to see it again.

"He's coming," Jarron said before Killian had a chance to fill us in, his arms tightening as if he was afraid I would drift away from his hold.

"Who's coming?" I asked, not that anyone heard. They all jumped to their feet, Jarron taking me with him before he began to run around and look behind piles of burning canvas.

He wasn't the only one. Drake and Killian were whispering about alligators, Suvi and Zoe about gems, or games, and scowling at the approaching emergency vehicles as if the glare alone could stop them.

I had clearly been sucked into a fourth dimension. Everyone was losing it, and I stood in the middle of it all looking like the only person with any sanity left.

"Who is coming," I tried again, louder this time. But it didn't matter anymore, because by then I had realized what Jarron had been talking about, or rather I had caught sight of the massive dragon-shaped shadows that were streaming through the liquid black of the sky.

"Oh shit," I snapped, frozen in the middle of the chaos, watching what were clearly dragons, streaking through the night.

They were so far away that they were little more than smudges of dark that were blotting out the sky, but that didn't make them any less terrifying.

So, this is how I was going to die. Well, unless I figured out how to turn the king into a cat, or a cantaloupe. Cat-a-loupe.

I was clearly doomed.

"Zoe, be the bait," Suvi grumbled through her pipe from somewhere behind me, her voice barely audible over the sirens now. "I'll shield you as long as I can. But get that bastard off my land before he catches on or I will end all of you."

I spun at the threat, but the old lady was gone, the sirens were gone. Holy hell! The hotel was gone. The parking lot was suddenly in the middle of nowhere, devoid of a few dragons, and a... whatever I was.

"Drake," Zoe whispered, giving me one look as she rushed passed me to the blood-soaked asphalt, shedding her clothes as she popped something in her mouth. "Hide."

Drake grabbed my hand to pull me away. Not that I could move, my feet felt like lead. My heart might as well have migrated to my toes with all the good it was doing me. I couldn't look away from the dark shadows that cut into the stars, the massive forms moving closer. Closer.

That one. The one I was sure was the king was massive. So much bigger than Killian had been in his dragon form. Forget the cantaloupes, I couldn't turn that into anything but an immortal.

Yes. Hide. Now.

"We need to go."

I didn't need to be told twice, clinging to his hand, we rushed away from Zoe who was now standing in her underwear in the middle of the pool of blood, the crimson lake lapping around her ankles. We ran away from Killian who looked at me with the saddest eyes I had ever seen. And Jarron, who was blowing me a kiss without a touch of a smile in his black eyes.

"Come on, Ellie," Drake hissed as I continued to follow him, although my soul was pulling me in the opposite direction.

"It'll be okay," Jarron said as Drake and I reached a large bank of fire, the massive remains of the burning tent the only safety that was within running distance.

My soul was screaming as he pulled me after him, the fire that was to be our only safety obscuring Killian, Jarron, and Zoe, the last of which was laying down in the blood as everything began to shimmer.

What in the world was she doing? Now was not the time to be laying down in a puddle of blood. I mean, I don't see any time being the best for that. But now was not it, she needed to be a million miles away. Away from the massive dark shadow that was practically on top of us now.

"Let's go," Drake hissed as he held me against him, plunging us through a massive bank of fire, and away from everyone that I needed to protect.

I sure as hell wish I had another choice right then. Dragon King? Run and hide. This time I wasn't going to question it.

My already ripped clothing began to burn away as we stepped through the tall violet flames, letting them encompass us like a curtain. It would have been the perfect hiding place, if those who were following us weren't dragons.

I had to pray that they hadn't seen our grand escape. Suvi was obviously hiding something, I hoped I was amongst those somethings.

Drake pulled me against him as we sunk into the folds of the smoldering canvas, sitting on the charred and boiling asphalt. I could feel the tar stick to my ass, the gooey mush feeling like gum on the bottom a shoe. The air against my skin felt like it was on fire, sweat streaming over my skin in rivers. I had never felt this hot before, everything after this was sure to feel like an arctic tundra.

I was desperate to move away, but instead we moved closer, letting the fire hide us as the ground began to shake in one massive thump, and then another, the deep boom of the landing shoving to the ground in a tangle of limbs, canvas, and panic.

Two. I had seen two shadows. But I didn't expect those two shadows to equate to fire-spitting tanks that were launched from a catapult. Sent from the sky to destroy me. I had no intention of seeing how big these two were. Especially considering that one of them wanted to boil me into a stew. Or something.

Now was not the time to think about it, especially with the heat that was rippling from Drake. Fire wasn't supposed to get that hot.

"Hi, Killy," A woman's voice raised above the creaking of scaffolding, hissing with the crackle of the flames and igniting a mine field inside of me.

Terror lived in every nerve ending, but that voice did some twisted gymnasts act to my heart, my soul perking up in a scream that I was sure everyone heard. Because, you know, now was the best time for me to work up into a jealous rage over two words.

I mean, if you are going to give Killian, who looks like the bouncer to the official sex-god club, a nickname, it sure as hell better be something better than Killy.

That sounded like something you named a goldfish.

Drake didn't seem to be taking it the same way. He was still drowning in fear.

"He brought her," he hissed, turning to investigate the fire that flickered behind us, as if he could see through them to whoever *her* was. "Of course, he brought her."

I looked to Drake in question, but he only wrapped his arms around me, his muscles tightening like a vice as he tried to tuck me into him. I wouldn't let him. I may be scared out of my wits, but I wouldn't cower.

"Who?" I asked, but Drake shook his head, giving the flames one last glare.

"You need to remain calm," he instructed, dodging my question. The normally melty-warmth of his eyes were smothered with a dark red flame as he stared at me, hand tight around my wrist.

I had seen that look before, seen the red of his fire drown his eyes. They burned into me with the same intensity as they had before; his dragon fuming right under the surface. The color was a stab in the chest now that I knew what he hid inside of him.

"If her dragon senses you, she can see into your mind. Keep your thoughts from your Phoenix, don't let her rise. Lock her away. We are just scared mortals, dying in the fire."

I think I would have settled for a name, I was even more confused now. He was talking about this dragon like they were some kind of secret weapon. Which, I realized, they probably were.

"A witch?" I asked, clinging to the only thing I knew.

"No. An ice dragon. They can read minds," Drake whispered as he sunk further into the flames, pressing me against him as he tried to settle his breath. It wasn't working, no matter how slow he breathed, he was still shaking like a leaf beside me.

Or maybe that was me.

"The king?" I asked stupidly, knowing beyond a doubt that the king was well... a king.

"No," He moaned, as some of the scaffolding collapsed, showering us in embers and singeing our already burned clothes. "Dabria."

I had heard that name before, where had I heard that name before?

"I didn't expect to see you here, handsome." The same woman from before crooned over the flames, whining in a weird baby talk that was bringing out an odd violence in me. "I've missed you the past few days. Haven't you gotten my texts?"

If Stacia was built of hell incarnate this is what her voice would sound like. Smooth as acid, sweet as poison. I cringed and clamped my eyes shut, trying to focus on the beat of Drake's heart and not on the painful stab of realization.

I knew where I had heard her name before. She was the woman Killian had been speaking about to Jarron.

The one I had thought was me, the one that had in some weird indirect way, started the dragon fight that had brought her here.

Awesome.

"I have received them. All of them," Killian growled, his voice rumbling with that same low moan I had heard in the alley, the one that always made my insides twist and tumble. Except this time, it wasn't directed at me, which made my twisting and tumbling more like a jealous rage. I could feel my already hot skin begin to smoke.

At least everything else was on fire, what was adding some more to that?

"I am sorry I have not returned to Rydaim as quickly as you had hoped, Dabria."

Ugh. Hearing him saying her name was certainly not helping the whole jealousy issue I was combating. I knew he was playing a role, hiding me and all that. I knew I should be as scared as Drake seemed to be, but this ugly monster was making it difficult.

"I have missed you, Killy," The pout in her voice was clear, and it made me want to punch her. Or better yet, burst through the flames and attack the whore.

Woah. That was harsh.

Not that she didn't deserve it.

I jerked a bit, my Phoenix pushing against my bones like she was going to burst out of me and go on a rampage. Probably would have too if Drake's hand hadn't tightened against my arm, pulling me back into him.

"He can't let her catch your scent, Ellie," He hissed, the flames smothering his hushed plea, and whatever interlude was happening on the other side. "Suvi is hiding you, but that only goes so far. He can't let her think anything is up."

I nodded. He was logical and calm, as always.

"I have been busy with the tasks that my father has commanded of our crown, Dabria," Killian said, his voice harsher than it had been a minute ago. "Find someone else to warm your bed."

Ice ran over my jealousy, calming it as the woman snarled, Killian's familiar chuckle rumbling right behind.

Yeah, put her in her place! I almost jumped up and danced in victory.

Almost.

"Stop this nonsense!"

Three words had never sounded so angry, each one dripped with malice and hatred, the ancient growl feeling like sandpaper against my heart. I tensed at the sound, even my Phoenix bristled and withdrew, scared of some tone, of some warning that I couldn't quite hear.

I wasn't the only one who reacted.

Drake flinched so hard that the canvas we leaned against crunched with the sound of a car crash, the movement sending a shower of sparks into the air. The shower of bright purples and reds were beautiful against the stars, if only they weren't quite so frightening.

With all the fire that we were surrounded by, it was doubtful that anyone else had noticed, but I wasn't about to hold my breath. Drake was doing that enough for both of us anyway, his eyes narrowed into the smoldering pile of canvas a few yards away, pure hate burning in his eyes.

"Is that the king?" I asked, even though I didn't need an answer.

Drake nodded, "Ceres."

Even the name sounded like that of a man that would find joy in ripping me limb from limb.

"We have business here," Ceres continued, with the same meat grinder voice, I resisted the need to flinch away that time. "I was informed of the boy's shift. My Fae felt his pathetic dragon rip free and struggle and writhe like the bastard he is. We came to finish him off. But it appears you have arrived here first, Killian. Wonderful. Wonderful."

It didn't sound too wonderful. Well, unless his wonderful was some sort of murdering sideshow. Which it very clearly was. I cringed and pressed into Drake more, I didn't want to give this man more murdering options. I hadn't even seen him yet, just heard his voice, and I think I was more scared of him than I had ever been.

And I grew up knowing this man was a monster.

Monsters are always more terrifying when you know they are real, and this man was suddenly very, very, real.

"Tell me, boys," He said, his voice growling eagerly. "Did he struggle? Did he cry for his mommy?"

The wicked mockery sliced against my heart and Drake flinched, the fire fading from his eyes as his arms tightened around me.

"He fought enough to take down the tent," Killian said with a growl that was twisted with the same mockery, the tone adding to the slicing and dicing that was happening to my heart. "He was working here, like a pathetic mortal. I ran into him on that tip you gave me."

Killian's tone twisted in a malice, an anger that was dripping in some hidden meaning, some secret. I tried to turn
around again, wanting to see him, as if that would somehow
help me figure out what the hell he was talking about, but I
couldn't move beneath Drake's grip, his eyes still hard and
far away as he shook his head.

At least his meaning was clear, "She's here. Block your
mind, Ellie. Block your mind."

I nodded once, as if I had any idea how to do that.

"Is that why you were here with your mortal hooker?"
Dabria snarled, the sound of her shoes crunching against
the gravel more akin to the breaking of bones. But not
hers. Mine.

My heart bones. Because that was a thing. I knew exactly
who she was talking about.

Blocking my mind was going to be an all-out impossibility. I would rather give her a very big, profanity-filled piece
of it.

"I saw her naked ass run away from you last week,
covered in ash like a good dragon's play thing," she continued, the glee in her voice heating against my skin like a slap.
"Did her flesh burn as nicely as all the others?"

"Better." Killian said, the single word grinding darkly
into the air. I could practically see the tight line of his jaw.

"My son, devouring women without me?" Ceres crooned,
his voice full of pride that somehow made everything worse.
"Next time save a little for me."

"There wasn't any left. I finished her off," Jarron said with
a laugh, the lighthearted sound zipping through my spine in
a line of painful electricity. I had nearly forgotten that he
was out there with the rest of them, pretending to be evil. It
was hard to imagine him out there, smiling with them. "We
watched her bleed over the sheets for hours."

They all laughed at that, their sounds rich and vibrant as they drifted through the crackles of the fire, combining to slice and dice against my soul like I was a hibachi bar. I sat there, staring into the fire, feeling the burn, feeling the pain, but too numb to even process.

It all came so natural to them, this nefarious mind-play. They sounded so evil, and the king who was just as wicked as they were, believed it all. I couldn't blame him, I was having trouble believing that these were the men that had vowed to protect me.

"Remember they have a role to play," Drake whispered in my ear, his hand running over the tangles of my hair as he tried to soothe me. "They are protecting you, and right now this is the only way."

I wasn't sure I could believe that. There had to be another way, like ripping Ceres' head from his body. He wouldn't even see me coming, he would think I was a boring mortal... and eat me anyway because they eat fucking mortals!

Okay, that plan needed some work.

"And then you finished off your pathetic little brother as well," Ceres continued, his voice as twisted as eager as if he was watching the horrific display.

Perhaps he still was. The sound of a bag of water exploding against a floor splashed against my ears and I cringed, fully aware that it wasn't water. I could smell the blood over the smoke. They laughed in a chorus of nauseating villainy, their glee twisting with the liquid like the bile that was twisting in my gut. I didn't want to know what they had done, or even how they had done it.

I was sure Zoe was someone disguising Drake's absence. Why else would she be standing in her underwear in a pool of blood?

My imagination ran wild, creating images of Zoe getting sliced open while she pretended to be Drake and twisted my anger in new and ridiculously dangerous ways. My Phoenix was as territorial of Zoe it seemed, and with one snarl it was clear that she was ready to raise hell. I would gladly join her.

"I'm sad to have missed all the fun," Dabria's icy voice cut in, the pout mixing with the crunching of pebbles against the tap of a high heeled shoe as she stepped closer to us, closer to our gold mine minds.

"Such beautiful golden lines. He is more beautiful in death than he was in life," The awe in the King's voice was so close I could hear his teeth clack together. I sunk lower against the smoldering canvas, Drake following suit as the king followed Dabria, both inching closer to where we were hiding. "He was always a weakling."

"I am surprised he lasted this long," Jarron agreed, the others laughing right alongside. But this time the high soprano of Dabria's forced laugh was gone, it was only the deep baritone of the boys, only more crunching of shoes.

And then, suddenly, it was silence. Not even the crackle of flames broke through the air, I could have sworn that the air was sucked out of it.

That the heat was sucked out of it.

"A mortal and your worthless brother," Ceres continued, his voice suddenly distant and far away. It echoed toward us as we sat amid the silent flames, a cold air blowing over our skin. "This circus sounds like a gold mine."

"Indeed," Jarron said, his jovial voice just as far away, echoing and out of place against whatever world I had become trapped in. "We can get you your own bendy mortal if you so desire, father."

The king laughed with his sons, all of them sounding deranged as their voices lengthened, as the sound stretched so far away that I was sure some beast was dragging them away.

Further. Further.

"It's all in your head."

Drake mumbled the words on repeat, his arms now so tight around me that I wasn't sure I could move, let alone take full breaths. I was starting to see the downside of having powerful dragon shifter boyfriend-mate-things.

I was trapped beneath him, and his focus was so far away that I couldn't do anything to pull it back to me. Not without gaining unwanted attention. His eyes were focused straight ahead, the wide orbs looking into the brightly burning flames, and reflecting his own right back.

"It's not here," Drake continued, his voice as lengthened and distanced as the others, although his hold was tightening to the point that I was having trouble breathing.

I could barely get in a breath. No wonder everything sounded so weird and far away.

"Drake," I said with a squeak, slapping my palm against his arm with as much force I dared to give considering that we were supposed to be silent.

Which I guess would be easy if I was unconscious on the asphalt, and I was quickly on my way to that.

He didn't even flinch at my attempts to pull him out of his stupor, however, he continued to stare forward, eyes locked with the flames as his dragon stared right back. My lungs began to burn with the lack of oxygen, my phoenix ready to explode. I didn't need someone to tell me how devastating that would be.

"I wish you hadn't destroyed the head," the King said, his voice echoing through my malfunctioning brain. I needed air. "I would have liked to mount that."

"Drake," I tried again, my voice little more than a strangled gasp as my lungs and head began to ache.

As everything began to go dark.

"Here, Kitty-Kitty," A voice hissed through the burning darkness, the acidic wisps of her voice pulling my oxygen-deprived mind pulling me somewhere I didn't expect.

The same long black hallway of my dreams.

2

ELLIOT

A DARK TUNNEL STRETCHED BEFORE ME IN RIDGES AND grooves of stone that unfolded as though I was looking through a telescope. At the end, or at least what I thought was the end, was the same quivering tapestry of lights I had seen the first time. The specs of light were so far away that the colors looked little more like smeared stars.

A window of stars. I tried to wrap my head around what in the world was going on. I could see the hall, but I couldn't move like I did last time, and even then, I didn't feel like I was standing.

I could still clearly feel myself leaning against Drake as we hid in the sweltering night air, the purple flames moving closer and closer to our hiding place. I could hear the heavy thunder of Drake's heartbeat echo in my ear, but I also heard her voice echo through the dark cave.

I was seeing something that wasn't where I was sitting, and I was sitting in the place that was clearly not where I was.

I had clearly been driven mad.

"You aren't crazy," the mocking female's voice came again. Although, this time I recognized it.

I knew the acid and sour-sugar sound, even if had never seen her face.

Dabria.

"What a purely pathetic thing to think," Dabria continued, a mocking laugh lacing her words. "How very mortal of you."

"What thought?" I asked without thinking, or rather, I thought without saying. I heard myself speaking, but no sound echoed over this weird stone hall.

Yep, I was losing my shit.

If Drake had experienced even a bit of whatever dementia I was stuck in, it was no wonder he had begun to blubber. I had a feeling I was probably doing the same thing.

Something about cats, and halls, and colorful stars.

"You aren't going crazy," she said with a contempt that chilled me to my bones. "Most mortals would think that, wouldn't they? Especially when they don't understand how weak and insignificant they are."

Every word she spoke was like spitting acid against my pride, or at least that's what she wanted it to be. Instead, it sparked strong against my soul, and the Phoenix that I was trying desperately to conceal perked her head in a need to pluck this woman's eyes out.

Not that she wasn't alone in that desire, but it wasn't something we couldn't do right now. I mean, I couldn't even see her. There were no eyes to pluck. She was nothing more than a faceless tunnel, poisoning my mind.

Reading it.

Reading all the precious little nuggets of information

that were swimming on the surface, waiting to be plucked like little secret roses that could destroy everything.

Okay, shield your mind. Obviously easier said than done.

If only I had a box I could stuff everything into.

Or maybe I did. One metal box coming right up.

"I am not weak," I said with far too much snarl, hoping the idiotic threat would be enough to mask what I was really doing: shoving every damning thought and secret into an imaginary mind box.

I was aware how ridiculous it sounded, but right then I was willing to do anything.

"Oh, you pathetic little underling. You will learn, and then I will make sure you 'go mad'," she crooned, a sliver of cold running over my cheek as though she was touching it.

Yeah, let's make this whole thing ever weirder. Mind boxes, cold invisible fingers, and Drake's warm arms holding me tight as he battled the same things I was.

It's not real, I reminded myself, the same as Drake had been doing, as if it would help.

It didn't, the long stone hallway didn't budge, not even when I tried to force my eyes shut. Which was also as point-less, seeing as I didn't have eyes to force shut in this weird mind prison.

"Trying to leave are you?" She said with that same mocking laugh. She was really grating on my nerves. Yeah, I was totally trying to blink her into oblivion now, something that made her laugh more. She better hope we never meet face to face. Eye plucking would occur.

"It's pointless you know," she continued with a sigh. "You're too weak to fight my magic. All mortals are. You won't be able to get rid of me until I find what I am looking for."

This whole mind box thing better be working, she was clearly digging through my mind with all the force of a bull-dozer. Even as the heat from the flames around my body burned hotter, my insides were beginning to chill with the cold, everything freezing and shivering as she dug her way around.

Ice dragon my ass, she was more like a 'burn your insides with liquid nitrogen' dragon. Why don't you come in and make yourself at home?

"What are you looking for?" Even in my mind, my teeth were chattering.

Dabria laughed at that, the sound twisted and full of as much acidic evil as her voice was.

"What makes you tick," she said with a hint of a snarl, "and why the man that should be mine alone is hiding a stupid mortal from his father. The king."

All my work of locking away every damning thought was pretty much useless at that point. Like hell if I was going to let her waltz into my mind and claim one of my dragons as her own. They were mine. All of them. Including Killian and his bull-headed, self-centered...

My thoughts froze as thoroughly as if she had touched them with her long, icy finger.

Mortal.

She has been calling me a mortal.

I was sure if I had a face in whatever mind dungeon this was it would be smiling. No amount of stellar acting ability could hide my shock.

Screw the box. If she couldn't sense what I was, then I was going to let that charade continue. And maybe mess with her a little bit while I was at it.

I had a feeling she would deserve it, too.

"A mortal?" I said, shooting a quiver into my voice. "Are

you talking about Killian? He said he would turn me immortal. That I could stay with him forever."

I didn't even know if that was a thing, but I was going to go with it. I was officially a naive, simple, dumb blonde. Well, red-head, but that's all in the semantics. I was going to get a freaking tony for this.

"He wants me with him forever," I continued over her mocking laugh. "That I would be the most beautiful dragon he had ever seen."

What started out as a laugh toward my idiocrasy turned into a scream of frustration that rattled the dark hallway enough that I could see the flame-filled parking lot.

"I believe we have another lead," I heard the twisted depravity of Ceres voice before the dark tunnel snapped back into place and blocked everything about the real world from view.

"He can't have said that," she continued through the scream, each word grinding through what I imagined to be perfectly straight, white teeth. "He wouldn't want you when he has such powerful dragons yearning for him."

It seems I had hit a nerve, a nerve that opened her twisted mind prison right open. Oh, I could use this. I tried not to rejoice at the fact and kept the whole pathetic mortal routine going, even though the air had gotten much cooler.

"He said he loved me, that he wanted me for his mate." I said, putting a fair bit of whine into my voice as I once again tried to both move and blink away the long stone tunnel. "That we would make little dragons together. Kings and Queens."

If I thought she was throwing a hissy fit before, it was nothing to this. The cave she had trapped me in shivered as she screamed, the growl more dragon than human as the cave once again flickered and faded back to the fire filled parking lot.

Drake's worried face hovered before mine, his hands warm against my face as he whispered something I couldn't hear. Well, not over Dabria's shouts from the other side of the flames.

It seems her anger had left the weird mind-cave and existed in the real world as well.

"He doesn't need a mortal when he has me," Dabria pouted, her voice even more irritating in real life than it was in my head. "I can give him all he needs."

"I am sure you can," Jarron cut in, his voice loud as it raised over what was clearly the growl of Killian's dragon.

"Ellie," Drake whispered, his fingers running softly over my cheeks as the cave flickered back over my eyes. The dark stone was clear in my mind for one sharp inhale before Drake's furrowed brow came back into focus.

My vision, my mind, flickered between the cave and the burning parking lot like a broken television set.

"I've got her," I whispered to Drake, my voice strained as he left and the cave took back over, Dabria pulling me into the dingy cave that was suddenly starting to make sense.

I had not been able to banish her from my mind, because I wasn't in my mind.

I was in hers.

I needed to get her upset enough that she kicked me out.

"He was going to make me into a dragon," I said into the cave before the snarling dragon had a chance to make herself known. "He said he was going to make me his mate."

A yell cut through the cave, shivering over the stone and through my spine as everything shifted and the heat of the real world slammed against my skin like hot flashes against the chill of her mind.

"He said he wanted you for his mate?" she mocked, her snarl having turned into a full blown laugh now. "Dragon kings don't have mates."

"But he said..."

"You foolish little girl, you are even stupider than the mortals I eat for breakfast." She laughed again, and a wave of pure ice ran over my skin, sending me shivering against whatever I was leaning against. Drake's arms had gone, replaced by something far too pokey and uncomfortable. A bed of nails, or maybe the jaws of a dragon if I had to venture a guess. Seeing as I was still stuck staring at the dark tunnel I couldn't know for sure.

"You don't eat..."

"You believed him, didn't you?" She interrupted me with a snap. "You believed all those lies, and all those pretty words that he wanted you forever."

It was a schoolyard mockery, and I wanted to call her out on it. Play the game and tell her how wrong she was, complete with some remark about how lame her shoes were, but the words were as frozen as the truth in my mind. I couldn't tell her how wrong she was without revealing the truth, and I couldn't do that, not yet. Even though the screaming, rampaging phoenix in me was nowhere near onboard with that plan.

"He does want me forever," I retorted lamely, fighting against my bristling temper.

She laughed again, the sound the same cold trill of devilish prodding that chilled me to the bone.

What I wouldn't give to punch her, lay her out and sit on her or something.

Okay, that made it clear that I really needed to learn how to fight, because obviously that wasn't a thing that would work, especially not against an emotionally manipulative and terrifyingly powerful ice dragon.

"I have known Killian my entire life, and I have shared his bed for nearly as long," Dabria continued, a fog of grey smearing over the glittering colors that I had been staring at for far too long.

It was a shapeless mass, a blip in the specks of light, but I knew it was her. I knew she was staring at me, just as she had in the dream. Staring, prodding.

It did nothing to help me settle my temper. She didn't have more than a faint ghost-in-a-sheet shape and it was taking everything in my power to stop me from rushing her. You know, if I could.

"I know his secrets, I know his desires, I know his plea-sures." Each word of her sleazy voice melted against me like ice on a spoon. They should have helped me chill out, but no, instead they were like freaking gasoline on an open flame. "You know how to lay still and make coffee in the morning."

That was it.

That was fucking it.

I tried to rush her, but there was nothing but her laugh. I was still trapped. She was lucky, because right then I don't think a herd of dragons could have stopped me.

"At least I know him well enough to see when he's using me," I poked deep, and hard. Letting my words stab as the dumb blonde routine slipped away.

The cave shivered before I had finished, the deep growl that I recognized at once as dragon rippling through the icy air and sending a shiver up my spine. I hadn't heard that before.

The growl grew as the cave began to shiver, the edges rippling like they themselves were responsible for the tumultuous sound. A shimmer of blue and violet painted over the stone like an oil slick, the colors shimmering smooth against the rock. It was beautiful. The same way that Killian's green sheen had glistened in the night, these glistened in waves of color that moved in time with the growl, as though they were the dragon.

No, not as though. They were. I was in the dragon.

Well, shit. This plan had backfired.

Fear snaked over me as the temperature began to grow, and for the first time ice dragged through my bones that the ice dragon wasn't responsible for.

"I would rip you apart. I would burn you to pieces," The deep rumble echoed around me, the burning walls dripping with bright blue flame that snaked toward me like ribbons. They would have been beautiful if not for the growing heat that made it clear she truly thought she could burn me alive.

I really didn't need her to find out that that wasn't possible. Even if it was possible inside a mind-fuck-meld thing. I really didn't want to find out.

"Killian would kill you if you tried!" Yeah, good one.

"It would be worth it," the creature snarled with a growl. "If only to watch you writhe."

I was sure she would be the one writhing, but I wasn't about to tell her that. Instead, I stayed silent, every muscle in my back wound so tight that I was fairly certain I had entered rigor mortis.

"It would be a beautiful thing," She snarled when I didn't respond. "To make you hurt him, and then watch him writhe when I expose his folly in keeping you. In lying to the king about you."

"I..." I was really lost, making me hurt him? And here I was thinking I was the one off my rocker.

"You are going to work for me," She hissed, that same icy

touch running over my skin, but this time over my neck and over my collar bone, like one would a lover. The touch twisted in my stomach, my phoenix rising in a white-hot heat that I did everything in my power to control, to hide.

I would have pushed the woman away, pushed her hand and went in for the kill, but there was still no one here, only the grey mass that was steadily growing closer.

"I am going to use you to make Killian hurt," her voice was a whisper now, the sound soft in my ear. I tried to turn to it but there was still nothing, I was still under her control. "I'll teach him to humiliate me. And you will help me do it."

Like I hell I would! Yeah, she was in my mind, but she thought I was a mortal. Some whiney little lovesick girl that she could control. Because I was going to let that happen.

I was going to let her keep thinking she could use me like some dog on a leash. Too bad for her, I would burn the leash and bite her hand off before she would be able to get too close.

"I will visit you soon, little mortal."

Oh, I sure as hell hope so.

The cave began to shimmer, but instead of falling away, everything began to shake, an icy heat running through my veins, threatening to burst out of me. A scream bubbled in my throat. but I fought it, writhing as the cave faded to black, and Drake's arms pressed me against him, his hand smothering my mouth and whatever sound had been trying to make an appearance.

Lashing about like a mad man I fought both arms and burn, only to find myself heaving on the ground beside the canvas, flames licking over my skin as though they were butterfly kisses. Drake hovered over me, a look of fear on his face as his hands pressed against my bare arms, sending his familiar soothing warmth through me.

27

"Did she see?" He said in a whisper so hushed that the laugh of the four dragons on the other side of the fire smothered it.

"No," I hissed, a smile spreading over my face.

She didn't know I was a phoenix, and I had gotten a couple of good jabs in, so I was considering that a win. I still didn't know why she thought I was a mortal, but I guess Suvi's shield just worked that good. I would have to get her some pipe tobacco for that, maybe something that doesn't smell like socks.

I almost stood up when a deep rumble of a laugh I barely recognized sliced against my heart.

Ceres.

I had been trapped in the looney bin for so long, I had forgotten that the lusty dragon wasn't the only danger here.

But after that, he didn't seem quite so scary. I had conquered the ice dragon, the king seemed like a walk in the park after that.

I turned ready to lunge through the flames, but I couldn't see well enough to know what was a person, or a dragon. That shape there looked like a donkey. There was nothing but smoke, the ashen wall growing heavier as the flames grew smaller.

"From one joyful task to another," The king crooned with a clap of his hands. "You boys have done brilliantly! Now, Killian, we have work to do. Come."

The kings voice dropped, and any calm that had been left in the air dropped along with it. I couldn't even see them, and I could feel the tension that had taken over. Drake reached up and pulled me away from the wall of smoke with enough force that for a moment I was sure someone had seen me.

"Shouldn't someone stay here and clean up the mess?"

Killian said with a growl that sent the smoke over our heads swirling.

I wasn't sure what was happening over there, but even I could tell that Killian was on the edge.

Didn't know him, my ass.

"I believe that your brother is capable of doing that on his own," Ceres said, his voice grinding through the air in warning. "You and I have work of our own."

"But I--"

"Is there something you need here?" Dabria cut in, her heels snapping against the asphalt as I assumed she walked toward Killian. Hearing her voice here, in the real world was doing weird things to me.

I hated her. I knew that without a shadow of a doubt, but there was something that was smothering it, an ownership that made me want to protect her. Oh, that was not a thing. I had clearly been in her mind too long.

I guess I did go crazy if I wanted to protect that snooty little bed-hopper.

There were four people I would protect, and she was not on that list.

"Is there something you need," She continued, cutting through the emotional tug-o-war I was battling. "Something you are hiding."

She whispered the last part, but she obviously didn't whisper it enough to hide it. Everyone heard, and the growl that followed it was enough to silence whatever Dabria had done to me.

"What is this? What is she talking about Killian?" All of the false joy in Ceres was gone, the hard grind of his sand-paper voice rubbing against my soul and evaporating the last of Dabria's chill with one long note of phoenix song.

Drake gave me a fearful look, making it clear he had

heard the song. Dabria hadn't been able to tell that I was a phoenix, but who knew if Suvi's spell was enough to block it from the King. It was already too late to take it back.

But, whatever was happening on the other side of the flames sounded much, much worse.

"What are you hiding?" the king snapped with a roar that sent me cowering, and I couldn't even see him.

I had thought the deep grind of his voice couldn't get any worse.

I was wrong.

I was so very, very wrong.

It was the same low growl, the same hate filled commands, but the undertone of his words had somehow caught fire. They burned through the air with a heat that I had never felt before, and for a moment I was sure my flesh was melting from me.

"It is nothing father," Killian said, that same hard edge in his voice that normally sent me on an emotional roller coaster. "You know the jealousy of this one. She's still fuming over the fact that I chose a mortal over her. A pathetic tirade from a weak little dragon."

Killian's anger bleached the air, a thunderous growl following behind. I cringed and moved into Drake, his hand running over my hair in what I was sure he thought was comforting. And it might have been, if there wasn't quite so much danger in the air. If I didn't know exactly what she was saying.

Luckily, the king was oblivious to all of it.

He laughed in a deep echo that cut through the growls of Dabria and Killian, silencing their dragons and leaving the crackle of fire to take its place.

"Don't worry, Killian," Ceres said through the deep warning of his laugh. "I'll put her in her place. Now come, we have work to do. I know I have left this task in good hands."

"You have, father," Jarron said, his voice so strained I was sure I could have jumped on it like a trampoline if given the opportunity.

"Clean the bastard from the earth," Ceres said with a snarl. "I want no trace that the pathetic disappointment every existed."

"Consider it done."

Drake's muscles rippled against me, his arms pulling me into him as though I was a life line. I was glad to be. I held him back, listening to the ripping of flesh and the flap of wings as Killian soared away, Dabria at his side.

Imagining that hurt much more than I would like to admit.

The sound of wings had barely left when Jarron jumped through the flames after us, skidding against the ripped up parking lot in his need to get closer.

"What happened?" Jarron hissed, pulling me from Drake and into him, his touch soothing away some of my frayed edges and loosening up the muscles in my back, just a bit. He was safe, and given everything that had happened, I hadn't realized how much I had been holding my breath.

For both of them.

Ripping myself away from his tight hold, I twisted toward the flames, toward the spot in the dark night sky where three large shapes were disappearing. My heart pulled tightly with every flap of those wings.

Darn bonding phoenix thing, he had just got back. We had just recovered from the whole balls-meet-stick thing. I wasn't ready for him to leave.

"What does she know?" Jarron asked again, his hand soft as he pulled me back to face him, his eyes wide.

"Nothing. She thinks I am a human," I replied with a shake of my head. "I think it's Suvi's shield. She knows Killian is hiding me, but I told her he wants to mate with me."

"So, the truth?" Jarron said with a slight twitch of his lips. "You did good, Ellie. I had a feeling she was baiting him. The bitch."

"I would love to see her burn." Drake mused as Jarron held me, the three of standing in the middle of the dying dragon fire.

"Don't worry. I can make that happen." I let that smile stretch.

Dabria thought she was going to take Killian down, and that I was going to help her.

Wouldn't she be surprised when I burned her to a crisp instead.

3

ELLIOT

THE CROWDS WERE STARTING TO FILTER IN, HORDES OF onlookers that were pressing against the yellow police line like a wall of overly concerned grandmothers. If there had been glass there you can rest assured that their noses would have been turned up against it.

Watching. Staring.

As it was, they stood in the light of the dying flames, halos of smoke lingering over their heads, dripping through the air like the tears of the performers who had come to watch their home burn.

I was with them. I may have been standing on the other side of the police line, covered in ash and blood. I may have been branded as a witness, as a suspect, but it didn't make it hurt any less.

Scattered amongst the rubberneckers the performers from the circus stood with tears streaming down their faces, watching as the tents continued to smolder and collapse. Everyone else had been staying in the hotel, or worked in the surrounding businesses and had come for a different kind of show. Interest, intrigue, curiosity. Gossip. They didn't seem to care that so many people's livelihoods were going up in puffs of unnaturally colored smoke.

Paraffin oil burns funny.

Or at least that's what Suvi had been telling the officers for the last hour, elaborating on some story about an audience member who had been stalking Zoe and tried to corner her. Suvi told the story dutifully, Drake following behind her and Zoe as they spoke to each eyewitness and investigator, Drake's expression growing more and more sour with every person they talked to.

I didn't like this, and not just because the story sounded like something a ten-year-old would make up to get out of doing the dishes, but because all of this was really my fault.

The fire. The dragon king. Drake's supposed death.

And all because I had thwacked Killian in the balls.

I was torn between laughing at the ridiculousness of it and groaning in frustration.

I went for the groan, but either sound would have been drowned by the screeches of fear, frustration and scaffolding as the last standing piece of the tent began to come down in a shower of sparks.

The black sky above the battle zone Jarron and I stood in filled with thousands of falling stars, the embers spinning and twirling as they began their descent. The crowd gasped in horror, but I stood still beneath the heart wrenching beauty before Jarron grabbed me and pulled me away from the waterfall. Large specks of flame and burning rubble crashed into the black top, adding to the layer of ash that was already there.

"Mortals get burned by flame," Jarron said with a wink, rubbing his hand up and down my back as he held me against him, the touch sending lines of electricity through my bones.

Even here, in the middle of the battlefield his touch was like the best kind of drug. If only it could stop the guilt, something I was sure was going to get worse. We were still waiting to talk to the cops about what we had seen. *Love sick fan with a knife, and a large dog,* I repeated to myself, knowing that there was no dog on this planet that could pass for a dragon.

Luckily, I had the skin of a bull or I would probably be spouting the truth all over the place. Or, at least I hoped I did. I had never been interviewed by the cops before, I had always soared away before it got that far.

For all I knew I was going to collapse under pressure and start raving about dragon kings and wicked ice demons who wanted to control me.

Okay, maybe the story of the obsessive fan was a bit more plausible than I thought.

"I wish I had never kicked Killian in the balls," I said without thinking, I didn't think it was possible to make a sucker punch to the groin sound quite so depressing.

Jarron, however, didn't think so. The prince began to laugh, the sound loud and very out of place amongst the rubble. Even some of the crowd that was barricaded on the other side of the police line was giving us bizarre looks.

"Don't laugh, Jarron," I grumbled, nodding toward the eavesdroppers and smacking him on the arm. Didn't matter, he continued to chuckle, his dark eyes reflecting the flames. "It's not funny."

"You kicked my brother in the balls and the tent exploded." he continued to chuckle, the sound grinding against my guilt uncomfortably. "Trust me, it's funny."

I didn't have to trust him, I knew it was. But I was far too stubborn to admit that right now.

"Maybe in ten years," I scoffed. My furrowed brow was

easily becoming so deep that no amount of lotion was going to fix it. Thank god I was immortal "But not now. Right now, I just feel bad."

"No use crying over spilled milk." I gave him a look for that one, it was very easily the oldest saying in the book, so of course it would be used by a two hundred-year-old dragon.

A dragon who was now fixing me with that same crooked half smile that popped his dimple in that perfect way and sent me into all sorts of twitterpated palpitations.

I swallowed, he smiled more, and held me into him. The last place I needed to be was right next to him, next to his warmth and soft electric touch. Feeling the tips of fingers drag over my arm as I pinned him to the rubble of the teeter-totter behind us. Holding him in place as I let my tongue explore his...

Oh god. My brain was running wild. It was late enough that I was sure Suvi's tea was wearing off.

"It's already happened, Elliot," Jarron said, oblivious to the R-rated movie that was playing in my head and tracing his fingers over my spine, sending more of those little electric shocks through my bones.

Oh lord, this was so much trouble. I wanted to tell him that he was playing with a horny fire, but I really didn't want him to stop either. So instead I groaned and leaned into him, something which he dutifully misinterpreted.

"You can't fix it," He continued, "so stop letting it fester. Breathe, let it go, and then we can figure out how to move past it."

And there went my need to jump on Jarron.

I should have been glad, but the little electric shocks that Jarron gave me were now more like little pricks against my guilt and I cringed. I wanted so much to agree with him, to move forward and find a way past the last few hours. Suvi certainly had done so, she had even expressed how glad she was that I was alive before she dragged Drake off with her, lighting her pipe as though she was going to gentleman club and not to go talk to the cops about why her circus was on fire.

"I don't see how we can fix this," I said, gesturing wildly to the circus that was the closest thing I had to a home.

Home.

That stabbed deep, no wonder I was feeling so much guilt and hopelessness over a bunch of canvas.

"I lost my home," I whispered, hating that my voice cracked with the emotion, but not even trying to stop it. It was the truth, and man that truth stung like a bad wax job.

"We can rebuild this, easy...." Jarron said as the tent gave one last gasp, the powerful jet of water from the firefighter's hose drowning the last of the flames and sending a wave of ash and sparks over all of us.

"You were saying?" I mocked as the creaking of the collapse wheezed into the night. I coughed and gagged against the ash, trying to wipe it from my already ash covered face.

"This is just a place, Ellie." Jarron whispered, leaning close to my ear as the chatter of voices from the crowd behind us began to pick up again, a few of the rubber-neckers leaving now that the show was clearly over. "We can rebuild a place. We can even build a new home in a place that no one can take away. What matters most is that my father did not catch your scent, and that you are safe."

"Well, safe enough without Dabria playing a deranged game of chess," I began, only to be cut off by a snap and a screech from the middle of the crowd.

"I don't care who gave you your instructions, this is my

home, my job, and you are going to let me in there or you are going to be on the ground begging for your life."

Oh lord.

Of course she was here. She always had a way to seek out destruction and any place she could leave a wave of terror behind. Of course, now that I had been introduced to Dabria, I think the worst Stacia could dish out was a mildly flowing case of nausea. But that didn't make her any less of an irritant.

Stacia and her two lackeys stood on the other side of the yellow police line, a burly police officer standing between the contortionist and her destination. She glared at the officer as he calmly tried to explain something to her, her eyes hard little specks of hatred that made it clear she thought she was going to get her way.

"Idiot," I scoffed to myself, of course she thought she was needed over here, although who knew why. Her back bend may be good, but it wasn't going to single handedly put the circus back together.

"I don't care..." She began, before her eyes darted to mine at the sound of my scoff and twisted into a poisonous dart. I know she expected a flinch, but like hell if I was going to give her that.

"You," she snarled, and at least this time I had the decency not to smile or glare in return. Not that I didn't want to, I was witness to a crime and all that. The less incriminating things I could do the better. "What did you do? Start the fire?"

Ash coated my tongue, my phoenix snarling at the girl who still obviously thought she was my nemesis.

Yeah, I did, are you happy, the words buzzed loud in my head, but I thankfully kept them there. Unfortunately, I couldn't keep the smug smile as locked away that time.

That one blazed loud and clear.

Her jaw might have dropped, shock smacked hard against her eyes before she rearranged her perfect features and turned to the officer with a sweet smile. Well, if sweet was laced with arsenic.

"I'm with them, let me through," She snarled, her and her lacky's pushing past both tape and officer as if it was nothing. The officer didn't even try to stop them, he even lifted the tape before shaking his head and walking away in pure robotic fashion.

The two girls who were always on her heels followed behind her as if they were on a string, not a drop of fear or worry in their eyes. In fact, there didn't seem to be a drop of anything in their eyes.

Weird. I had performed alongside those two for years, and I had never seen them look so vacant. Penny, the curly haired girl that had joined us near Germany, had even stood up for me at one point in time. Well, before she had become Stacia's lackey. But even then, she possessed cohesive thought.

Now, I was sure that I could blow on her and she would fall over.

"Oh shit," Jarron mumbled from behind me, pulling me behind him as he angled himself between Stacia and I like a brick wall.

I had heard that fear in his voice before, probably a half an hour before when his father had been flying toward us. Directing that level of concern at bullying Stacia seemed a little bit excessive. I mean, you would think she was a monster with the way he was going into full on 'protect the princess' mode. I gave him a look that said as much, pushing myself around his wall, but he ignored me his eyes on Stacia.

"How did I not see it before," He snapped, his skin growing hot as the lines of gold began to string through his eyes, except this time they didn't have a drop of beauty there. They screamed danger.

"How did you not notice what before?" I parroted, but neither of them even looked at me, they were both staring daggers, the lackey's now watching the smoke as if it was a rare bird.

Okay, this was officially getting creepy. The flare of ash and panic that my phoenix was rippling through me wasn't helping.

"Jarron?" I asked, hating how my voice was shaking.

"She's one of them," He hissed, pushing me behind him again, and turning himself into a wall between me and the scowling ice queen who was now walking toward us. "She's a blood slave. Connected to my father."

4

ELLIOT

THE FIRE FILLED DREAD THAT HAD TAKEN OVER JARRON made sense. Although, I still couldn't wrap my head around it. I mean, other than the fact that Stacia was a vile manipulative bully, she couldn't work for the dragon king. I mean, why would Suvi let her stay here?

But then, watching her walk toward us in her ugly glittering shoes, making goo-goo eyes at Jarron and flipping her hair like a super model, I could believe it.

It really wasn't helping the inferno of flame my phoenix was raging in. She really needed to stop looking at him that way, well, unless she wanted to lose something.

Like a head.

What was with my phoenix and ripping off heads? I probably needed to get that looked at, because I really wasn't okay with it.

"Down boy," Stacia snarled as she reached us. "I'm not going to hurt her, and I'm not dumb enough to try to fight you. I mean, unless you want me to. Because I could pin you to the ground better than this virginal shifter over here."

She gave me a look of disgust before fixing Jarron with one that was pure greed.

Freaking bedroom eyes, she might have well stripped off all her clothes right then. The ash that had filled my mouth before turned into a full blown inferno. I could feel smoke tickle my nostrils as my phoenix practically screamed inside of me, the sound loud and angry and everywhere. I was suddenly very glad that Jarron stood between Stacia and I, or else I probably would have spit fire and ripped her head from her shoulders.

As it was I burped smoke and expelled the last of the flames in a belch that was nearly as loud as the scream of my phoenix.

And the winner for sexiest phoenix goes to. Sure as hell not me. Gross.

"I heard that," Stacia crooned, her voice like acid as she stepped even closer, trying to dart around Jarron the wall king.

"Excuse me," I began, but she cut me off with a laugh before I could say anything more.

"Not that, loser." She sneered, shooting me a scowl as brash and conceited as she was. "That screechy noise that your shifter is making. It sounds like you might be drowning, you might want to check that out."

She heard that? Oh my god, she heard that.

I froze as Jarron's skin began to smoke and ripple, his dragon growling so loud that the remaining mortals were sure to think that something else was going to collapse with how they began to screech and scuttle around like lost chickens.

"Seriously, sexy, relax," Stacia said, her laugh all but gone now, which was enraging me more. I don't know what was going on. Only I can call Jarron sexy, and I wasn't ready to call him sexy yet.

Even if he was.

And he was.

"If I wanted to hurt her, or you, I would have done it long ago." Stacia crooned, flipping her hair and taking another step closer to us. Luckily Jarron stepped back, if she had come much closer I couldn't promise any amount of control. "You didn't even know what I was until now, and even then it's because Suvi's magic is stretched so thin that she can't conceal us all. Xi is hiding in the courtyard, Ryn is in the pool, and you..."

She drew the word out, the mocking dragging through the ash filled air as she peeked around Jarron to see me. It was clear she expected me to be cowering.

I was not that weak. Oh, I was so over this staring match. I was ready to fight, or scowl, pull hair, or whatever it was she had planned. Jarron tried to push me behind him, but I wasn't having any of that. I knew Stacia's tricks, well I thought I did. Right then I was having trouble wrapping my head around what she had said.

Why the hell would Ryn be in the pool? He was scared of water last I checked.

"I can't tell what you are, Elliot." Stacia continued, cutting through my thoughts. "A shifter obviously, but since you are clinging to a dragon like a parasite you've got to be something weak and pathetic. Like a moth. Are you a moth, Elliot?"

Her smile was twisted with malice and disgust now, her eyes filled with a haunting red gleam that I hadn't seen before. I wanted to say it was just the fire, but there was something dark and twisted in her eyes, in the way she looked at me that made me want to get out of dodge.

And possibly shoot her with a fire javelin in the process.

Definitely that.

"I'm a bit more than that," I spat, letting the words slice and dice against her ego as I fixed her with a grin. "Something that would gladly rip you to shreds. Starting with that pretty little head from your shoulders..."

Great, my fury had brought me full circle. Yeah, I may have a problem.

I didn't get any more out before Jarron pulled me back against him, chest rumbling with a growl as he postured the petite blonde who was now looking at us with the widest eyes I had ever seen, the white ringed with a haunting red.

The look of shock lasted for a moment before it faded away, twisting into malice as she let out a single mocking laugh.

"You don't know what I am. Do you?"

And there went all my confidence.

"You work for the dragon king," I repeated what Jarron had said, but instead of balloons and streamers you would get in a game show, she laughed deeper, her mocking so loud now that everyone had turned to watch.

"*Worked*," she corrected, as if that made it any better. "Do you really think Suvi would let me in here if I still worked for those disgusting murderers?"

Well, no. But stubbornness dictated that I say nothing.

The red rings in her eyes flashed with the police lights, her smile tweaking as she took a step closer. A swirl of cool infecting the air as though she herself was a winter storm warning.

"Fangs and claws away, bloodsucker," Jarron growled, keeping himself firmly planted between Stacia and I.

Jarron had always been a bit on the protective side, but this manly-man act was starting to feel a bit excessive. I get it, it was his job was to protect me. But Stacia was more bully than powerful. I could take her. Even if she was something that Ceres would keep close by.

Like Dabria. Ugh. Stacia and Dabria, even their names matched. It made me want to know how the hell bitchy Stacia had ended up here.

"Your dragon bodyguard can feel it," She sneered, from the other side of Jarron. I peeked around him, looking right into her bloodshot eyes before Jarron blocked me again. "What's wrong with you?"

"You might be asking yourself the same thing," Jarron hissed, his hand warm against mine as Stacia's and her cronies stepped closer, their shoes kicking rubble around.

I tried to wiggle away, but this time he wasn't having it. He wasn't leaving my side as much as the Queen of England wasn't going to die anytime soon.

"Nothing is wrong with me," Stacia said with a flip of her hair. "Nothing more than you. You must have pissed off your daddy big time to be hiding here, *your highness.*"

Lust-filled prodding had made a return, and so had my need to knock some sense into her. First, she is some blood slave thing that worked for Jarron's dad. Suvi was hiding her, so she should be safe, except for the fact that she had been openly hitting on him and his brother since day one.

I would say I was going to be sick, but I think I was just getting pissed.

Mine. It wasn't Jarron's dragon that had growled that time, but my phoenix. The sound rang through my head, Jarron turning to fix me with a look of shock before he snapped back to Stacia, his brow furrowing.

"So, you know who I am," It wasn't a question, and Jarron's low growl was definitely not sending her running. If anything, she kept moving closer, like a moth to a flame.

Keep coming, bitch, I'll crush you.

"How are you connected to him?" Jarron continued to snarl, ignoring the lust that Stacia was practically painting on her face like a two dollar hooker. "When was the last time you saw that bastard?"

He growled with a sound that deepened and lengthened in ways that made me want to pull away. The warning in both growl and voice was hauntingly clear, but the threat bounced off Stacia like a dodgeball to the face. She flinched, yes, but her smug smile was back in place before anyone could react, flinging her sheet of blonde hair behind her with way too much flourish as she stared into Jarron.

I didn't think anyone could look like they wanted to eat someone, but she did.

It was only a mild improvement.

"I don't know which *bastard* you are speaking of, but I haven't seen any of them in years," Stacia hissed, her Slavic accent increasing alongside what I could only guess was frustration. It was hard to tell with her, she always looked at me like that though. "I don't know if you caught the memo, but I am in hiding. Suvi hides people like us. I'm hiding from my daddy, like you are. I've left that life behind me."

"Yes," Jarron sneered with a head tilt to the two women who were still staring vacantly into the space around him "Your mules seem to agree with that. Living up to your full potential, are you?" he continued, as if addressing the two, but they didn't so much as blink. "College education and all that?"

"They volunteered for the position," Stacia snarled, but even without context I didn't believe her. Jarron didn't either with the way he was chuckling darkly.

"You don't have to believe me, let me show you," She said, her voice a lure as she stepped closer, her hand pulling toward Jarron as the hunger in her eyes shifted, the lines of red in her eyes growing darker. "One night and you will forget all about your little moth. No sharing required. I can be all yours."

Ummm. Hell no.

I was so over this whole cat and mouse thing that was going on. I didn't know who was the cat and who was the mouse, but I was officially the dog, ready to step in and rip her fucking throat out.

My phoenix snarled, and I shoved Jarron away from her reaching fingers, the long white appendages looking more spindly and poisonous in the last of the flickering flames.

"Don't you dare," I snarled in a voice deeper than my own, my phoenix pressing against my skin with so much power that I began to smoke, waves of scarlet running over my skin until they looked like an oil slick. Eyes sparking with the rose-colored flames of my shifter, I stepped toward Stacia, and she flinched.

At any other time, I would have rejoiced in the fear I brought in the girl, whether it was from the threat in my eyes, voice, or maybe because she was secretly a coward I didn't know, and I didn't pause to question. I didn't let her get too far away. I snatched her wrist from where it hovered in its quest to grab my dragon and held it between my flaming smoking fingers like a vice.

Another flinch.

"What the hell?" She snarled, her face growing dark as she tried to pull her hand away. I wouldn't let her, or rather, my phoenix wouldn't let her. "Let me go."

"Don't touch my mate," My eyes narrowed as my grip increased, panic blanching her face as she fixed her blood shot eyes on me.

"Your mate?" she snarled, her emphasis on the word

freezing through me. "You aren't even powerful enough that Suvi's magic can't hold you. You are so weak her flimsy spell is still holding on. There is no way power as weak as yours would bond with the golden executioner."

Ummm. What? The golden executioner? That sounded like the name you give the head boss in a video game. You know, the ones I never play because I always lose.

And I would definitely lose at that.

I tried to lock away my confusion, but it didn't quite work. My grip loosened enough that she pulled herself away with a snap, her wrist covered with a boiling burn in the exact shape of my hand. Each finger was perfectly preserved. I waited for it to heal like I had seen so many times on Zoe and my boys, but the burn continued to grow. Stacia looked from her wrist to me with a glare that would have melted metal if given the chance.

It didn't even look like her. Her face had somehow elongated, her eyes narrowed as the red rings began to overtake them. If it wasn't for the growling of my phoenix, I might have backed down with that.

"You fucking bitch," she snarled, her eyes nearly pure red now, her already pale skin beginning to darken as shadows of spider webs began trailing over her skin in diseased veins.

The lines migrated over him as Jarron pulled me back into him, I didn't fight him, I couldn't even look away from whatever monster was transforming before me.

It was like she possessed. Or maybe she was the possessee. Like a demon. Oh god... please don't let demons be real, too.

"What the...?"

"You are weak and pathetic, and you will pay for this," She hissed in a sound that somehow sucked the light and heat from the air. The few breaths I was able to suck in twisted through my lungs like an infection.

Without a word, Stacia extended her hand to one of the drugged-out groupies. Penny, the girl who had been nice to me once, stepped forward as though she had been pulled there, her eyes glossing over as she extended her arm to Stacia, the thin skin riddled with dozens of little pock marks, each one twisting over her throbbing veins like battle scars.

No, bite marks.

I realized what I had been missing a moment before it happened, before Stacia sunk her protruding fangs into the tender arm of the vacant woman and the scent of iron and salt mixed with the burning of dragon fire and I knew I was going to be sick.

I couldn't even watch people bleed from an injury. This was about a million times worse.

"Holy shit," I hissed as Stacia pulled away from the arm, sighing as though she had done nothing more than had a little drink from the fountain of youth.

Which she had.

Oh god, don't think about that.

"You're a vampire," I gasped, looking from bleeding arm, to the red tinged fangs of the beautiful woman before me with so much shock there was no chance of hiding it.

This wasn't possible. It couldn't be possible. Vampires weren't real. Except, yeah, they very clearly were.

I obviously couldn't take anything I read online seriously. Dragon's don't have caves, vampires exist. What's next? A Unicorn that grants wishes. I would have looked around for the thing, but I didn't dare look away from the horror that was unfolding before me.

"And one of the worst kinds," Jarron provided, tucking

me back into him protectively. "She's a feeder. She needs a living host to survive."

Suddenly the two zombies behind her made sense. I wonder if they were always like that, or even if they knew what was going on. I was suddenly struck with an overwhelming need to grab them and run away from this monster.

I always knew that Stacia was evil, but this takes the cake.

"We aren't interested in the position." Jarron continued, shooing her away as we took a step back.

"I wouldn't want her weakness infecting me," Stacia snarled with a glare in my direction. "But you already know you are welcome to my bed and my side any time. It's been so long since I have feasted in the blood of a dragon."

I jerked toward her, not even caring that her fangs were still out, or that vampires were supposed to have superhero powers. I could so take her.

"Make sure to come and find me when whoever Suvi is hiding this one from finds her." Stacia continued, stepping toward us as Jarron held me still, heat and smoke rolling over my arms as I tried to break free and rush her. So much for not looking like an arsonist. "If you can't recognize me, you don't have much time in this world. When you are finished off, I'll be there to comfort your beautiful mate and soothe his broken heart away."

She looked at me with a gleam filled with so much pompous attitude that it was clear she thought she had won.

Like hell if I was going to let that happen. With a growl that vibrated over the smoldering parking lot, turning the heads of all the grandmothers, I broke free of Jarron, and I rushed her.

"Hands off my dragon," I yelled as my shoulder slammed

into her gut with the force of a battering ram. I stood, ready to watch her tumble back on her ridiculously glittered heels.

But no, she was freaking flying through the air in an inhuman arch, screeching like a banshee as she went. Bristles of pride ran over me, as she hit the ground with a thud and the shock of the crowd turned to shrieks as heads turned to stare at me.

Well, shit.

The one time I go and attack someone, it happens to be a vampire with an affinity for flight in front of a hoard of gossiping mortals. Half of which I knew.

Suvi was going to kill me, well unless the vampire got there first.

Especially considering that said vampire had jumped to her feet, red eyes burning into me as her blood tinged fangs protruded with a hiss. The shadows of dark webbing I had seen before spread over her skin in veins of the purest black.

"Damn it," Jarron snapped, rushing to my side as a crack echoed over the parking lot, and the vampire vanished from where she was.

I jerked, the crowd screamed, and Jarron rushed beside me as the undead monster re-appeared with a pop and a snarl.

"Do you really want to try me," she hissed in my ear, her breath so cold against my skin it burned. "Suvi's spell is weakened, which means my power has been unbound. I'm sure your blood would look beautiful spilled over the parking lot, and over my lips."

"Like hell if it would get that far," I snarled, turning toward her and attempting to get a good hold on the bloodsucker, my hands swiping through the air like claws.

Claws that she easily side stepped, laughing as I continued to fight against my bodyguard.

Damn it, she was fast. If Jarron would let me go then I could get one good hit in when she wasn't expecting it.

"I'd like to see you try," she teased, the dark veins popping against her skin until she looked like she was carved from marble. If marble was diseased and covered in death. "You have no idea what you are up against."

"Neither do you," I snapped, pulling out of Jarron's arms and lunging myself into the still laughing vampire like I was a bowling ball in the bumper lanes. Shock widened in her eyes as I straddled her, pinning her to the ground as we went down hard.

Her face was like ice under my fingers as I gripped it, pressing her skin and batting at her hands in what I was sure was going to be the grandest of all cat fights. Well, it would have been if I hadn't been pulled away from my clawing adventure by not one, but three pair of hands.

Drake's palms clenched my arms, holding me against him as Zoe let go of me and followed Suvi after the vampire, the old waddling lady practically dragging the snarling thing away with her as if she was little more than a bit of fabric and fluff.

I tried to fight Drake, just as Stacia tried to fight Suvi, her skin so webbed she looked like the victim of a plague. Maybe she was, I didn't know enough about Vampires to know how all of that got started.

Not that it mattered, disease or not, the girl looked horrifying, but in that horror movie way where you wanted to poke around and see what makes them tick. I couldn't look away, even as her lackeys turned as one, like they were mechanical wax works following their master on a string.

"Elliot, are you okay?" Drake asked as he turned me in his arms, his hands pressing against forehead, collarbone, and cheeks in an obvious attempt to check for injuries. Like it worked that way, unless he had some magic I didn't know about I am sure all he was feeling was some overly scalding flesh.

I nodded in response, well aware that both my Phoenix and I were still ready to spit fire, or rip heads, or whatever it was you do in a fight.

"What the hell was that?" Drake asked Jarron as Zoe sprinted back over to us, the woman looking out of breath for what I was sure was the first time in her life.

"One of Parris' coven," Jarron said, his dark eyes boring into Zoe as she came up behind her brother. "But what the hell she is doing here?"

I was pretty sure she was just a vampire, but Jarron's answer made it seem like more than that, and given the look that Drake was now giving Jarron, I had a feeling it was substantially more than someone who prefers blood over milk with their eggs and bacon, if they even ate that, which I doubted.

"Suvi hides non-mortals," Zoe said with an exasperated sigh. "I thought you knew that much."

"I thought that meant like wolf shifters, or faeries or something," I said through an exasperated inhale. "Not..." I struggled to find the right word. "That."

Yep, nowhere close to what I wanted.

"Vampires," Jarron provided.

I may not have grown up knowing about all the things that were hiding in this world. To me it was just me, Zoe, and a whole bunch of dragons that wanted my blood. But I had always assumed that the soul sucking dragon king was the worst of it.

I was clearly wrong.

5

KILLIAN

KILLIAN'S BODY FELT LIKE IT WAS BEING RIPPED APART. EVEN IN the reverse of his shift, everything felt pulled and stretched in unnatural ways. Bones twisted, muscles cracking, and everything grinding one over the other as his body returned to its human form.

He felt the burn of his wings as they fused back into his spine, his human feet landing easily on the cold stone of the cave that was reserved for the coming and going of his father, and in turn him. The soft slaps of his feet against stone mutated as his clothes returned, shoes wrapping over feet as his heavy foot falls rumbled the air as they walked toward the throne room, Killian dutifully following his father with his head held high.

Nothing in a dragon shifters existence hurt as much as a shift. You could feel every bone break, every muscle stretch into unnatural lines. The only thing that hurt more was having your wings ripped from your body, and although Killian had seen that punishment enacted on many, he did not plan on experiencing it himself. Even if he did, he doubted he would scream. Screaming through the pain of anything, including a shift, was not befit of the heir to the throne.

He had learned that young enough. Killian had cried and screamed enough in his first shift, only to be beaten further for any tear he shed afterwards. Beaten when his dragon shredded his clothes. Beaten when he couldn't harness the power of shifting and clothing and everything that came with it. If the pain of a shift wasn't bad enough, the pain of his father's lashings would easily put them to shame.

He learned quick enough in his youth to remain silent. Most dragons didn't have the sense and modesty to restrain their distress. Most didn't have the control and strength enough to do so.

Dabria being one of them. Her soft moans of agony echoed around his as he followed his father toward the throne room. She may think herself favored, but she wasn't the only woman to grace his father's presence. Her pathetic whimpers ensured that she wouldn't reach any higher than being an occasional pet, valued for her skills in manipulation and intrigue.

Which was for the best. The woman had enough gall as it was and putting her any closer to power could be dangerous. It was a miracle she hadn't realized what Parris was up to, her switching loyalties could spell disaster, especially if his suspicions were correct.

That hadn't been a slip of the tongue back at the circus. Dabria knew something, and Killian would rip it out of her if he needed to.

She had already made it clear she couldn't handle pain. No easier way to make a person talk, than to make them scream.

"Your highness," Parris' smooth voice slid through the icy

air of the cave as though it belonged there, the pale man slithering from the throne room to greet their arrival as though he was welcoming them to a house party.

The vile vampire's smile was spread wide, well, until he caught sight of Killian behind his father. Killian had never seen the blood sucker's face fall faster. He didn't even try to restrain the grin of success at that. The look enraged the vampire more.

"What is it Parris?" Killian prodded as he slid his suit jacket over his shoulders, and quickly fastened the buttons. "You don't seem happy to see me."

"I... I didn't expect to see you back so soon," the man managed to stutter out, although the lie was nearly as transparent as his skin.

Unfortunately, Killian's father did not seem to see, he was too focused on the door that Parris had emerged from, and the chattering of voices that was filtering through the crack in the stone.

"My son has defeated his treacherous brother!" Ceres announced, clapping Parris on the shoulder as he continued to peer through the crack in the door. "Such an occasion deserves a reward! Is that what I think it is?"

Ceres' focus pulled from the door, to the pale man who was still looking at Killian with a poisonous scowl. Killian let the daggers sink into him, but he didn't flinch, and he sure as hell wasn't going to look away. It had been a long time since his father's lap dog had dared look at him so wickedly. That alone was a dangerous line, but with the king right there? The look sparked warning in Killian, his beast slicing prods of warning over his spine, ready to shift back to its form if needed.

Something foul was filling the air, and it wasn't just the

smell of blood and salt that followed Parris around like a bad body odor.

The vampire swallowed, his Adam's apple bobbing beneath his pale skin as he shook away the scowl and finally turned toward the king with his trademark slimy grin.

"Yes, sire it is," Parris said, his voice drawn out as he attempted to turn the king away from his son, his voice dropping low enough that Killian was sure the man thought he could not hear him. The fool always underestimated him. "It took some time, but we have found all of the others as you requested. We are waiting for you, but from what he has been saying I feel that this meeting should be only for you."

Parris' eyes lifted to Killian, the bloodshot rings that circled his pupils making it clear that the little man thought he had won, which made his father's laugh that much more enjoyable, the cutting grind ripping through Parris' confidence.

"Nonsense, Parris!" Ceres said with a darkness that flicked between the wiry vampire and his son so quickly that Killian was sure the old man would have caught sight of the vampire's glare. As speedy as he was, however, Parris had already twisted his smile from distaste to eager servitude. "Killian is my most trusted adviser, and quite skilled in getting information out of unruly mortals. I wouldn't dream of doing this without him."

Killian didn't need to hear much more to know what Parris was hiding behind the door, although who they had found that needed torture was a twisting worry over Killian's spine. His father had mentioned a new lead when they stood beside Zoe disguised form outside the ruins of the circus tent, and now, standing beside a vampire, and an ice dragon as the hallway filled with twisted laughter and muffled screams, made him worry as to what that lead truly was.

And how much closer Parris was to discovering Ellie, and his connection to her.

Dabria, and now Parris, appeared to be far too close to sniffing out the truth.

Killian didn't like that, and his dragon liked that even less. His beast lifted its snarling head at that, ready to destroy the two pathetic underlings to keep Ellie safe.

"I am never one to say no to some fingernail pulling in the name of information," Killian said with as much eagerness he could force into his voice, which was much more difficult than it should have been. "If it gets us closer to that damn Phoenix, and to my father's true role in our clan, then so be it."

Every word physically hurt to say, his need to protect the girl fueling the dark fire that was now buzzing in the back of his throat.

"Then it's settled, let's begin the fun," Ceres smiled at Killian's proclamation, clapping him on the back as Dabria finally stumbled up to join them, her face twisted back into defiant servitude, even though the streaks of tears were still clearly staining her ebony skin.

Parris however, was beginning to look like he was the one being prepped for torture. His scowl deepened, the red rings around his eyes darkening until Killian's skin prickled in expectation of a fight. He had never had to fight the monsters, the treaty between their kinds had been signed long before he was born. But seeing the scowl on the man's face was increasing the already heightened alarm in Killian's mind.

His muscles were pulled so tight that they were in

danger of snapping. The blood sucker was clearly hiding something.

"Well, you have heard the king. Show me what treasure you would like me to break," Killian said, purposefully prodding Parris and fixing him with a grin that the vampire had no choice but to return.

Perfect, the pale bastard needed a reminder of who he was serving and why. Killian was glad to provide it. The blood sucker may think he had the upper hand, but Killian and his brothers already had the girl. He would do anything to protect her. If Parris had new information about that in the room, then Killian would be in there. Even if he had to destroy Parris to do so.

"I really don't think this is a good idea, Sire," Parris said, the Vampire staring at Ceres as he blocked Killian's advance, the tiny points of his teeth barely visible behind his lips. "This news should be for your ears only."

"Do you really wish to defy your king, Parris?" Killian snarled, letting his voice echo off the stone as the deep growl of his dragon followed behind. "Perhaps you need a reminder of who you serve."

The vampire flinched, his eyes narrowing at the reminder, and the threat. He had clearly lost, but still, he didn't move. Killian was not ready to give himself away just yet, but this man was making that difficult.

"Would you like me to see if there is a problem?" Dabria hissed from behind them, her voice eager, if not a little out of breath. Who knew shifting took so much out of her.

"Patience lovely. Do we have a problem?" Ceres said from behind the showdown Killian and Parris were locked in. His voice had lost all humor now, the hard disappointment stabbing into Killian's back.

"No, sire," Parris muttered, his eyes narrowing at Killian before he stepped away and opened the large stone door to the throne room for them and flooding the entry way with sound.

Laughter, sobs, and screams melded with the aroma of blood, sweat, and urine and slammed against them all in a wall that twisted and nearly upturned the contents of Killian's stomach. Not because of what he saw, he had been privy to far too many of these late-night torture feasts. Just the smell of blood and fear, sent a pleasurable twist through his stomach, the saliva swelling in the back of his throat as his dragon's hunger overtook him. It had been far too long since he had let the creature feast, and he probably would have if not for who was in the room.

He had expected the clan of mingling vampires, waiting for their own precious taste of human blood. It was the humans that was sending a pulse of fear through his heart, his dragon suddenly desperate to destroy each of them, and the information they carried.

No wonder Parris had not wanted him here.

He recognized every one of them as the mortals who had witnessed Elliot's spectacular *fall* from Angel's Landing in Zion National Park.

The night he had met Ellie behind the hotel, Dabria had told him of the fall and he had tracked them down. Listening to them ramble about a girl who had stripped to her underwear and jumped. He had barely listened, his mind three hundred miles away with the girl his dragon had bonded to. Twenty-four hours later he had discovered the Ellie was the Phoenix and these pathetic mortals had hardly mattered.

Now, they mattered.

A couple clung to each other as they cried in the corner, two vampires smelling and taunting them with their fangs.

A young man clutched a backpack as he stared around him in shock and fear. There were at least twenty of them, and in the middle of the room, huddled amid at least ten vampires was a bulk of a man, his muscles rendered useless amongst the undead. This one Killian knew. It was this man who had soiled himself, it was also this man that Killian had spoken to before.

Brayden, the man that had walked with Ellie up the mountain. If Killian remembered correctly, he did not know her name, but he knew exactly what she looked like.

Thankfully, no one in this room had seen her. Only Dabria, who had seen her ash covered nakedness run down a hallway that same night. Dragon's covered their lovers in flame, they played with their food. If Killian was lucky Dabria wouldn't realize that the ash Ellie had been covered in was from her Phoenix. She would not put two and two together.

He was, quite literally, playing with fire. His heart may well burst from the pressure with how it was pulsing.

"Beautiful," Dabria sighed as she stepped beside Killian, her hand cold through his suit as she let her palm press against his arm, the touch revealing how tense he was. "Eager are we?"

"Of course," Killian growled, letting her roll with her assumptions, even as he carefully blocked his thoughts. He certainly wasn't going to give Dabria easier access to the secret that was now feeling like a time bomb. "It's been quite some time since I got to feel the pleasurable crack of bone in my jaws."

Killian smiled, forcing eagerness into the look as he turned toward the seductress. Although, with the pressure of his dragon and the gentle lift of her eyebrow it was clear he had not done the look justice.

Killian was used to being powerful, in control, and with the upper hand. This time, Parris may have won. He had no choice to play along, and hopefully get a message to Jarron if anything was revealed. Fire was burning Killian from the inside out, and it wasn't all his.

"It's been quite some time since I have seen a feast this abundant," Ceres crooned, clapping Parris on the back as the two stepped past Killian, looking over the whimpering mortals as if they were picking a lobster from a tank.

Killian needed the upper hand, and he knew one way to do that, he had to choose the first lobster.

"My mouth is already watering," Killian said honestly, before turning toward his father, carefully picking his words through the thunder of his heart. "Why don't you pick whose cries you would like to hear first, father."

Killian had never been so nervous, he had never felt fear this powerful, the emotion was nearly crippling. It was only made worse knowing that Parris was staring at him, his own panic at losing echoed back.

"I know many of these from when you sent me down to southern Utah," Killian continued before either Parris or Dabria could cut in. "The couple there were not ones I questioned before. I am sure any new answers from the others would rip wide open as I rip them apart."

Dabria laughed maniacally, Ceres smiled greedily, and they all began to walk toward the poor mortals with eyes that screamed death, giving one single nod of approval to Killian. The answer may be in the room, but Killian would keep his father from it for as long as possible.

Killian stepped forward, ready to follow his father and begin the work that he had mastered so long ago, only to find an icy hand over his chest, blocking his way.

"I know what you are doing," Parris sneered, his iced breath chilling Killian's ear as the man leaned into him.

Killian side stepped the monster, turning toward him with a scowl as he straightened his jacket, as if he could wipe away the icy filth that the vampire had infected him with.

"Do you?" Killian said, keeping his voice dark as he stepped closer until Parris was a minuscule spec standing in Killian's shadow. "Because it seems to me that you are following my footsteps and picking up any clues I leave behind."

The deep rumble of Killian's statement had meant to be a threat, but instead Parris' pale face twisted into a maniacal smile.

"Perhaps if you stopped dropping them there wouldn't be anything to find."

Killian did not like the way the vampire was twisting his words, the way his eyes glistened. The man had obviously found something, but how? Killian had always been so careful to cover his tracks. Well, before Ellie. These poor souls may know something, they may give Parris what he was looking for.

Killian wouldn't let that happen.

"You will not find the phoenix before I do," Killian warned, knowing that there was only truth there. Confidence infected his voice, knocking against Parris, who didn't even flinch.

"Who said I am still looking for that nightmarish creature?" he hissed under his breath as Ceres began yelling for them from across the hall. "I can get what I want simply by taking down the one thing that stands in my way."

Parris stepped away from him, but the air remained icy

and chilled in his wake, a panic gripping Killian that froze him to the bone.

"And I have already done that," Parris said with a grin so wide it could have easily sliced his face in half.

Parris didn't wait for Killian's response before he slinked away, joining Ceres and Dabria who had now began tracing the veins of their prey.

Dread ripped through Killian, his dragon screaming inside of him in a need to flee that Killian had never experienced. He had never lost, but he couldn't ignore the desire to run, to message Jarron and hide the girl who was very clearly in danger.

It pulled him back, even as his mind pulled him forward, knowing that there would be more danger in leaving without knowing what the Vampires had discovered, and how close that danger truly was.

Ceres called to his son with an eager hunger in his eyes, the look pulling through Killian until he knew there was no other way but forward.

His shoes slid against the blood-soaked stone as he walked toward his father, past the kid with the backpack, a girl with grey eyes, and Brayden, who had very clearly already been tortured.

6

ELLIOT

I should have known they would be staying in a suite.

Even without Killian's obviously way-to-expensive suits, Jarron was always a bit too perfectly coiffed for the morning, like he had taken a bath in lavender oils and given himself a facial with slugs or some shit. Not that I was complaining. If I could get super model smooth skin like Jarron by bathing with slugs and goldfish I would probably do it too.

Given the size of the bath tub that was tucked into the corner of their bathroom I would gladly take that opportunity right now.

I had stolen a few minutes to "relieve myself," which mostly meant turning every fluffy white towel this room had to offer into dark grey masses that were covered with ash. It probably would have been easier to take a bath. I had scrubbed every bit of exposed skin I could find, but it really didn't do much. I was still streaked with ash, blood, and some sticky white substance that I didn't want to know the origin of. I looked like a child's drawing of a kitten.

You know what it's supposed to be, but you can't quite

tell if it's a cat, a windmill, or a fairytale princess on a ski trip.

That's kind of how I was feeling right now, too.

Phoenix-Fae-Dragon hybrid. I wouldn't be shocked if Zoe was going to tell me I was part Vampire too. Everything and anything was on the table now.

"Are there any other surprises we need to be aware of?" Jarron snapped as I opened the door to the bathroom, revealing the three siblings sitting in what the hotel was trying to pass off as a living room. You know, if living rooms were where you conducted board meetings.

A small couch and two chairs upholstered in the same fabric as the bedspreads faced each other, or rather, faced the massive vase of flowers that someone had placed on the low coffee table between them. Long stemmed flowers shot into the air like fireworks, bursts of fake blossoms adding color, and dust to the room.

It was ridiculous, and they looked ridiculous as they all bantered, scowling at each other from behind the azaleas.

Three powerful dragons, and none of them with enough sense to move a vase of flowers.

"Nothing more than I told you," Zoe said, twisting herself to look at Jarron. "Not that I can promise something else won't pop up. We are kind of in uncharted territory."

"More so than me being a Phoenix-Fae-thing?" I asked, relocating the vase to the floor before collapsing onto the couch next to Jarron, the guy jostled right into me in a not so accidental action, his arms wrapping around me as he hoisted me into his lap.

Into his hard, soft, muscular lap. With his body pressed against mine, his muscles against my back, his hips pressing into mine.

Pulling me into him, into his fire.

A low purr rumbled in my chest, my fingers clenching into couch and thighs as a dragon growl echoed from the other side of the room.

Drake wasn't usually the one to get all hot and bothered over me being with Jarron, and sure enough it wasn't him. He sat, fixing us with the tiniest of smiles, eating jerky and sipping water like his life depended on it. Which it probably did, near death experience and all that. Whatever Suvi had dragged him around to do after hadn't helped either.

He looked pale, and seeing him there made me want to rush over and fix it, which probably wouldn't help ease the frustration of the dragon who was growling.

Zoe sat with her hands clenched around the arm rest of the chair, her face twisted into one of the most severe of scowls I had ever seen.

The savior of my virtue to the rescue. Yeah, I totally rolled my eyes.

"Chill out, Zoe," I said, letting my grumps run free. Yeah, I knew it wasn't safe to be here. But I didn't want to move away from his warmth, from the way the seam of his shirt felt underneath my fingers, the way he shivered underneath me.

Oh damn. Yes, moving needed.

"We are wearing clothes and I have no plans on kissing him with you in the room, because I am sure you would explode."

Well, actually, I would be the one doing the exploding, but it was probably wise to keep the dropping bombs to ourselves for the moment. We already had enough to deal with. Like Fae. And Stacia. And the freaking King and his floozy of a side kick.

"Well, it's more important now than it has ever been." Zoe said, her brow furrowing even more, if that was possible. She looked as much like the disgruntled mother as I had ever seen her. But, of course, of the MILF variety. "We don't know how you will react with three mates, and we sure don't know what a Dragon will do if it mates with a Fae."

"Make a Phoenix, obviously," I grumbled, sliding from the comforting heat of Jarron's lap to the couch beside him, sagging against the floral upholstery with a sigh.

I may have been grumpy, but Zoe and Jarron looked like they had been slapped upside the head, Jarron's arm was still extended out toward where I had been a minute before. If it wasn't for Drake's slow chewing and Zoe's shivering pupils I would think I had frozen time.

"What?" I asked, looking between them.

"Don't tell me you two haven't put that together," Drake said behind a mouthful of jerky, his eyes smiling as he smiled and downed the rest of his water. "I mean, she can't be Fae without some Fae in her bloodline. And since we know who her father is, he must have mated with a Fae to create the egg. I mean, we do know that Elliot is the father, right? Zoe?"

Zoe shook her head as though emptying it of butterflies, meanwhile those damn bugs moved into my stomach like they owned the place, buzzing around and twisting my heart into unnatural positions.

"Are we really going to start discussing how I was created and by who?" I asked dryly, my mouth feeling like a cotton ball. "Because this feels like it should be a private conversation."

With me, and me, and no one else but me. Not this weird almost a reality TV show alternate universe I had clearly been sucked into. I swear if someone produced a manila envelope with the paternity results I was going to lose it.

I forced myself to swallow back the flames. No wonder my mouth was so dry.

"Yeah," Zoe gasped out, her eyes sliding in and out of focus as she stared at the flowers. I half expected them to burst into flames. "I mean, he brought her to me before we even started the coup. He said she was his, and that father was hunting her."

"She?" Jarron asked, the confusion catching me off guard. I mean, he had seen me naked so there shouldn't be any question of my gender, right? I wasn't that good at covering myself in the steam room. I was pretty sure I had experienced more than your standard nip slip.

"You can't tell gender before hatching," he continued, confusing me more.

"She wasn't an egg, she was a child. Maybe five years old?" Zoe whispered, looking from the flowers, to Drake, to Jarron, but not at me. She looked anywhere but at me, which certainly wasn't helping the whole furious confusion that was starting to make my skin prickle. "We had her in an orphanage in Italy, and then I took her with me when I faked my death, we traveled for about a year before I found Suvi and she was able to hide us more securely."

"So, perhaps she was not sired by a dragon?" Jarron asked, his arm tightening around me in comfort, or what he thought would be.

But I had had it.

"Will you guys knock it off!" I snapped, ripping myself from Jarron's side and scooting myself across the couch, which granted, didn't get me that far. "I'm sitting right here. And besides, none of this is making sense. I mean, obviously dragons hatch from eggs, and that's weird enough on its own. But if I was five, and then in an orphanage and then traveled the world with you," I nodded to Zoe, "don't you think I would remember that? I mean, I don't even know what my dad looks like, and I sure don't remember Zoe before she came to the circus *after* me. And even then, I got here when I was five. Not ten or whatever."

The guilt on Zoe's face was equal to the look you get from a five-year-old that was caught in a lie. And not some little, I painted my little sister blue lie. Like a life changing I'm really a vampire princess lie.

And good grief that better not be true, because seeing Stacia go all demon-Rambo had given me the fill I needed of vampires for the next century.

"Oh my god," I gasped aloud, "what did you do?"

"*I* didn't do anything," Zoe promised, although I wasn't having it. "Suvi bound your powers, but even she doesn't know what happened to your memories. They were there when I left you here, and gone a few years later. You didn't remember me when I got back."

"Bound my powers?" I asked as I tried to weed through Zoe's rant, looking from Drake to Jarron in hopes of some back up, except that this clearly wasn't as shocking to them as it was to me. "Wait."

I knew I should be dwelling on the whole bound powers' thing, what with all the time stopping, fire javelin breathing I was doing. But for me, days away from my eighteenth birthday, there was a much bigger problem.

"How old am I?"

I didn't think the guilt on Zoe's face could get any deeper, but it did. She might as well have been grey with it.

"Zoe," I prodded when she didn't answer, the boys at full attention now.

"I don't know for sure," Zoe began, all fire devoid from her eyes as she looked right at me. Everything about her was soft, as though it would help to ease the blow of whatever bomb she was dropping. I had a feeling it was going to make it worse. "You are definitely older than eighteen, possibly older than twenty. Maybe twenty-three?"

Talk about being hit in the face by a truck. I couldn't move, I could barely breathe, which was good because with the level of fire that was running through my veins I couldn't promise that I wouldn't burn down the mother fucking hotel.

"Happy Birthday," she finished lamely, waving her hands in the air in a silent celebration that was somehow a mockery.

Oh, I was gonna kill her. To think a few days ago I was celebrating having gotten my first kiss before I turned eighteen, and now, I was skipping a few birthdays as though I was playing a deranged game of chutes and ladders.

My instinct was to run, and with how my phoenix was bristling and pulsing against my heart, it was probably the safest bet.

But, I guess I was an adult now.

Just thinking that was like adding gasoline to a flame. Talk about adding a nail to my coffin. Well, not literally, because I am immortal, but you get the idea.

"Okay," I began, working very hard to regulate my breathing, which I was sure made me look like a mad man. "The second the sun is up and the cops are gone we need to go to Suvi, ask her to unbind my memories, and my powers. Then we will know what's going on. I mean, if I was that old, I have to remember something."

Even if it was what my father looked like, I would take it.

"I suggested the same," Drake said calmly, as he threw an empty bag of jerky in the trash and pulled another out of the brown bag Jarron had given him. I think that was bag number five, now.

"Great, then it's decided," I began, cutting him off and jumping to my feet. "Forget first light, let's go now. Track her down, end all of this now."

Instead of running head first into Suvi's trailer, if it was even still standing, Drake stopped me with a finger and a look that cooled the melted butter in his eyes to a dark caramel.

"There is a problem," he said, and I instantly sunk back into the couch, my stomach shifting to my toes. "With your power bound our father can't track you, for right now we need you safe."

"I think I would rather be able to protect myself and know who the fuck I am than be safe," I was illogical, and I knew it, I hadn't even seen the king, but the memory of the way the earth trembled beneath him, and the terrifying tremor in his voice made me want to hide in Suvi's protection forever. But I couldn't do that, not anymore.

I needed to face my own problems. Like the freaking adult I apparently was.

"You don't know what you are asking, darling," Jarron whispered, sliding close to me and gathering my hands into his. He dark eyes sparked with gold, reflecting the pink light of dawn that was filtering through the window. "We need to come up with a plan on how we are going to eliminate the king before we do that. It will be easier to take him down without him knowing you are here. But once the threat is gone, so is the binding."

"So, let me take him down with you. I am a Phoenix-Dragon-Fae thing, I've got to be pretty powerful," I said, squeezing his hands between my own. "Maybe I have a super-secret ability that will turn him into a hippopotamus or something. It can't be that hard."

This would be so easy. I could already imagine the epic

battle with me shooting fire bombs and glitter nets at the hippopotamus king. The rainbow of fear and concern that was painted on Jarron and Drake's brows, however, made it clear that it was not.

"There is something standing in our way," Jarron whispered and I quirked an eyebrow.

"I have seen Killian's dragon, unless whatever is 'standing in our way' is a nine-hundred-pound Tyrannosaurus Rex I am pretty sure we got this."

"It's not the brawn but the brains that are the problem in this fight," Jarron said, glancing at Zoe who gave him a slight head nod, like he was getting permission. I looked between them, but Zoe wasn't looking at me, and even Jarron was looking at his hands in anxious tension.

Oh god, it better not be a Tyrannosaurus Rex.

"There is a particularly meddlesome Vampire and a slut who likes to bed royals who seem to have their own agenda." Jarron began, his eyes digging right into me as both his words and the intensity of his stare sucked all the air from the room. "If we were to simply remove Ceres, it would not be a smooth transition to Killian's rule. Many people, both dragons and vampires alike, would rise up to challenge him. We have to eliminate the underbelly before we eliminate the tyrant."

I didn't know exactly who the vampire was, but after seeing Stacia go all full demon, and having Dabria in my head poking around like a masochistic therapist, I had a good idea who, or what he was talking about.

"If its Dabria," I said with a scowl "I can take her. That bitch is all talk..."

"And fire and spite and an affinity to backstab unlike anyone I have ever seen," Drake cut in. "I can only assume how much worse she has gotten in the last few years if she has climbed to the heights that she has. Of course, it helps when you can manipulate people's minds against them."

"Exactly," Jarron said with a snap of his fingers, "And who knows what lures she has implanted inside of Ceres' mind. I don't think she is foolish enough to poke around and manipulate him. But I wouldn't put anything past her, either. The last thing we need is her skills in Parris' hands. We have to play this very carefully."

"Fine," I interrupted, not wanting to hear much more about it. Dabria already grated on my hide, and thinking of her with Killian right now in whatever cave or city the dragons called home was bringing on a whole new level of jealous rage. "We leave my phoenix bound. That doesn't mean we can't unbind my memories. Because I would really like to get to know myself."

And perhaps my father too. The thought that I had somehow forgotten years of my life was already upsetting enough, but to think that I had some memory of my father locked up tight, that I had always known who I was, and perhaps even who my mother way made me all sorts of jittery. Well, jittery in the way that I wanted to know everything, run away from everything, and then throw up.

I was pretty sure I could avoid that last one.

"Suvi has tried to unbind your memories before," Zoe said with a sigh. "But like with Drake's dragon, only Fae magic can unbind Fae magic."

"So, you are saying a Fae waltzed in here and erased her memories, and no one stopped it?" Drake asked, his jerky forgotten in his lap.

"I feel like this is something you should take up with Suvi," Zoe mumbled, no longer looking at anyone.

"Who did Suvi let in here?" Jarron asked, his voice as

dark as his eyes were becoming. "I don't see that old bat letting anyone in here to wipe memories or otherwise."

"As I said," Zoe said with a tone as dark as Jarron's as she faced him head on. "You will have to take it up with Suvi."

I had thought the air had been sucked from the room before, but now it was downright toxic. I could taste the tension and anger, and the steam that was rippling from Jarron's skin wasn't helping.

"Stop it," I growled as I jumped to my feet, placing myself between Zoe and Jarron with my hands extended as if stopping dragon fights was my calling. Which it might be, I was getting a track record.

"I'm a Fae," I began, looking between the three of them. "I can freeze time. I used glowy hands to turn Drake back into a man. I am sure I can create purple sparks or something and bring back all my memories."

I dropped my hands as the daggers in their eyes began to fade, the animosity replaced by confusion. Which seemed fitting seeing as I had used the term "glowy hands" like it was a scientific term.

Maybe it was, not like I would know. Faeries had stolen my memories.

"Glowy hands?" Zoe repeated with a snort. "You sound ridiculous."

"You think I don't know that?" I hissed, holding my hands before me and staring at them intensely, well aware that I didn't know how to make them smoke, let alone glow, or bring back my memories. "I don't see you giving me many other options. So, sit back and watch the show."

Zoe sighed in that exasperated way that always drove me nuts and sat back in her chair, arms folded over her chest intent on watching the show. Which was fine, the more fuel to my fire the better.

I stood with my hands held in front of me as though I was holding a precious egg. *A dragon egg,* my subconscious provided, much to my surly displeasure. My skin warmed and buzzed as my phoenix bristled in agitation. It was a sensation that I had felt probably a million times before, uncontrollable heat rippling under the surface of my skin. This time however, I tried to control it and push all that buzzing fire power into my hands.

"Come on, glowy hands." The only thing that happened was that my hands began to smoke, and I looked more than a little constipated.

"Darling," Jarron whispered, wrapping his hands around mine as he stood in front of me, pulling my focus and thankfully dispersing the smoke, which smelled a bit too much like rotten eggs for its own good. Rotten eggs and constipation face, what a great and perfectly attractive combination.

"Please calm down, darling. There is always another way," I opened my mouth to retort, but he stopped me with that warm smile of his. The beautiful thing melted into me and sunk to my belly to reactivate all those damn butterflies. "And yes, I think I have another option."

He led me back over to the couch, Drake already waiting there, his lean muscle looking so welcoming as he leaned against the arm rest. I swallowed and looked away, I think I had enough on my plate with the whole Fae thing, I didn't really need Chastity Belt Zoe to add any more to that.

Of course, it's not like I could really get away from it. Jarron tucked me against him as he sat down, while Drake slid into the narrow space on the other side of me, effectively making an Ellie sandwich. A warm, melty, gooey Ellie sandwich. Including all the skin scalding horny heat that went with it.

Oh god. Talk about being slammed in the chest with hormones.

I took a deep cleansing breath, knowing that fresh air would do me good, and it may have if it didn't smell so much like smoke, pine, and whatever pheromone they were doused with.

Breathe. You're an adult now. You can handle an Ellie sandwich.

That sounded wrong.

Oh my god.

I can't believe I said that.

Breathe.

"What's the option?" I said, aware my voice sounded like it had been run through a meat grinder.

Zoe sighed exasperatingly and stood up, scuttling over to a weird looking end table near the front door, "Will you two back off and let the poor girl breathe?"

Zoe gave them one look before she opened the cabinet looking thing and pulled out a teapot. It might have been the best thing I had seen all day. You know, after Jarron's smile, and Drake's sinewy muscles. But it was better than psychotic vampires.

"The last thing we need is a hormonal explosion," Zoe said with her back turned to us, and I barely contained the snort.

Jarron, however, fixed me with a knowing wink as he scooted away, well inched away. It was as much as the tiny couch would allow, and gave me breathing room while not much else. Drake lifted himself to sit on the arm rest, although his fingers remained on the back of my neck, lazily coiling around the strands of my hair and tracing the lines of my neck.

Jarron saw the lingering touch, and leaned back into me,

his fingers trailing over the ash residue on my warm up pants.

"Just because I am suddenly twenty now doesn't mean you are going to get in my pants any easier." I had said it without thinking, each breathless syllable escaping my lips and increasing my blush until Jarron laughed, Drake pulled away, and Zoe dropped the teapot, sending the blue tea over the floor in a spot that looked like a bloody stain.

Great. I was going to have to defeat this hormonal origami on my own.

I can do that. Yeah, just try not to focus on soft fingers, and dark eyes and...

"Oh my god," Zoe groaned, giving both us and the teapot a look full of all the blame. Not my fault if she can't hold onto a teapot. "I'm going to have to put a nanny cam in your room."

"Jeez, Zoe, chill," I sighed and tried to scoot away from both Jarron and Drake, not that I wanted to, but I also didn't need Zoe spying me.

Well, that and breathing sounded like a really good idea right about now.

Not that it helped, Drake may have given me space, but Jarron was still tracing a dozen invisible lines on my back, well until Drake batted him away. "Let her breathe."

"What's your idea?" I said to Jarron, ready to move the conversation back to somewhat safer territory and ignore Zoe's keeper of the virtue look.

"Callay." Jarron said simply, and thankfully this time I knew enough to understand.

So did everyone else, it seems, and they weren't about to sugar coat it.

"You mean Killian's slave?" Zoe snarled, as she walked back over to us, a tiny teacup in hand. I guess there was more tea or leaves or whatever. or maybe she scooped it up off the floor. I didn't really care enough to question.

But I also couldn't drink. I knew Jarron had tiptoed around the word before, but hearing it now with so much hatred was burning my heart in a new pain. Slave was so much worse than servant. So much more painful.

Jarron had told me how Ceres had enslaved the Fae. But now I was one, my mother was one, and that foul word cut deeper than it ever had before. My phoenix prickled up at the pain, sparks of fire twisting through my veins as my heart seized.

"Yes, but she is sympathetic to our cause. she can help," Jarron said, his voice as tight as the line in his jaw.

"I don't care how sympathetic she is, she is still bound to Ceres," Zoe said, shoving the teacup at me as she towered over us, hands on her hips. "She chose to tie her power to him. She chose to keep her power to serve him. You can't trust the slaves, Jarron."

"We can trust her. Not all those who have vowed slavery remain loyal to him," Jarron said, his hand winding over my waist protectively. The touch sparked a million little fires over my skin, the heat of our connection blending with the rage that was already smoldering until it felt like a white-hot heat inside of me.

The same as it had when I had seen Drake's dragon lying there, covered in gold and blood.

"If we want to unbind Ellie's memories, she may be our only chance," Jarron said with a snap, his voice suddenly a million miles away.

My heart pulled toward him, my magic pulled toward some unfamiliar history, a past that I hadn't know was mine. But I sat still, feeling the pulse of power in veins, watching the water in the teacup begin to boil.

7

ELLIOT

"I saw that," Drake said the moment the door had closed behind Zoe and Jarron.

Zoe insisted that she needed to get more tea from Suvi after I had refused to drink what she had recovered from the now stained carpet. I had wanted to go with her, demand info on Fae and memories and everything in between, but considering the last six hours. Now was not the time.

Well, that's what Jarron had insisted, and I had insisted he get as much info as he could from her while he retrieved the tea with Zoe.

I think he wanted to get rid of Zoe, not that I was going to fight him. It was late, or early, or something. The sun was coming up, the smoke had cleared, and the view from the large balcony looked like something out of a post-apocalyptic movie. The smoldering remains of my life.

Like a phoenix from the ashes, I will rise.

The phrase was something akin to a cruel irony now.

"Saw what?" I asked innocently as I sunk back onto the couch, curling my legs onto the tiny thing, fully intending to sleep like a hibernating bear. Well, sans snoring. I hope.

Drake fixed me with a look and glanced at the still steaming tea cup, the tiny porcelain thing sitting in the middle of the flower exempt table. Steam curled from the surface in perfect spirals, the faint pink lines as unnatural as they could get. Or rather, as unnatural as I could get them.

They had been chattering about some plan to get Callay and I together, but I had been creating interesting boiling patterns in my teacup.

Jarron may have been oblivious, but Drake was far more observant than his brothers.

"How did you do it?"

I shrugged, which was quite a feat seeing as I was curled into hibernating bear mode. "I'm not sure."

I'm sure I looked ridiculous, not that Drake cared, he settled down into the tiny sliver of couch that I wasn't occupying and pulled my feet over him, the same as we had done on the nearly identical couch in my room at least a dozen times before.

"Do you feel hot when your dragon is angry?" I asked, twisting until I lay over him, my feet dangling off the edge of the couch, and keeping my filthy shoes away from him.

"Yes?" he said, obviously confused as he began to poke at a hole in my warm up sweats that I hadn't seen before. I mourned the loss of the comfy pants, but everything I was wearing was officially toast. Again. "Does your phoenix?"

I nodded, trying to swallow away the twisting steam that the gentle touch of his finger against my thigh was infecting me with. It wasn't working.

"When I am angry. Jealous. When you and your brothers touch me," or look at me, or smile at me, or are near me, or think of me from a hundred miles away, I continued internally. He may already have an idea about how out of control my hormones are, but I don't think I was ready to openly admit that yet. "She's an emotional creature."

"So, this?" he asked nodding to his fingers as they began to move over the now frayed seam of the pants, trailing toward my knee as he flicked at a dozen more pin holes. Each time I felt the warmth of his fingers a million little sparks of fire ignited in my veins.

So much for hiding the extent of what he was doing to me. I was officially having trouble breathing.

"Ecstasy," I gasped out, and he smiled, his eyes shining with the yellow light of the sun as it began to clear the mountains. The warm brown burned into me, even as his hand left my knee and a tiny smile twisted over his lips. "I won't push you too far."

He said it, but I could tell he didn't want to. Just as I didn't want him to stop.

Well, didn't want him too and needed him too were two different things. I had burst into flames when I kissed Jarron, I wasn't ready to play with fire again, especially with no tea in my system.

I had already been partially responsible for burning down a building today.

"Is that how you did it then?" Drake asked, nodding to the teacup. "Your phoenix?"

"I have no clue," I said, sinking back into the couch. "It's like with you..." I froze, not sure how to continue. "I don't know how I did that either, it just happened."

Drake was no longer looking at me, he was staring at the teacup as though the thing was going to sprout wings and take off into the dawn. Something that he could no longer do, I realized. Not with his wing like that, not with his father ready to kill him. He had told me that silks had been the closest he had been to flying in years.

I was starting to understand what that meant.

"Did it hurt?" I asked, biting my cheek the moment the words had left my mouth.

I don't think I had ever regretted a question more.

"It hurt when they did it," he whispered, still not looking at me. "It hurt in the beginning when I couldn't block my dragon. But it got better. I learned to lock that part of me away. I learned to forget who I was."

"Who you are," I corrected without thinking, his focus finally leaving the teacup to stare at me, the honey brown of his eyes glistening. "I had to lock my phoenix away, too. I did until I jumped off Moscow Tower. I shifted before I hit the ground. I still had to hide her, but she was still part of who I am. Just like your dragon is part of you, and part of me now too."

"You jumped?" He asked, his eyes wide as his hand wrapped tightly around my leg.

I swallowed and looked away, my phoenix screaming in pain as my eyes began to burn in threat of an emotional downpour. I was not interested in letting him see those tears. Any tears really. But these are the worst.

"I was thirteen, or I thought I was thirteen," I corrected, "I was alone. It wasn't an accident."

The desire to run hit me loud and clear, but I ignored it, needing to be here

"I had planned my first climb of El Capitan to be my last." He admitted, his thumb trailing over my cheek and wiping away the lone tear that trailed down my cheek. "It's the hardest free climb in the world. Every time I have climbed it, I have planned to fall. And every time something pulled me forward. My dragon pulled me forward."

His fingers left a trail of heat behind, the touch lingering on my cheek like glitter. I gasped at the touch, at the pull I felt for him, but for the first time I didn't want to jump him. I didn't want to meld myself into him. I wanted to be here with him, loving him.

"I'm glad you didn't give up." I said with a gasp, the tight bind of emotion making it hard to get the words out.

"I'm glad you didn't either." His own tears burst from his eyes, two tiny tears training over his cheeks like little drops of melted honey.

I leaned closer, brushing the wet away, ready to risk it all and kiss him. I would have too, if memories of burning tents, flesh, and everything else wasn't quite so close to the surface.

"I'm glad I found you," he said, his voice haunted as he began to untie and remove my foul sneakers, the things were so caked in blood that I didn't want to think about what was gluing it to the rubber and canvas.

Except I knew.

I knew because the way Drake was sitting gave me the perfect view of the long scars that covered his arm, and the gentle tattoos that tried to conceal them. Long spindly lines, that cut into my heart as effectively as they cut into his skin.

"Why did you tell me they were from a climbing accident?" I asked as I reached forward, my now removed shoes hitting the floor with a thump.

"I wasn't ready to tell you what really happened," he whispered, his voice breathless as he stared forward, each muscle of his arm tensing and flexing under my touch. "You saw my dragon. You had bonded to someone who can't really protect you. I can't shift, I can't save you. I didn't want you to be disappointed."

"I am not disappointed," I said, touching his shoulder and pulling his focus. "And you aren't useless. I am, however, going to find a way to fix it."

I gave him a smile as my fingers continued to trace the lines of his tattoo, to trace the deep gashes that were hidden far beneath.

"Elliot," Drake whispered, placing his hand over mine, trapping our skin and the heat together until the fire from his dragon began to roll over me in waves. "I know you mean well, but these gashes. There is no way to heal them."

"Well, I don't know if you've heard, but I am a Fae-Dragon-Phoenix. Who knows what I will be able to do," I tried to smile, I tried to let the hope in my heart infect him, but the look on his face was so devastating that I could feel it infecting me.

Like hell if I was going to let it.

"I'll fix it," I promised. He clearly didn't believe me.

"You can't fix this, Ellie," he gasped, his eyes swelling with tears. "There is no way to stop them from spreading. From killing."

"What are you saying?" I asked, the last word a stab against my heart, trying to pull away from his hand as he held it against him, the fire fueled heat of a minute ago having shifted to the burn of ice and failure.

"The fire that is burning away my dragon, it doesn't go away. Nothing can stop it. It will burn me until there is nothing left."

I had about enough of bad news for the day, I had about enough of the ugly fates of the world trying to take away the things that were important to me.

It may be my stubbornness talking, it may be the last of my teenage foolishness, but I wasn't going to sit back and let the world take away one of the most important things in my life.

My skin burned in waves of gold as I jumped to sitting, pressing myself against him until we sat in a bubble of heat, his dragon purring in the radiated warmth as his flame blended with mine. My phoenix burned between our hands, the fire in his eyes burning in the brightest red as his hands heated, and his skin began to smoke.

I was sure that he wasn't alone in that, but I wasn't about to check. I had more important things on my mind than if I was about to burst into flame.

"You climbed a mountain, determined to die, and something pulled you forward..."

"And you jumped from a building, determined to--" he cut me off, but I served it right back to him, snapping loudly as I stopped his retort.

"And something in me wouldn't let me give up that easy." I said, leaning into him until all I could see where the soft tears rolling down his cheeks, the tiny drops of water that clung to his eyelashes reflecting the fire in my eyes. "I won't let you give up that easy, Drake. I will find a way to fix it."

"Are you always this stubborn?"

"Oh, all the goddamn time," I smirked, he laughed, and before my brain could think better of it, I leaned forward, pressing myself against him, pressing my lips against his.

The heat that was already buzzing through my veins erupted at the touch, the burning fire of phoenix and who knew what else consuming me. I pulled away, panic nearly extinguishing the flame as I looked at my arms, expecting the same gold and pink flames of before, but there was only ash streaked skin.

"What is it?" Drake asked, his hand running down my thankfully normal arm, threatening to ignite me all over again.

"Nothing," I gasped, my hand on his chest as I stared at him, as the beat of my heart thundered in my ears, and my heart pulled me forward.

I knew I shouldn't. I knew I was already playing with fire. But I was already playing, I might as well win the game.

Clenching his shirt, I pulled him toward me, coaxing him lower as I lay back on the couch, his hips pressing against me, his lips crashing into mine.

His forestry aroma assaulted me, drowning me in images of mountains and soaring through the trees. I lifted myself to him, dragging my lips over his jaw and closer to his ear, my smile spreading as he began to shiver.

Pressing my lips against the hollow of his jaw, I shivered as a low moan drifted from his throat, the sound driving me mad. I trailed my lips and tongue back to his, the sound growing deeper as his dragon joined in.

That sound, the way his eyes where heating into me. It was going to be the end of me.

He turned before I could get closer and captured my lips with his, the tip of his tongue tracing against mine as I let my fingers trail down his back, touching the tiny strip of exposed skin at his waistline.

I lifted his shirt, ready to pull it over his head when the door to the room burst open, and Jarron charged in, thankfully with no Zoe on his heels.

I didn't want to know what would have happened with her, it was bad enough with Jarron standing there, a knowing smirk on his lips. I had never seen Drake move faster than he did in his attempt to get off me.

"I guess I should have been quicker with the tea," he teased, giving us a wink as the door to the room snapped shut behind him.

"I... ummm..." I began, but Jarron stopped me with a smirk and a wave of his hand. Drake was now sitting on the other side of the couch, straightening his shirt as if it would make him look less incriminating.

My ashy fingerprints all over his face were bad enough.

"No, worries, darling. My baby brother is part of the bond as I am. Enjoy him tonight. I'll be with you tomorrow," Jarron teased, leaning against the table where bags of blue and green leaves were now piled.

It looked like the spoils of a drug deal, you know, if Dr. Seuss was a drug dealer.

"This isn't a competition, Jarron," I scolded, but he smiled, blew me a kiss, and began to walk toward what I assumed was a bedroom.

"Come get me if she explodes," Jarron teased as he left us with a wink and walked into one of the side rooms.

"Oh my god," Drake said, collapsing back onto the couch, his eyes full of shock. "Is that a concern? Exploding?"

I sighed, leave it to Jarron to ruin this for me. He probably did it on purpose.

"That was one time!" I called after him, Drake's face filling with even more alarm. "It was one time," I repeated to Drake, it did nothing to settle his nerves. He was now checking the couch for scorch marks.

"Awesome," I grumbled, climbing off the couch and chasing after Jarron. "No competition my ass."

"You did that on purpose," I ranted as I slammed the door open, the wooden entry swinging to reveal Jarron, shirtless, standing in the middle of the room.

He was in the middle of changing, his shirt balled on the floor, his pants unzipped and partially pulled down, revealing the narrow v of his hips, the checker print of his boxers. It was all too much. I had seen him in the steam room, seen every muscle and every deep chiseled line of his supermodel body. But this was worse.

Because now it was mine, and the need to feel every one of those lines felt like an addiction.

"I.... I..." I couldn't get anything out more than that.

In fact, it was close to a miracle that I was still dressed and standing in one place. I should be in his arms already, all wrapped up in Jarron.

No. I needed to get out of here. If only I could make myself move. I was pretty sure my feet had been stapled to the floor.

"Ellie?" He asked, obviously concerned, even

"Sex..." I gasped, shock spreading his face into a smile as all blood was drained of mine. I did not just say that. "Your sex... I mean. You're sexy..."

Oh. My. God.

Can I please disappear right now?

"So are you, darling," Jarron whispered, his dark eyes drawing me in as he stepped closer, the muscles that clung to his hips flexing and pulling with each step, drawing me closer. "I think we need to get you some tea, darling. We don't need you to explode."

No, don't need tea. I needed to take off those pants the rest of the way.

"Again, explain the exploding," Drake said from right behind me, his hand moving to my back as he joined us. His touch was the last thing I needed. It was like a freaking nuclear bomb against my already frayed nerves. "And for Christ's sake put your shirt back on, Jarron."

Or keep it off forever. Your choice either way.

"Are you okay, honey?" Drake whispered as he turned to me, his breath running over my neck as his fingers pressed against my back. As Jarron's eyes began to spark with lines of gold.

Too much. It was too fucking much. Heat. Muscles. Smiles. Eyes.

"Sexy," I said again, I was clearly delusional, and Drake's embarrassed smirk was so not helping to ease that.

"Let's get you some tea, darling," Jarron said as he reached me, his hand inches from my own.

"No!" I nearly yelled, side stepping both his and Drake's touch, my alarm sliding into place as the buzz of heat began to take over.

I really couldn't take much more, one more touch and I would explode. I was amazed I hadn't burst into liquid flame already.

"I'm... I'm going to take a bath," I gasped out, the words barely making an appearance as I made my way toward the massive tub I had seen before.

If I was going to explode I might as well be near water.

I could really only afford to destroy one hotel room a month.

I was already at my limit.

8

JARRON

Nothing about Rydaim felt like home to Jarron. Not anymore. Not since Ellie.

The air stuck to his skin, the aroma of smoke and death that clung to the stone that he had once found so comforting was now a shadow across his heart that reminded him why he was here, and what he had left behind.

He hated being here as much as he assumed Killian did. Neither of them wanted to be away from her, but being away from her was the best form of protection they could give her.

He had rushed here with the intent to bring Callay to Ellie, and after a few minutes here he could smell the lingering panic that always infected this city.

"Jarron!" The shout rippled through the crowd of the morning market, adding to the cloud of noise as hundreds of dragons mingled and wandered from shop to shop and to the slave market near the center. Even through all the noise, and the muddled haggling he was surrounded by, he recognized the shout.

"Good morning, Sebastian!" Jarron announced as the pre-teen reached him, his lanky frame busting at the seams of his previously well-tailored shirt and trousers. His family was nowhere near hurting, but the closer a boy grew to shifting age, the more they grew, and if Sebastian's growth was any indication, his dragon was going to be huge.

"How is the market this morning?" Jarron asked, ruffling the dark brown shag of Sebastian's hair and taking an apple from a vendor who was openly ogling him. The balding man had owned this stand for nearly four hundred years, his family even longer, and Jarron knew him well.

Not because his apples where widely considered the juiciest grown in the caves, but because of what he hid in orchards. Jarron had recently discovered that the long expanse of trees was one of the keys to the underground that was smuggling both the forgotten and the slaves out of Rydaim. Jarron was still working to gain his trust. He had been content to take his time before, but now the timeline felt smothering.

"Thank you, my friend," Jarron uttered, pressing more than double the amount of the apple into the aging dragons' hand and continuing on his way, the prattling teen still right on his heels.

"Busy," Sebastian provided, stepping before Jarron like an escort and breaking apart at least seven chatting woman who instantly started batting their eyelashes at him like oddly deformed butterflies.

Jarron's heart tensed at the lustful looks the woman gave him, at least two he recognized of having wooed previously. His dragon growled at the way one of their hands attempted to wander, reaching toward him as he attempted to pass.

His heart was no longer on the market. He would give anything to alert these women to that fact, but any hint to him having been taken would alert his father, so instead he winked, tossed one of the girls his untouched apple and tweaked another on the cheek, his heart and soul screaming even as they swooned and giggled.

"They say there is to be an execution soon," Sebastian continued, blushing as one of the women tapped his cheek, whispering something about how cute he was. "Is that why you are here?"

"No, and I believe the execution was last night" Jarron said, wracking his mind as to what the kid was talking about. He hadn't heard anything about an execution, of course he had only landed in Rydaim about an hour before. He hadn't even been able to make it home and speak to Callay, as that was the whole reason for his visit. He had been making his rounds through the market, checking with every contact, and hearing any news he may have missed.

Even through all that, there was nothing about an execution. Well, unless you counted Drake's death, and that news was everywhere.

"My bastard brother was killed last night," Jarron said, choosing his words carefully as he began to make his way toward the slave trade that always built up around the fountain this time of day. He needed to get there before Matthias sold his bounty. One of the silk sellers spoke of one of The Forgotten that had been found with their magic still intact. All magic was cut from the Fae that did not swear to the king. But, this one was uncut, unsworn. They would be sold today, and Jarron needed to be there.

Judging by the crowd around the fountain, the news had traveled faster than expected.

Luckily the grey-haired man still stood in turn, at least five Fae bound and gagged beside him.

"Perhaps that is the execution you were hearing about?"

Jarron finished, his mind already drifting to the slaves and from the still hovering kid.

"I guess," Sebastian muttered, tugging at the too short sleeve of his linen shirt. "They did say it was the king's son."

"Yeah, we found him in a circus," Jarron said, making his way toward the front as the seller before Matthias began to finish up, Sebastian still glued to him. Luckily, as a prince it wasn't too hard to reach his destination. Most of the dragons shrunk to the side, eager to make way for him.

"A circus?" Sebastian asked in awe as they made it to the front and the last of Lorna's slaves was sold to Sasin. "You mean with like clowns and elephants and stuff?"

"Sure kid." Jarron wasn't even listening anymore, he was staring at Sasin, trying to decide if the man had heard about the uncut Fae or not. The man was a slave collector, his estate full of Fae in deplorable conditions. He didn't want to know what the man would do with a Fae with raw magic.

Jarron, however, knew exactly what he would *do* with them.

Get them the hell out.

Sasin already held five red slips that he would exchange for his purchased slaves after the close of the market, he may have already spent his daily allotment, but judging by the number of gold rings on the man's fingers he doubted.

He was ready to fight, and he never backed down his bids. Not against Jarron, not against the King. He was ruthless. This would be a fight.

Matthias took to the fountain, dragging his slaves behind him as the crowd began to murmur, fingers pointing, and wide eyes stares all directed at the same person, a young girl of about seventeen, if he had to guess. Her mossy brown hair was matted and clumped together, her pouty lips cracked and bleeding, she was tiny beneath the oversize rags the slaves usually wore.

But all of that was normal for these poor souls. It was her arms that was causing all the interest. The skin had obviously been scrubbed clean, revealing the perfectly smooth uncut forearms that you saw in the slaves distributed and trained by the palace.

Uncut Fae didn't exist outside the kings' control. The knowledge of where this girl had come from was dangerous in the wrong hands.

Matthias began a show of re-shackling his wares to the post, showing teeth and breasts and everything else before the chattering crowd fell silent, and Jarron's father emerged right beside him.

The appearance of the king and his entourage sent Sebastian and a few others scuttling. Jarron however didn't even move, even though the air had become filled with a chill that wasn't from the icy soul of his father.

"Father," Jarron greeted him without looking. "Parris."

"Young prince," Parris said as he came to stand on the other side of him, the slime that Jarron had come to associate with him dripping from his voice. "Welcome home. How does it feel to be the youngest son?"

"Wonderful," Jarron said with a grin that sliced against his heart. The lie weighing heavy as he played right into the sadistic pairs' hands. "I burned the bastard until there was nothing left. I am sure the mortals will never be able to remove the stain."

Ceres laughed with a rumbling sound that cut through the whispers of the few dragons who were pressing in on them, desperate to be close to their God. Parris, however, fixed him with a smile that did not reach his eyes, the deep color twisting uncomfortably through Jarron.

He had never seen the vampire look so vicious. He must be hungry. No wonder he was here. Fae blood, even the blood of the Fae without magic was like a drug to his kind. And to have magic here... the thought twisted in Jarron's stomach like a sickness. He couldn't let the bastard get a hold of the girl.

"I assume you have heard of the female," Jarron said, happy to pull his focus from the twisted Vampire, and nodded toward the girl who was now stripped to her under-things, her arms still clearly on display.

"Indeed," the King snarled, a hungry greed taking over his stare, his tongue darting out to lick his lower lip as the girl cried.

Perhaps it was more than Parris that he needed to save this girl from. This was beginning to feel like a fool's mission.

"I would love to know where they found her," he said, still looking at the girl who was now looking directly at him, her silver eyes bright with fear.

It was clear she knew who he was.

"I trust you will secure the girl for me," Ceres said, turning to stare at his son, a hunger in his eyes that made Jarron's stomach seize.

He needed the girl for himself, not for his father. His father clearly saw Jarron's desire, but Jarron had no other choice.

"Of course," he said with a nod, his spine in twisted knots as he stood before the king, fixing his face into the nearest form of platitude that he could.

He had never defied his father before, at least not to his knowledge. Over the last few years, he had success-fully hidden his espionage, and he would not falter now. Not in that way. Not now when everything was littered with landmines, and the most precious thing of all was at stake.

Thinking of Ellie calmed his nerves and he smiled, the joyous thought of his mate twisting into the deep grin that his father easily misinterpreted as malice.

"Wonderful," The king said darkly, the tone in his voice so vile that Jarron fought the need to step back. Assisted by the fact that the Vampire still stood behind him. "See that she is in my chambers before nightfall."

"And see that I get a bite before you do," Parris hissed in his ear, the king laughing at the request before they both walked away. The crowd behind them parted like the sea, the heads of his people bowing like a wave.

Jarron's heart pounded in his chest as they left, heart aching at the thought of the girl, and what was sure to happen if he did as his father asked.

The auction began with a roar, prices called out as the auctioneer rambled through them all, selling one slave after another, edging closer and closer to the girl. Her tears flowed freely as she looked around her, pleading with some-one, anyone to save her.

But there was no one, not even Jarron could save her now.

The girl was pulled forward as the auction began, Sasin out bidding everyone, even the few half-hearted bids that Jarron was able to stutter out.

"Twelve hundred," Sasin called out in reply to Jarron's eleven-fifty, the older man's smug face painted with the chal-lenge that they had both been wrapped up many times before.

Twelve hundred was a pittance for both of them, they were probably both wearing jewelry that was worth more. Sasin just on his pinky finger. Jarron had bid against the collector enough to know that if he wanted something bad enough he wouldn't stop bidding until he got what he wanted, no matter who was against him.

And he really wanted this.

This girl with the tear stained face, and the wide eyes that were now looking right into Jarron, pleading for him to win.

He knew why. He had a reputation. He was kind. The golden prince. She knew of him, but she also knew of Sasin, unbeknownst to her, however, Sasin was the lesser of two evils.

She would survive with him.

She would survive.

The thought slammed against Jarron's chest, the guilt already pulling through him with what he was about to do. It had been decades since he had defied his father so openly, and he would pay for this choice, but the girl would pay less, and that was the best outcome she could hope for, even though she didn't know it.

He gave the girl one last sad look as he made two more bets for her life, and then, with a solitary tear sneaking down his cheek, he turned and walked away.

9

KILLIAN

A CRASH RUMBLED THROUGH THE AIR WITH THE FORCE OF A bomb, the impact smashing against Killian's already sore muscles as the stronger than iron pool ball hit against the dark mahogany walls.

Killian loved those walls, he loved the color and the way the light reflected off them in waves. He had chosen them specifically for the game room to give the space a dark, earthy feel. Living in a cave, in a house with hardly any windows, the pull from nature was needed. It was desires. But with one throw the heavy wood cracked and splintered under the impact of the black eight ball as though it was plywood, the wood nearly shearing in two.

The ball, however, fell to the tile floor with a thud, cracking more tile, and rolling away completely unharmed.

Damn dragon bone. The stuff was practically indestructible, which made it both helpful and irritating in his current need for chaos and destruction. Anything to diffuse his anger. The emotion was practically dripping from him. Cracking the walls of one of his favorite rooms was not calming his frustration as he had hoped.

He would give anything to see the ball explode alongside.

"Feel better?" Callay asked, her smile wide as she walked in, balancing a tray piled with a teapot, cups, and a few cakes. Afternoon tea. How very European of her. He had missed this while in the states, but now hardly seemed like the time to reintroduce it.

Callay didn't even seem phased by Killian's explosion, or the accompanied dark-eyed glare. Unsurprising, since she had served him for the last hundred and fifty years. She knew him well, which was often a good thing. In this situation he wasn't too sure.

She had spent the last hundred and fifty years as his slave. A gift from his father on his hundredth birthday. He had always trusted her before, he had no reason not to, but after the hours spent torturing mortals and hiding information he was questioning it.

That alone made him more irate. He didn't like his father under his skin, and the monster was most decidedly there.

The thought ground deeper and he let out a roar, throwing another of the dragon bone billiard balls into the wall, the impact slicing the air apart with another forceful boom.

This time the ball lodged in the wall, sitting amongst the already cracked wood like an ugly boil. Still, Callay did not jump, she walked past Killian as he fumed and heaved, placing the tray on the low antique table and dislodged the ball with a flick of her wrist.

"I thought you liked these walls," She said with a smirk, handing Killian the ball. He took it without even so much as a thanks. No matter what he would have said it wouldn't have sounded very thankful anyway.

"I can replace the walls." It was true, but it didn't stop his frustrated rumble. At this point, the walls didn't really matter. After what he had heard during Parris' party, none of this mattered.

The house. The city. He needed to get out of here. Which wasn't going to happen with how Parris was watching him. Although stalking seemed a more fitting word with how many of his minions Parris had set around his house.

"How many of Parris's little bloodsuckers are watching the house today?" He asked, bouncing the ball in his palm before throwing it again, his heart cracking as deeply as the wood did.

"More than yesterday," Callay said with far too much cheer given the situation. "But I still think your plan is possible, as long as there aren't too many more added complications. Oh, and I found the map."

Callay smiled brightly, her eyes shining silver as she snapped her fingers and a long roll of parchment appeared in her hand, the old thing was faded, ripped and even stained in some places.

Killian should have been overjoyed at the added instrument to his arsenal. He would have been if the Faerie didn't seem so giddy and her words choice so ominous.

"What do you mean by 'many more'?" He asked, carefully taking the map from the girl who smiled and turned to the tray, beginning to arrange the cups and cakes like she was going to host a little party. Knowing her, she was. "And why are there three cups?"

Killian had barely asked the question when the slam of a door echoed from the kitchen. The powerful dragon jerked at the sound, turning toward the door in preparation for attack when the irritating bubble of singing began bouncing over the stone and tile walls. Even if he hadn't dismissed the rest of his staff for the week he would know who it was.

There was only one person who was this irritatingly enthusiastic, and loud, this early in the morning.

"No." Pain twisted through him. Callay still arranging tea in eager party preparation, although he didn't understand why. There absolutely couldn't have been a worse time for his brother to make an appearance. Getting himself out while under Parris' smothering eye was proving hard enough.

There also wasn't a worse time for his brother to leave their mate alone with a broken dragon and his irritating sister. That he needed to fix first.

Everything in his life was so out of control that it was making his dragon unfurl in rage. Normally the beasts awakening would be a warm reminder of strength and power. But not lately. Lately, it had been nearly impossible to control his beast.

Having Jarron here was going to be a challenge.

"We are in here!" Callay called through Jarron's ruckus, her voice echoing to him, as his irritating whistles made a return to them.

Killian's brow furrowed even deeper, the look attempting to take over his face as he threw another ball into the wall. Now was not the time for this level of cheerfulness.

"He can help," the Fae continued in a low voice, the hushed declaration adding to the tension that was ripping through Killian's chest.

"Unless he is going to lay himself down like a sacrificial lamb, I don't see how that is possible."

She gave him a smile and began pouring tea, filling the room with the gentle aroma of mint, orange and cinnamon.

It was a mixture that only Callay made, he had tasted something similar once, nearly eighty years ago on a trip to Russia. The aromatic combination flavored the room in its attempt to make the stress float away. He was sure that the warm liquid was meant to do the same to him, but he wasn't sure how it would. His out of control dragon was already rumbling in both fire and fear.

"Drink," Callay said, handing him a teacup before turning to pour the next one. "And don't break the cups, it took me twenty years to convince you to buy them, and they happen to be my favorites."

Her smile was wide, the calm that radiated from her mixing with the tea and the fire in his chest loosened, well, until his brother charged in so excited he was practically glowing. One look at the damage that Killian had caused, however, and his face fell his joy blinking into worry before he began to laugh.

"I take it you know you are being watched," Jarron said with a nod to the splintered wall. "I always knew you would find a good use for those billiard balls."

"I can always think of another one," Killian warned, taking a sip of the tea, thankful when his dragon continued to lull.

Faintly, he wondered if this was what Ellie's tea felt like. This warm bath of calm and understanding. Killian sighed and took another sip, he didn't need to think about that now. Reminding himself about Elliot when the man who was supposed to be guarding her was here, and clearly not besides the girl.

"You mean like taking out Parris' men?" Jarron asked, gathering his own teacup from the tiny Fae and giving her a smile that instantly pushed her into a blush.

Callay had always had a soft spot for his younger brother. Any other owner would beat the emotion out of her, but Killian let it stay. He may not have always been that person, but he wanted to be it now. It wasn't all because of Ellie, either. Besides, Callay's little crush wasn't hurting anyone. Well, not yet anyway. He hated to think of the sting she would feel when she found out that he was officially taken.

"Why are they following you, Killian?"

"Why are you here?" Killian countered, not quite ready to answer his question. He didn't like failure, and this time it would be turnabout to that. So much for the tea, his dragon was up and bristling again.

"Something happened," Jarron paused, casting Callay a side glance, his worry clear.

He waved his brother off, "She knows. Well, she knows enough. She can put two and two together better than anyone, even without her superpowers."

"They aren't superpowers," Callay sassed, although it was barely loud enough for anyone to hear her. "And to answer your question, Jarron, you can trust me."

"No superpowers, eh?" Killian said, chuckling as he sipped his tea from the tiny little cup, grateful for the break in tension, even if his scowl hadn't decreased from the intense scowl of a super villain.

"I know we can." Jarron began, stepping closer to the Fae. Killian was amazed she didn't take one giant step back. But then, with the wide orbs of her eyes, she might be incapable. "You are the reason I am here, Callay. Our girl is in danger and I need you to return to the circus, both of you."

Killian slammed his own cup down on the pool table, some of the remaining content splashing over the edge and seeping into the green felt.

Callay gasped, hands flying to her mouth as she promptly dropped and shattered the tea cup that she had filled for herself. The shock was unsurprising, the Fae had never been out of Rydaim to his knowledge. If Killian had to guess, however, it was a bit more than that.

Jarron had said 'our girl.'

Her cup hit the tile with a clunk, tea spreading through the deep grooves of the grout in its plot to escape the now shattered porcelain. Callay jumped, diving down to clean it. Killian could have cared less if it had stayed there forever.

"What happened? Is she okay?" His dragon growled protectively, the danger blazing through Killian's eyes, but Jarron didn't back down. He didn't even flinch, just drained his cup and set it beside Killian's.

"She's fine. She's safe. But you two have more in common right now than I would have expected."

"What do you mean?" he wasn't even trying to control his dragon anymore.

"You both are surrounded by Parris's vampires."

One simple phrase had never enraged him more.

"What!" The few pool balls that remained on the table rattled under the anger in his voice. Jarron smiled and very nearly got himself punched.

Wouldn't have been the first time he smacked the smug look off his brothers' face.

"Calm down brother. I assure she is safe."

"Then explain." There was more growl than words to his voice. Jarron understood anyway.

"You know that strumpet at the circus? Stacia. She was one of those Russian acrobats. She has ties to your little friends." Jarron began nodding toward the shuttered window.

Killian had closed the wooden screen and drawn the

drapes the second the blood suckers had appeared. At least ten of them, posted in the crevices and window sills of every home and business that faced his estate.

"He's found her already."

"Who? Parris?" Jarron asked, with a shake of his head. "No, it appears that she was in hiding as well, used to work for the beast himself."

He said it as if that made any difference. Killian wasn't sure if it did anything other than make it worse.

Killian could have flipped the god damned pool table right then. His dragon screamed, fire boiling in his throat and he turned, ready to release it, only to find himself facing a very worried Callay, her hands waving at him.

"Don't, master," she pleaded, but the use of the disgusting title made him fume more.

"We have to get back to her." He growled, turning from Callay as his monster boiled in his chest. He was not willing to let the tiny Fae face the brunt of his anger.

"Which is why I came to get you, both of you."

"Why both?" Killian said, the words grinding between his teeth. There was no use trying to control himself, any answer that Jarron gave him was going to rile him right back up anyway.

"It's a long story," Jarron said, with a tone that deserved more than the shrug it received. "Much like your escorts, I assume? What are they doing watching you? I came from the market and the whole place is swarming with vamps. Although, everyone is talking about Drake's execution, so it looks like we shouldn't have anything to worry about there."

"Maybe not everyone," Killian said, grabbing one of the balls off the table and lunging it at the already shattered wood paneling. It hit the wall with a thwack, sending splinters of mahogany through the air as though a bomb had gone off underneath it.

No one flinched. Callay had busied herself with the tea set again, but Jarron was looking right at him, his eyes showing the faintest shimmer of his dragon, the lines of gold feeling like a death sentence.

"There is a chance they know about Elliot," He said, using his words carefully. He was sure Parris' men weren't listening, Callay had promised him the house was secure, but he had been through too much, had too much at stake to accept that as fool proof.

"Explain."

"Remember that lead father spoke of?" Jarron nodded, and Killian let one growl out before continuing. "He had Parris capture every eyewitness of that fall in Southern Utah a few days before we found Drake."

Careful wording, knowing glances, and Jarron's expression transformed from confusion to a dark anger that Killian could feel radiating from him.

Good. Let his brother be mad. They would need that if they had any chance of getting out of here.

"How sure are you?" Jarron hissed, careful to keep his voice low.

"They haven't arrested me yet. But," He waved his hand, indicating the dozens of Parris's disgusting minions that were stalking his every move. "*Yet*. I never got to interview the guy that *the jumper* walked up to the cliff with before they fell. I spoke to him the day after it happened, but one of Parris' little buzzards bit him and they carted him off before I could make my way over."

"So, we need to get out of here."

"Or destroy them all. Go down with a fight," Killian

growled, grabbing another one of billiard balls and wrapping his hands around it. "Time is no longer on our side."

He hated admitting it. It felt like a dirty failure, but there was no other truth right now. Everything in Rydaim had drifted further and further into chaos over the last few years; but it was the last few days that those strings of chaos had begun to show.

"Well, I vote we leave. Get back to Elliot. She might have a power inside of her that could help us win this fight," Jarron said, picking at the frayed edge of the rolled-up map that Killian had set inside of the pool table.

"Unless it's fire stronger than yours I doubt anything could stop the blood that is about to soak this place, Jarron."

"Well, we won't know until we get you and Callay out of here." His brother leaned closer to him, even as Callay took a step back, the tiny girl looking out of place for the first time.

"Don't worry, we are way ahead of you," Killian's dragon prickled against his skin as he snatched the map from underneath his brothers' hand and unfurled it over the table, pinning the corners down with the multicolored balls that attempted to roll away over the green felt.

He had seen many maps of Rydaim, but this one was special, this one was unique. He was surprised that Callay had been able to find a copy at all. Let alone in the hours after he requested it. The old thick parchment was trying to simultaneously disintegrate and roll back in on itself. Judging by the state of the paper, he wouldn't be surprised if the copy dated back to when they were first building the caves.

"What in the world is this?" Jarron asked, stepping to the other side of the pool table and leaning over the old parchment. Their heads cast weird shadows over the yellowed map, which wasn't helping in his attempts to read the thing. Besides the fountain in the middle of a large empty cavern, nothing about this was making any sense.

He may have never seen anything like it, but he had also hoped he would have been able to read it.

"It's the schematics from when they first began to build the cave." Callay said popping up beside them, sipping tea from her now repaired mug. "All the service tunnels. All the hidden alcoves. Every way you can get in and out, every place you can hide."

"Oh my god," Jarron gasped, reaching toward the parchment as though it was sacred. Perhaps it was, Killian might be mistaken, but he was fairly certain that the signature in the corner belonged to his grandfather.

The man who had started this all, nearly a thousand years ago.

"I didn't even know this existed."

"It doesn't, not officially," Callay said, "It's on loan from a friend and we can't keep it here long. It's too dangerous even without those leeches hanging around outside."

"Where did you get it?" Jarron asked, his voice still lowered in awe, his hands still fluttering over the surface.

"It's on loan from a friend," Callay repeated, emphasizing each word as she stared Jarron down. She had never been so forward with either of them, especially Jarron, who was now chuckling.

Killian, however, was staring intently at the lines and squiggles, trying to make sense of the lines, to find the connection from what Rydaim had been, to how the city was today, trying to understand it. But more than anything, he was trying to commit the entire thing to memory. Callay was right, the map couldn't be here long, he may never have another opportunity to see this, he wasn't going to let it go to waste.

"All right well make sure to tell this friend thank you," Jarron said, his voice spelling mischief. He didn't need to look up from the map, Killian could see the look his brother was giving her just in the tone of his voice. "It will be all their doing when we get out of here alive and someone's memories make a grand return."

Killian's head shot up, his stomach dropping to his toes as Callay choked and sputtered on her tea, the cup dropping to the floor for the second time. It survived as well, the shattered fragments of the porcelain chattering over the ornate tile and cutting apart the stunned silence.

"It's a long story," Jarron said, holding up his hand. "But it seems she is missing a few years of her life. We need Callay to unlock that. We need the magic of a Fae to reverse the magic of another."

Killian glanced at Callay at the mention of magic. He wasn't quite sure he was ready to reveal that bit to the girl quite yet, but too late now. A weird shock lined the Fae's face, the girl staring between the two of them with wide quivering eyes.

For the first time in decades, she looked scared. Perhaps she feared the world, Killian couldn't tell. But the haunting depth of her eyes, the lingering shimmer of her magic that so many Fae had lost when they were forced into slavery, it slammed into his chest and he gasped, the sharp intake catching both Jarron and Callay's attention.

"We need to leave here tomorrow afternoon, when both Vampires and Dragons are lazy and asleep," Killian commanded, putting his full strength behind each word.

Jarron straightened, meeting him head on, but the

younger dragon did not defy him, even though the gold flame of his beast had nearly overtaken his eyes.

"Good," Killian continued, turning to Callay. "I need you to text our two dead ancestors." He chose his words carefully, unsure of how to refer to the two. Callay grinned knowingly, her eyes shining, and she nodded enthusiastically. Killian was beginning to wonder exactly how much the girl knew. "They need to stay with Elliot, tell them where to meet us and about the tourists."

"I can do that," she said with a nod.

"So, we leave tomorrow night." Jarron was determined, the same fire was practically consuming Killian.

"And if we can't get out. We turn and fight, take out as many of the things as we can. For her."

"For her." Jarron agreed.

"No!" Callay interrupted as the light above the pool table began to flicker, the sparks of the girls magic surging through it. "You need to get back to her. You need what is inside of her."

Light flickered around them as Killian turned to the tiny Fae, ice drenching his spine. The girl looked stern, powerful, dare he say it dangerous. Callay had always been so kind, serving, obedient. The look she gave him now was a slap in the face.

"What is inside of her, Callay? What do you know?" Killian said, fire burning in his eyes as he looked at the girl. She didn't even flinch.

Smoke filled the room as Jarron's dragon began to growl, the beast inside of him ready to erupt but Killian did not turn. Jarron could handle his dragon on his own. He wasn't about to let Callay out of his sights.

"Tell me." Killian's demand shook the walls.

"I wasn't placed with you on accident, Killian," She said, her voice an echo in the shock she left behind.

"Do you work for Ceres?" Jarron snapped, his panic going to the exact same place that Killian's had. "Parris?"

Callay shook her head, looking at Jarron before she smiled. "No. I wouldn't get near that bloodsucker. It's that damn Unicorn. She's the one who brought me here."

10

DRAKE

EVEN THOUGH THE HOTEL HAD A MEETING ROOM, IT WAS clear it had not been used in a while, the aroma of dust clung to the air, blending with a lingering body odor that called attention to the fact that the room was not built for this many people.

Every chair at the five large circular tables was filled, every inch of wall space was leaned on, or sat, or stretched against. Even some of the floor was occupied, an especially large part taken up by Xi, who had the lead in the show. She was spread out on the floor like a bear skin rug, her nose so far in the book it might as well have mutated on to her face.

The aroma of smoke, chalk, rosin, and paraffin oil that Drake associated with the circus was conspicuously missing. If it wasn't for the perfect pancake split that Xi was in, and the pair that was doing some kind of hand-balancing act in the corner, the group would look like nothing more than mourners, and in many ways, they were.

Drake had only been a member for a few precious weeks, but even he felt the sting of that loss.

"By now you all know of the incident that destroyed our

precious home two nights ago," Suvi began, and Drake's heart tensed painfully, the guilt nearly ripping him apart.

'Incident' was a cruel understatement to what had really happened. That wasn't the source of Drake's guilt however. When Suvi said that they had heard about it, she meant that Drake had visited each and every one of them over the last few days and convinced them that there had been no dragon, and that the fire was an accident.

He had regretted using his gift against a few mortals at a climbing gym a few weeks ago. Now, he had melted the memories of every person in this room, and at least twenty public servants. The stench of guilt was all over him.

Drake sunk back against the wall beside Ellie. He knew it was needed. If any of them truly knew what had happened at the circus it would spell danger for all of them.

But it didn't make his actions any easier. He had switched out the memory of a dragon for a disgruntled stalker, and changed his name for another. He had changed their memories, and without permission.

Ellie gave him a look as he sighed in a low growl, but he shook his head, not willing to dive into his abilities quite yet. He could only really handle sharing one secret at a time with her, and over the last few days far too many had been exposed as it was. He kept waiting for the exposed secret that would cause her not to trust him.

He didn't want this one to be *the one*. His dying dragon was one thing, but manipulating others was drawing the line for him.

Ellie gave him a sad smile and wrapped her hand around his, leaning against him as Suvi continued, the accent of her voice feeling like sandpaper against his soul.

"I want you to know that this incident is not the end of our circus," Suvi said, her announcement gaining her a few confused looks from the performers. "This was a tragedy, but I cannot express how glad I am that everyone who was involved is alive."

Suvi paused, looking right at him as Ellie squeezed his hand, hers heating until it felt like he was holding a hot water bottle. The heat buzzed through his veins, pressing against his heart in an attempt to soothe him. Instead, his dragon grumbled in a low growl that was thankfully disguised from the chattering crowd. The beast was as frustrated as he was.

"Luckily, we have savings and insurance, so we will be able to go on," Suvi chuckled before anyone caught the exchange, well anyone but Zoe, who was still looking at him with all sorts of pride in her eyes.

Normally, a look like that would make him uncomfortable, but with Zoe it was a given. She always looked at him like that. Even though part of him rebelled against it, he would always be her baby brother.

"Becky and Alan will be meeting with each one of you today to discuss touring plans, any contract concerns you might have, as well as answer any questions. You can sign up for a time to meet with them on the papers located right outside this room," Suvi said with a nod to the haggard looking woman and the tiny, and slightly balding man that Drake didn't know beyond the angry tirade he would receive when bursting through his office every time he had been to see Suvi.

He had assumed the increased number of intrusions had made the man grumpy, but seeing him now it was clear that he was simply like that all the time.

"Speaking of the tour," Alan mumbled stepping up to join Suvi who promptly stepped back, Zoe pulling her aside so fast that she might as well have been saving her from assassination.

So much for his guilt. The emotion vanished, Drake's nerves kicking into overdrive as Zoe's wide, beaming smile disintegrated into an anxious grimace, the two women staring at a cell phone with an intensity that could raise the dead.

The scrapes of their indistinguishable whispers picked at the back of Drake's mind, like mice looking for cheese as Alan's announcement faded to a mumble.

Something was wrong. Zoe was growing more concerned the longer she stared at the device, and even Suvi seemed apt to begin raging over the group. Ellie's hand tightened around him, making it clear that she had seen whatever was happening on the other side of the room, not that he could provide her with any answers, which was clearly what she wanted with the stare she was giving him.

A simple shake of the head would never satiate the tenacious girl.

"One of the big changes that we will be implementing in the coming months," Alan said, his disgruntled voice cutting through the fog of anxiety that was smothering Drake. "In regard to the tour. We will be foregoing our stop in Arizona and instead stopping in..."

His words raced to a stop as Suvi gripped his arm, pulling him back. The old woman's eyes glowed with a weirdly dark light as she hissed something at him, the tiny man nodding once before turning back to the crowd.

Drake's hackles went up, his skin prickling painfully as he watched the pair, picking apart every action in a hope of finding answers. As the youngest, he had become used to being out of the loop, but that was always in things that didn't directly affect him. He was sure this did not fall into the same category.

"We will be going to Denver, Colorado," Alan finished lamely, the break in his voice making it clear that had not been what he originally planned to say.

The group broke into chatter, the mumbling buzz of voices an angry hive around them. Drake, however, continued to stare at Zoe and Suvi, waiting for some glance, some head nod that would hint him into what was going on. Nothing could interrupt the old biddies conference, it seemed.

"What in the world is happening over there?" Ellie said as she stepped forward, ready to drag him over to where Zoe was now madly texting.

Drake held her back, pulling her against him as though they were in a dance.

"We are going to Denver," he said calmly, Ellie twisting in his arms to give him a look.

Facts and redirection never worked for her. She was too quick, and too smart for that to fly.

"You know what I mean." Yes, her concern was valid, but this meeting wasn't over and running over in the middle was going to create more problems.

"I do, but I don't have answers for you."

"Which is why we should go over there."

"Not now," he advised from behind the clench in his jaw. "Wait until all this is over. We don't want to frighten the mortals."

And he didn't want to be forced to change any more memories.

Ellie's face fell into a scowl, her eyes sparkling with a playful prodding. Her stubborn spontaneity was going to get her in trouble if she wasn't patient. He had once been the same, acting without thinking. Give her another hundred years and she may not jump into trouble quite as often. But not too much, he hoped, he would miss her bright, feisty naivety.

The chatter began to die down, Alan settling the crowd into silence. Drake wasn't going to give her a 'told you so' look, she did that well enough on her own, her playful pout gleaming in her eye as she leaned into the wall next to him.

Drake would never tell her, but that tiny frown was one of his weaknesses, the way it sparked mischief in her eyes and ignited a very particular kind of light made him feel warm and needy. He knew it was an exaggerated show, but it didn't stop him from wanting to kiss her lower lip back into a smile.

It didn't stop him from wanting to pepper her in the soft touches.

He must control himself. If running over to Zoe in this crowd was a bad idea, kissing the dickens out of Elliot was possibly even worse in this crowd of gossips. No matter if he had bonded to her or not. These mortals didn't even know what that meant.

And the way he wanted to kiss her wouldn't really be deemed appropriate.

Besides, there was the whole exploding thing that Jarron had neglected to go into detail on before he left for Rydaim.

It was best not to risk it.

Drake pushed his desire for her away, only to have it vanish as his own phone began to buzz. He looked up to Zoe, half expecting the stare of expectation that came with secret emergency texts sent across the room, but she was still staring at her phone, Suvi now whispering to the dowdy stage manager, Becky.

Ellie pulled into him as he pulled the phone from his

pocket, her eyes growing as she stared at the message that filled Drake with as much ice as if the Vampire were right there.

Parris has eyewitnesses. Meet in Denver. DO NOT leave her side.

Cold was everywhere, Drake immediately checked both crowds and door as if the maniacal undead monster would be sitting amongst them. He hadn't seen the demonic blood sucker in more than a decade, but he would never forget the way his smile twisted, his blood shot eyes bored into him.

Parris may not be here, but there was one vampire who was, and she happened to be staring right at him, her two lackeys at her side. Her hungry eyes added to the chill that had bathed the air and Drake instinctively pulled Ellie tighter against him, ready to carry her from the room, or even bust through the wall to get her away from the vamp if it came to that. Zoe had promised that the vampire was not a threat, but right then he wasn't having it.

She looked like a threat, and that was enough for him right now.

"Who is Parris?" Ellie whispered in his ear, her hand tightening around his as she tried to get his attention.

He jumped at her voice, the icy chill that spread over his spine growing, even as the warmth from her hand radiated over him. The only thing that Drake could do was shake his head. If rushing over to Zoe in this crowd was a bad idea, giving this explanation was out of the question.

"Make sure you sign up for a time today, as we will be beginning our move to Denver tomorrow," Alan said, peering at his clipboard as though he was having trouble seeing it. "Thank you for coming this morning, and for being part of our family. Remember that we are always here to answer any questions you might have."

Well, okay now he didn't have any excuse.

Everyone jumped to their feet, shouts and questions bouncing off the walls and releasing even more dust into the air. Ellie, however, was looking at him, her wide eyes staring him down as if she would somehow force any answer out.

"Who is Parris?" Elliot asked again as the volume in the room increased, everyone talking as they began to filter out. Her eyes sparked with frustration a she stood, hip popped, waiting for a response.

"Do you remember that 'particularly meddlesome vampire' Jarron was talking about before he left?" Drake asked under his breath as Zoe charged over, her dragon peeking out so cleanly from her eyes that if his dragon didn't know hers so well he might have attacked.

The heat that blazed from his sister, however, was not in battle, it was in the protective instinct that appeared to be as strong in Zoe as it was in him.

"Do you mean the..." Ellie began, her eyes scared little saucers as her mouth fell open into a wide "o".

"I take it you got the same message?" Zoe said, cutting off whatever Ellie had been about to say, if she had been able to form the words. Considering she was still attempting to pick her jaw up from the floor, it didn't appear she was close.

"About our favorite little snake?" Drake asked, giving the room a cursory glance. Everyone had mostly cleared out, except for Ryn, Xi, and Stacia. The tall Asian man was speaking with Suvi, the girl was still buried in her book, although she had moved from the floor to a table. The blonde vampire was still staring at him.

Her pale eyes were unwavering, the intensity of her blood-soaked glare igniting the flame in Drake's chest, a low growl rumbling through his bones as heat spread through his mouth. He wasn't about to risk being this close to one of the blood suckers right now, and he pulled Ellie closer, jostling her back to reality.

"What does that mean, he has eyewitnesses?" she asked, a hint of panic in her voice. "Like from the other night? From when..." She began waving her hands around like she was trapped in a game of charades, odd exploding noises rumbling from her.

"I have no clue," Zoe said, clearly frustrated as she held out her phone so she could compare notes with his, but they were perfectly identical. Nothing besides a warning and a demand to keep Ellie in their sights.

Drake had no problem with that. Not that he enjoyed being away from her in the first place. He wished the reasoning wasn't as ambiguous as it was.

Drake's ability to protect her was as limited as the information they had. He and his dragon may like having her close, but this situation was dangerous for both of them.

"If it was, I am sure the message would be much more world-ending." Zoe said, a dark scowl wrinkling her brow as her eyes sparked dangerously. Thankfully the look was not directed to them. Best friend or not, Ellie did not understand what the true heir was capable of. "If Parris knows about the truth of that night, then Rydaim is the last place that those two want to be."

Danger dripped from her voice. Drake really didn't need her to go on. Rydaim had been his home, but it was also a fortress. Even the Fae were trapped within the mountain that they were forced to call home. When Drake had been captured after the failed coup, it had been because he had not been able to find a way out in time.

He couldn't imagine the same happening to his brothers. Especially with Jarron --

"Well, they aren't going to stay there are they? I mean, they can still just leave, right?" Ellie asked in a panic, putting words to the fear that was already aggravating Drake's memory. His dragon was near boiling point anger now, the ash and blood that was coating his mouth adding to the painful reminders.

He breathed deeply, letting the beautiful creatures anger flare was not a good idea.

"Jarron and Killian don't run away from danger," Zoe said with an irritated snarl, folding her arms over her chest. "They run into it, flames blazing like morons. And they will be even more idiotic if Parris is involved."

Ellie jerked in Drake's arms, stepping away from him so fast, that he couldn't stop her as she snatched the phone.

"What are you doing?" Drake tried to get the phone back from her, but Ellie kept dodging, twisting around him as she tapped against the screen like a child poking a snail.

"Texting him, telling them to come home," she said, still tapping and opening a photo ap, making Drake question if she even knew how to use the device.

He would laugh, if there wasn't a risk of the text falling into the wrong hands, she was causing way too much of a scene, especially with that fucking vampire still staring at them.

"Honey, this isn't the way," Drake whispered as he grabbed her waist, stopping Ellie's fight and carefully removing the phone, that was now recording their conversation, from her hand.

Her eyes swallowed him, pulling his heart toward her and he almost gave in to the silent plea, gave into her heart and promised to fix everything. But he couldn't, not the way she wanted to anyway. The best he could do now was hope, and plan.

"We will get them out, Elliot," Zoe interrupted, "but this

may not be the best way if they are in danger. We don't know what's going on there, and jumping off the cliff without a clear plan is dangerous, we need to make a --"

"Excuse me," A snide voice broke over their hushed conversation, Stacia's harsh whisper drifting over to them, bathing the tension in an arctic chill as she and her two shadows sauntered over. "I couldn't help but overhear."

"You stood staring at us and you couldn't help but overhear?"

Stacia's sneer was nearly as powerful as the distaste Drake felt for her. The vampire's eyes blazed red, and Drake moved his mate behind him as much as the stubborn girl would allow; which wasn't much. Now was not a time for Ellie to pick a fight, not that he could tell her that.

Or that telling her would stop her.

"You are going to fight him," she said, flipping a strand of long hair behind her back. "If that's true, there is something you should know about the coven."

"You mean beyond them being a bunch of prissed up blood suckers that are high on Fae blood?" Zoe snapped, folding her arms over her chest, a clear glare in her voice.

There had never been a better time for Drake's powerful sister to play backup. Especially with Stacia's skin growing more ashen, her eyes more bloodshot as she met the scowl head on.

"Well, yes, little dragon queen. I would love to say you are right. But this is about Parris specifically."

"I thought you told Suvi all that you knew when you joined us?" Zoe asked, stepping between Drake and Stacia, which was good because Ellie was really not having this whole protection thing. Drake could battle her all day, but not when it comes to vampires.

Stacia scoffed, tossed her hair back, and nodded toward her two lackey's who instantly moved for the door.

For one terrifying second, Drake was sure they would lock them in and they would be stuck with the twisted vampire. Something that even with Suvi still in the room and giving them some serious side eye, didn't give him the greatest confidence. He hadn't been able to master the ability of fighting Vampires when they were training for the coup ten years ago, and he hardly doubted years of rock climbing had helped him with that skill. Instead, the two girls walked out as if they had been remote controlled there, moving into a banter about some TV show that Drake had never heard of.

"I told her all that *she* needed to know," Stacia emphasized as she turned toward Ellie, her blood shot eyes digging into the girl with throes of threat and malice. Drake's dragon didn't need any more of a reason to awaken, his spine straightened, the creatures head lifting in preparation for attack. Ten years ago the posturing would have been welcome, now it was frightening, and he worked to keep the powerful shifter restrained.

He didn't need to put Ellie's magic, or his father's tracking ability to the test. Again.

Looks like Ellie was either going to try his patience or her dragon reversion skill. She muscled past him, her chin raised as she faced the vampire head on. Good lord, what was she thinking? He tried to pull her back, but she would have none of it, which was doing nothing to calm his need to protect her.

"Do you really want to do this again?" Ellie taunted, taking a step closer before Drake pulled her back. She was really testing his limits. "Because I think I proved last night that I can take you."

Ellie cracked her knuckles in what Drake was sure she thought was ominous. Instead, she looked like she was ready to engage in a playground rumble. Zoe chuckled under her breath, but Ellie continued on in her true pig-headed fashion and returned Stacia's glare, the girl scoffing as she pursed her lips.

"You can, you little moth," Stacia sneered, the response nothing like Drake had expected. "And that's part of the problem."

He had thought the girl had doused the air in ice on her arrival. It was nothing compared to the shock that was now soaking them. Zoe's entertained smile dropped as fast as Drake's worry, both exchanging a confused glance.

"Why is that a problem?" Ellie said, her question broken apart in bewilderment.

"Because dragon's *can't* defeat Vampires." Stacia said with a grimace, stepping closer to Ellie. Drake pulled her back into him and as far away from the demon's fangs as possible, there was a repugnant hunger in the vampire's eyes that he wasn't willing to let anyone get too close to.

"Explain," Drake said, keeping his voice in a low rumble and his warning clear.

"Step back, pretty boy," Stacia snarled, even as Ellie began to muscle her way through the protective wall he had been trying to build. He wasn't going to let her get away as easy this time. "She doesn't need you to protect her. She's stronger than you are on your best day. Even if she may not know it yet."

"Don't worry, Drake," Ellie said with a strength that at any other time he was sure he would be proud of. Not then, not with both an ominous text and a foolhardy vampire staring him down.

He didn't care if her connection with Parris was ancient

history. She was dangerous, and he didn't want her anywhere near them. His chest rumbled, nostrils flaring with a tiny bit of smoke. The normally fearful warning did not have the intended effect, however. Stacia scoffed and rolled her eyes.

"Seriously, Elliot," Stacia said with the tiniest bit of a prod, "You gotta learn to control your men. I mean, I didn't take you for a tramp, but I guess even you have a naughty side."

"She's not a *tramp*," Drake interrupted, the word a rumble of distaste in his chest. He didn't want to attack this woman, but if she was going to speak about Ellie that way, he was not going to try so hard to restrain himself.

"Oh really?" Stacia taunted, "Because I seem to recall that she is your brother's mate, so what in the world are you doing standing so close to her?"

"If you really want to fight, then by all means, continue digging your ugly little blood hole." Ellie's threat didn't make much sense, but Stacia still flinched and stepped back anyway, the frustration in her face fading.

Well, that was unexpected, and thankfully enough to calm his already aggressive dragon.

"Why can't dragons defeat vampires?" Ellie prodded when Stacia didn't continue

Drake restrained a scoff of irritation. Vampire or not, the statement made no sense, if not a little ridiculous. He may not be an expert Vampire fighter, but had killed enough vampires in his life, he had watched them burn. He had ripped them limb from limb. The woman was obviously delusional.

"They are too big, too slow, and even though their fire burns, we can still survive it."

"Vampires can't survive dragon fire," Zoe interrupted her with a scoff, Drake nodding in agreement.

The vampire in question though, just stood and smiled until the tips of her fangs pulled at her lips.

"Well, you're right," Stacia said, stepping closer still and lowering her voice until Drake was sure that not even Suvi could hear, magical witch hearing or no. "Or at least you were. Did you ever wonder why the Vampires were so eager to pair up with your kind all those centuries ago? I mean, Dragons are medieval. You haven't adapted. We can do better than you."

"We?" Zoe asked incredulously, but Stacia only smiled.

"You happen to have a resource that gives our kind the upper hand." Stacia continued, the red in her eyes glowing. Drake tried to pull Ellie back into him, but the foolhardy girl stood her ground, refusing to look away from the blood sucker. "As I said, dragon fire cannot destroy vampires. You *think* it can, you think it is the only thing keeping you safe. But you," Stacia said, her focus boring into Ellie with all the strength of a jackhammer.

"You are not a dragon."

She held up her wrist then, the pale flesh raised and bubbling from a wound that appeared to be growing and spreading through her skin like a disease. Drake didn't understand what it was at first, until Ellie raised her hand, her eyes nearly popping out of her head as she stared from her bare palm to the raised and boiling skin of the vampire.

"I burned you," she whispered, more to herself than to the vampire who gave a scratchy laugh in reply.

It didn't matter who she spoke too, it had the same effect. The burn bubbled and waved over her skin like a living thing. Drake's heart twisted as he looked to Zoe, but her eyes were nearly as wide as his, and nearly as telling.

The burn of a Phoenix.

Ellie's powers were still bound by Suvi's magic, nothing like this should have been able to happen. Ellie pushing him back into his human form, Ellie burning a vampire. None of it. Either Suvi was growing weaker, her magic stretched too thin after the last night. Or Ellie was growing more powerful, and if that was the case nothing would be able to hold her after much longer.

He didn't know which he preferred, especially now, as he stared at the boiling skin on the wrist of a vampire that claims she cannot be burned.

If the legends were to be believed, Phoenix flame could burn anything in its path, it could destroy anything. There was something about the way this burn moved, however. This was more than what the books said. It hadn't just burned the victim, it was consuming her.

Either the books were wrong, or Ellie's hybrid blood was a bit more than they bargained for.

"I came here after I betrayed my coven. Parris was conducting experiments to help make us stronger, but his techniques were too appalling even for me," Stacia continued when no one said anything. "I hid because I had information that would change the wave of destruction that always follows that idiot around and turn it into a tsunami. I like my food source the way it is."

Stacia finished with a sigh and a smile that sent an even colder wave of ice through the chilled air.

"So, you have a soul..." Ellie began, but Stacia cut her off with a laugh. The sound was a high mocking that made Drake uncomfortable, the growl of his dragon filled with enough warning to say as much.

"No one has a soul," Stacia said, peeking behind her again, as if she was checking to see if Suvi was tuning in.

Knowing the old woman, she wasn't missing a moment. "But I do have a conscious, and even I can tell when something is wrong. Like you."

The points of her fangs that were peeking out from beneath her lip as she smiled, and even Ellie stepped back into Drake's arms that time. Drake let his dragon growl louder, gaining the attention of the girl with the book, who was now fixing them with a curious look.

"There is something different about you," Stacia sneered, "and I would have to guess that Parris knows exactly what."

"Parris doesn't even know I exist," Ellie retorted with a snap, "I am..."

Drake cut her off with a growl, pulling Ellie into him so fast he was nearly afraid he had given her whiplash, not that she couldn't survive it. But this was not the person she needed to let in on their little secret. He was sure, given the scowl he had fixed her with, that she wouldn't have said anything, but he wasn't going to take the risk.

There would be time to apologize later. His sole need was to protect her, even if it included accidental whiplash. Good thing he knew how to give a good massage.

Something they could both look forward to once they get rid of their hovering friend.

"It's okay, you don't have to tell me. I am sure I can guess," Stacia said her voice taking a dark undertone that made Drake shiver. "If I'm right, Parris was the one to create you, and even if he doesn't know exactly *what* you are, he knows what your blood can do."

"Don't be vile," Zoe snapped, stepping closer to the vampire, nearly pressing herself against the snarling woman.

Seeing Zoe stand against her was twisting his nerves. He wouldn't dare to pull his sister away, but he would destroy the vampire if it came to that. He didn't know how, but he would have to figure it out.

"I knew her father, he gave her to me to protect..."

"And where did he get the child from? Was it really his?" Stacia interrupted, echoing every question they had broached the other day.

They sounded so much worse when dripping from her twisted tongue. He couldn't imagine how much they would cut and slice against Ellie, he couldn't imagine the pain. He could sure feel it, however, as her skin began to burn like a furnace.

"You don't know do you?" Stacia's red eyes reflected the fire that was in Zoe's until the daggers that were flying between them were boiled in flame, the accusation twisting in the air.

This woman was depraved, Vampires were not to be trusted, but the lines that were deepening on Zoe's brow told another story, one that Ellie was burning inside of. Fear and pain were swimming in her eyes and Drake wrapped his arms around his mate, his heart thumping with worry as his skin touched her, and the fire that usually sparked at the connection burned through his veins.

"I don't care what you are, Elliot. But I think you can stop Parris and his deranged vision better than I ever could hiding in this ridiculous circus." Stacia peered around a now smoking Zoe, red eyes digging into Drake and Ellie, fangs pulling at her lip with every word. "He created your blood, little moth, and if I am right, he wants it back. Your dragons can only protect you so far. Instead, you need to give him your fire."

"I think that's the last thing I want to give him. Unless I am burning him."

"Exactly." She smiled, "Parris and his minions have

found strength in the blood of Fae. But they have also created children to feed from, children who give them even deeper power. You need to figure out what you really are, Elliot. Because you sure as hell aren't a moth. And if you can control this," she paused, holding up her wrist again and letting the ugly burn spread and bubble before their eyes.

"Then you might be the only one who can stop Parris from turning the earth into his own personal blood bank."

11

ELLIOT

I was starting to get really tired of that pipe.

My entire childhood and Suvi keeps the thing, and the smell, hidden. But cue my three sexy dragons and suddenly the pipe is everywhere; stinking up my mind, and my clothes. I was pretty sure I was starting to smell the thing in my dreams, which wasn't a good thing. It smelled like feet, sweat, and a dead animal in the forest.

It was not a good combination.

I don't know how Zoe handled it, she sat there as though it was nothing. Drake, however, looked ready to rush from the room. I was ready to puke.

We were quite the pair.

"I take it Denver was a last-minute change of plans?" Drake asked, his voice tense as he tapped his fingers against the singed seam on his chair.

The discolored fabric was faint, the burned hem almost hidden against the usual organized chaos of Suvi's office.

Almost.

To the naked eye Suvi's trailer had been mostly

unscathed in the dragon battle, well, the inside. The outside was so battered that I was amazed it was standing.

Inside, everything was in its place, the silks still covering the walls in kaleidoscope waves, the sun still streamed in from the window in its usual too-bright glow. It looked perfectly normal. Expect that everything was a little too singed, a little too cracked. Even the legs of her desk appeared to be clinging for life.

It looked as though the whole thing had been thrown through the air like a match box and taped back together.

In fact, I was sure that was exactly what had happened. But with dragon's and her magic instead of matchsticks and tape.

Shifting in my own, perfectly singed, seat I twisted my hands in my lap, staring at the appendages for what was probably the millionth time in the last twenty-four hours. I half expected the skin to start glowing white, and glitter to burst from the tips of my fingers while angel song filled the air. Ridiculous yes, but I now knew it wasn't impossible, sans angel song of course. I was determined to make it happen again. There was still nothing but calloused skin and a few ripped blisters.

And smoke. But that had become a given. I really needed to figure out how to control this. I tucked my hands under my thighs before they exploded. Zoe gave me a look, making it clear she had seen. Not that I cared.

I was over hiding that. I was a Phoenix-Dragon-Fae-Possibly Vampire mega-tron. I wasn't hiding anything, anymore.

Suvi on the other hand, she deserved the glare I was throwing her way. I was ready to get some answers.

"Denver is where you need to be, so it is where we will go," Suvi said, ignoring the elephant in the room and shuffling through her drawer as she spoke between both pipe and clenched teeth. "The circus will protect you and hide you for as long as you need."

"You say that as though you are going to disappear," Zoe said with a laugh.

Well, if you could call it a laugh, the chuckle was dripping with nervous energy. And for good reason, no Suvi, no super witch protection. I didn't want to think of what that would mean for us.

I thought the smell of Suvi's pipe was bad enough, but the weight of the toxic pressure that was now taking over the air was enough to cripple me. I gasped and sat back in my chair, still safely keeping my hands tucked away.

"I may not," Suvi said, no longer looking at us as she began to arrange what I was sure were Tarot cards.

I had never seen them before, well, not officially. Suvi had always done Tarot readings at every cast party, but when you know someone is a witch, like a real, honest to god legitimate witch, you don't go over there and ask her to look at some cards and tell you when you are going to die.

Because it could be true. And knowing of my impending decapitation or death by falling piano was not something I had on my to do list. Can we leave that ticking clock off the table? Literally.

The way Suvi's eyes were starting to fade to white, however, was making it clear she had other plans.

Umm no.

"We can stop right there," I said, jumping to my feet and putting my hands over the Tarot cards to stop whatever she was about to do.

Over, but not touching, I had made that mistake that before. Accidental bone throwing was part of the reason my powers were still bound. Or at least, supposedly bound.

"I don't need to know when I will die," I said, earning me a confused look from pretty much everyone. Oh yeah, that conversation had all been in my head. "I don't even know when I was born, can we start with that?"

Suvi snapped her teeth around her long wooden pipe as the scowl faded to a smile. "Zoe told you, I take it. About the little Phoenix child."

"She told me that I was at orphanages and stuff," I said, flipping my hand to the side. It may have looked like I was being dramatic, I was mostly clearing the foul-smelling smoke from the air. "Why don't I remember it?"

Suvi's smile grew, it stretched so wide that the pipe looked like a sieve, her face twisted in wrinkles and lines that I have never seen before. "Because it was taken from you."

"Wow, helpful," My voice may have snapped, but my shoulders sagged so low that I ended up looking like a little sea cucumber, all tight and anxious, standing in the middle of the room. I would be concerned that my poor phoenix couldn't breathe with how she was pressing against me, except she was clearly as freaked out as I was.

Calm. I'm getting all the answers I need.

"Do you know who took her memories from her? Jarron went to get Killian and Callay. Will that work?" Drake asked, his hands a warm weight on my back as he came up behind me, his touch loosening the straight jacket of my spine, just a bit.

The old woman's smile twisted as she removed the pipe, setting it to smoke on a small tray before throwing the bones over the cards. Great. There was no getting away from it now.

Reverting dragons to people with weird glowy hands,

that was obviously fine. I draw the line at looking into my future with some old dames' knuckle bones.

Sick.

"That future is unclear, but your time with me is on a clock. As it always has been."

"And when does that end?" Drake asked, his fingers taut little points on my back, holding me steady even as I tried to back up.

"Denver holds more than answers," Suvi whispered, her eyes now completely white as she looked straight ahead, past me and into some great unknown. Or, at least, that's what I would assume.

"It holds an end, a beginning, and a demon," Suvi continued, her fingers hovering over the bones before she picked up a card and held it out like a diabolical banner. Which was strangely fitting seeing as the picture of the whimsical devil was front and center.

Massive horns, pale skin, and a pitched tail. Add to that, the bright red eyes and she was looking a bit too much like Stacia for my liking.

"Stacia," Drake said with a growl, his fingers tightening around me.

I guess I wasn't the only one to think so.

"That demon is in your lives, but she is not the one I speak of," Suvi continued, putting that card down to throw the bones again. "This one is hiding inside of you. This one has the power to destroy you all."

Well, that sounds promising. I guess my exploding was good for something. Like killing everyone.

I leaned closer to Drake, grateful when the color began to return to Suvi's eyes, although it did nothing to calm the weight of doom and destruction that was smothering the room.

I mean, she was staring straight at me. The little Phoenix-Dragon-Fae-Demon Super-bomb.

This title was getting too long.

Which made sense considering I was the only one in here who had mystery powers of some kind hidden inside of them. I mean, unless Zoe was secretly a Werewolf, which I doubted. Werewolves would never be so flawless at night, full moon or otherwise.

"If you say I am a vampire too I might lose it," I said with an unmistakable snap, leaning toward the old witch, whose face twitched.

I didn't know how she could be enjoying herself right now. I mean, demons, and vampires, and blood experiments? I was still trying to wrap my head around it.

"Not that I know of," She said, stuffing some more of the rancid leaves in her pipe. "Although I would love to know what the only vampire amongst us told you. Between her intelligence and the text Zoe and Drake received I think the demon may be a little more than some alter ego waiting to escape."

"You know of Stacia's former position as an errand runner for Parris' clan," Zoe said, pushing herself from the wall she had been leaning against and sending the silks rippling around the room in a wave. "And that she had information she wished to keep from Parris. Unfortunately, she wasn't truthful in what that information was. From what she said, Parris has been breeding supernatural creatures in an attempt to build some kind of super blood. She thinks Ellie is a result of those experiments, and based on the rumors I have heard over the years, I would have to agree."

"You believe that... thing?" I nearly screamed the word as I jumped back, suddenly feeling a bit too dangerous to be standing next to Drake. To be standing next to anyone, really. "You said you were sure my father was Elliot, that I was a Phoenix-Fae thing. Can't we focus on unlocking my memories and go kill the bastards?"

Saying it aloud made it seem like a shopping list for supernatural creatures. Bread? Check. Eggs? Check. Make sure you don't have a secret vampire daddy? Well, who the fuck knows anymore.

"That would be the goal, child," Suvi sighed, in a tone that was more condescending than calming. I sunk into my chair with a sigh, I think we had already established that I was not a child. "But seeing as I cannot do this you must wait until Jarron returns from Rydaim in his search of the help of the Fae?"

"Yes, and now it seems that he has promptly gotten himself stuck there," Drake provided, returning to his own chair. At least he could sit down in it without pretending to be a boulder.

"Don't be dramatic," Suvi said, nursing the pipe back to life. "The message said that there were eyewitnesses, not that they were being burned at the stake. Not that the act would do anything to a dragon."

She smiled, and both Zoe and Drake laughed at some joke that I was clearly missing. Not that I minded, I was watching them all from the bubble of my own self-pity, trying to pretend I wasn't worried about Killian and Jarron, or upset about the whole Maury Show Paternity Test failure that had become my life.

I was caught somewhere between fuming, confused, and hurt. So, I sat in a cloud of the pungent aroma of burning leather as the chair begin to burn under the now smoking flesh of my hands. And I thought Suvi's pipe was bad, this smelled like ass. Everything around me began to ripple as though I was in a mirage. Or maybe I was the mirage.

"I do not sense much in the way of danger for our boys..."

Suvi's voice quivered as the air did, my own shivering nerves cranking up a notch as the air continued to dance, my hands burning as my skin began to burn. As my hands rumbled in preparation to explode. I held my hand up, to the smoking skin, to a bright circle of white that had appeared in my palm.

It was no longer the leather that was burning. It was me.

Perfectly round, the ring appeared to be cut into my skin, the glowing light cutting into the flesh, spreading over it. Much the same way that the burn on Stacia's wrist was spreading over her.

Phoenix fire, bursting out of me.

"I'm the only one who can stop him," I whispered to myself, Suvi and Zoe's conversation fading to nothing as the light on my hand grew, as it spread over me.

It was beautiful. It was consuming. It was like looking at myself from the inside out. My light. My fire. Just like the light that had saved Drake.

Phoenix song swelled to a scream as I slowly stood, staring at the light as it burned, as it pulsed.

"Elliot? Honey?" Drake whispered from beside me, his figure edging itself closer.

I saw him out of the corner of my eyes, but I couldn't look away from the light, from the way it pulsed and burned against my skin, as though it was part of me.

"It's beautiful," I whispered spreading my fingers, letting the light burst from me in a beam that shot into the ceiling with a crash that shook the room, before the white light fell like sparks and smoke.

White stars collided as they fell, whipping into a

whirling wind that circled around us, spreading the specks of light as though they were dust.

Hair, clothing, yards of silks, they all whirled through the air, spiraling in a storm of color. The tornado circled the beam of light that burned the air, infecting everything until each particle of dust began to glow, swirling like stars.

Little specks of magic.

I gasped at the imagery, looking from the light to Drake who stood still, his hands reaching toward mine as though he wanted to take the light, or perhaps he wanted to hold it.

"It's part of me," I sighed, my voice sounding far away as Drake stopped in his tracks, his eyes quivering as he froze, his hands still reaching.

I didn't know what was happening, but I knew he couldn't take it. I knew he couldn't take me, not yet. That didn't stop me from wanting him to be with me, to feel this warmth, to bring him into this light. My heart pressed me toward him as my phoenix continued to sing, the brown sugar in his eyes beginning to melt as his dragon lifted to reach my shifter, he wasn't even touching me, and I could feel his fire.

I wanted to melt into those eyes, melt into him, but before I could move the light swelled into a bomb of light that consumed everything. Brilliant white washed the color from the room, scrubbing the walls from existence until it was only Drake, Zoe, Suvi and I standing in the middle of the bleached world.

"Child. You need to dim the light. It's too strong for you now," Suvi muttered from somewhere in the light, her voice tense. I knew I should be afraid, I could hear her fear, I could feel my own buzzing around in my mind, but I couldn't grasp it.

The world had turned into light. There was only light,

only the burning fire that had taken over Drake's eyes, his dragon so close I could feel him wrap around me, feel his scales against my skin.

I stepped closer, my heart pulling me into him as I placed my hands over his, needing to share the light with him. Needing to feel him inside of me.

Instead, the moment his skin pressed against mine, the room exploded.

The beam of light erupted, turning into a tower of flame. Massive tongues of the brightest red swirled through the pillar to consume the white. Consume everything.

The room drifted back into focus, but instead of the slightly disheveled office, we were surrounded by fire.

Holy shit!

I screamed as Drake did, his hands falling from mine and thankfully extinguishing the fire. Well, at least the fire that was streaming from us like some mother fucking cannon.

The room wasn't so lucky. It had turned into nothing but flames, and with the way the walls, and the silks were melting it was far hotter than your everyday arson fire.

Not saying this was arson, but god damn it was really getting out of control.

"Oh my god, put it out!" I yelled, as I jumped away from Drake and grabbed some of the silks that lay crumpled on the floor, swinging them around as if one strip of lowly fabric would extinguish it.

But no, it caught fire, the entire strip or purple lycra erupting into a whip of flame. Which is exactly what it was as I covered everyone in bits of burning ember, screaming as I continued to fling the fabric around.

"Shit! Ellie," Zoe said, nearly knocking me down to get it away from me.

"What the hell," I cursed as Drake pulled me away from the fire as a wall of wind ran through the room, the sparkling breeze swallowing the flames as though they were never there. Suvi's deep mumble whispered through the breeze, the words sounding like gibberish.

Well, gibberish that extinguished whatever the hell had happened.

"I'm getting really tired of this," I mumbled as Drake released me and I sunk to the floor. "I'm made of fire, you would think I would have at least some skill on controlling it."

"It's okay, Ellie," Drake whispered as he collapsed beside me, gathering me into his arms. "You will soon enough."

"Not before I take down a few more hotels in the process," I mumbled to nobody in particular.

"What the hell happened?" I demanded of Suvi, pulling away from Drake, he felt more dangerous than he had a minute ago.

I kiss Jarron and explode into flames, and that....

"What the hell happened!"

I may not be a teenager anymore, but I was sure any adult with a shred of sanity would react to what happened the same way.

"You created a conduit," Suvi said, focusing on lighting her pipe again.

"That tells me nothing," I snarled, pulling myself to my feet and extinguishing the last few smoldering bits of carpet with the sole of my shoe. "What is a conduit?"

"It's a charged linking of your powers," Suvi said, her eyes narrowing into me, as though she was studying me, which I was sure she was. "Think of taking your abilities and combining them--"

"Into a bomb?" I finished for her. I suddenly didn't feel safe being around anyone just then.

Suvi nodded, "I am surprised you were able to create one. It is difficult magic, even for a Fae."

Dragon-Phoenix-Vampire thing I finished silently.

"Are you quite sure she's not ready for you to unbind her powers," Zoe said, slapping her jeans as she tried to push the ash and a few burning embers away. "Because if you don't do it soon, we won't be able to train her--"

"Forget training me," I interrupted. "If you don't unbind my powers soon there is a high chance I am going to do it for you, and I doubt any of you will like the outcome."

Hell, I already wasn't liking the outcome. I was done with fire and exploding and not knowing when each one was going to happen.

Suvi only smiled, puffed on her pipe and gave me a look that only set my blood right back into a boil. If it wasn't for Drake's hand wrapped around mine, I am sure I would have.

"There are answers in Denver," was all she said.

"Well, I hope they don't like their hotels in Denver, because if the answers aren't there, I can't guarantee I won't burn them all down."

12

ELLIOT

I STRIPPED MY CLOTHES OFF UNTIL I STOOD IN ONLY A SINGED set of lacy underwear and threw everything else I had been wearing in the garbage, right on top of the last pair of clothes I had burned so badly they couldn't be salvaged. Unfortunately, the underwear wasn't that far behind.

"You know," I said to Zoe as I removed my bra and pulled a hoodie over my head, throwing both bra and panties in the trash. "I liked those. Hell, I liked all of them, and I would really like to stop throwing away all my clothes. I'm running low as it is, and I don't want to have to start walking around naked."

"Why not?" Zoe teased, pulling my suitcase out from the wardrobe and onto the bed. "I am sure my brothers won't have any objections."

I froze in place, one leg in the pair of leggings that I usually wore to bed. At least those hadn't been damaged.

"Hold up," I said, recovering quickly and pulling my pants on the rest of the way. "What happened to the no sex, no touching, no looking at each other with googly eyes that could remotely make anyone under the age of fourteen blush?"

I said it all so fast that I was fairly certain she had only heard part of what I had been saying. Or worse yet, she had misinterpreted everything.

Instead, she shrugged. "We have bigger problems."

"True," I said, although I didn't quite agree with her. I mean, I had a habit of exploding when kissing or touching the boys, something I had proven was getting worse - not better. It was already bad enough that Suvi seemed content to let that continue to happen.

Which was awesome, because who doesn't like a best friend who literally erupts into flame?

Zoe may have moved on to the whole, 'Parris is conducting weird genome experiments' thing but I was still going to keep a safe 'clothes on' distance. Lips, hands, and everything else away. At least as much as I could, I swear between needy phoenix and lusty imaginations it was getting harder. But it needed to be the new rule until I stopped exploding, because I really didn't have enough clothing to support that habit.

Heaving an overly loud sigh, I grabbed a handful of shirts, underwear, and whatever else I had thrown in the top drawer after the last wash day. With a well-placed toss they landed in the now open suitcase, Zoe scowling at it with a glare that that was more fire than fury.

"Can you please not turn my clothes into ash with your angry dragon glare?" I said, throwing more clothes on top of the others. "I really do need them."

"What you really need is to start folding your clothes," She said with a sigh, grabbing one of my leos and prepping to fold it.

Oh god. Mom-Zoe was making an appearance. I

snatched the leo from her before she could even get one crease into the wrinkled swatch of fabric.

"If anyone is going to fold my clothes, it's going to be me." I tossed the leo back into the now cluttered suitcase with way too much flourish. "And it's not going to be me."

"Seriously?" Zoe was incredulous, I just gave her a smile. One of those smug know it all ones that always ground on her nerves.

And it did, her nostrils flared, and she made a sound that was part growl, part snort. Like a human-dragon hybrid instead of a shifter. I wanted to tell her that there was only enough room for one hybrid in this town, but I wasn't going to risk it now.

I had put on my favorite pajamas and would rather not scorch those too.

"This is becoming a problem," she said through a clamped jaw.

"Really? This is a problem?" I said gesturing to the cluttered suitcase. "And here I was thinking child experiments, exploding best friends, and vampires with spy networks was going to take the cake."

Zoe opened her mouth, I raised an eyebrow, and the dragon backed down, although not without a bit of flame in her eyes.

My phoenix boiled under my skin, ready to rise and meet her, but I wasn't about to let that happen. Partly because Zoe couldn't see my phoenix anyway, but mostly because I had already won that little showdown. It may have been won on a technicality, but I wasn't going to put it in danger.

Elliot, one. Zoe, zero. It even had a nice ring to it.

Although, as far as wins with Zoe goes, this one was the worst. Everything grew silent and that same dead weight that had been haunting me that last few days flooded back into the room like Jack Frost with PMS.

"You know," Zoe began, breaking the silence as she attempted to secretly fold more of my clothes and place them into the second suitcase. We had done this enough that we were both on autopilot. She didn't need any help. Well, other than the reminder not to fold my clothes, but that one was a constant. I already had a trademark 'stop that nonsense right now' glare, which I was currently giving her.

"When you say it all together like that," she continued after a moment. "It sounds awful."

"Welcome to my life," I mumbled under my breath, closing suitcase number one, which sent a few articles of clothing soaring over the bed. Just about as many peaked out of the sides of the case and I ceremoniously stuffed them back in, zipping and stuffing the entire way around.

Yes, Zoe was right, as usual. I should fold my clothes. But even with my usual stubbornness I wasn't going to concede that fact to her.

"I thought I had a handle of things when I was throwing myself off buildings once a month," I said, sitting on the case to get the last of it closed. "Easy. Hidden. I was managing."

Zoe gave me a look that was very clearly reminding me that I was not 'managing'. Which was true, but I sure as hell was managing better than I was now... whatever this was.

"Managing as in not exploding all the time," I clarified. "At least, those time freeze things have stopped, but I think I would gladly see those make a grand return after creating a tower of flame. At least I can use it to explode things now."

You know, if I could control it.

It sounded like something out of the Bible. Flame and pillars of salt and death and everything. I mean, I had never read the Bible. But I had heard enough to know some crazy stuff went down. A pillar of fire had to be in there.

"It was a conduit," Zoe corrected and I rolled my eyes at her.

"Doesn't matter what it is if I can't control it," I said looking at my hands again, which I instantly regretted.

I mean, they were perfectly fine, but I had been creating a track record of having my hands burst into flames with a glance. I shook the troublesome things and jumped off the suitcase, there had to be something else here I could pack. If only to get my stuff in the hopefully indestructible suitcases and away from well... me.

Maybe I should be the fire eater, not Zoe.

"You can control it, you just have to concentrate and keep your mind clear," Zoe advised, handing me the last of the clothes and stepping into the bathroom. I could hear her messing with hair dryers and toothbrushes in her attempt to create order, but I froze in the middle of the room bundled clothes in my hands.

"You do hear yourself, right?" I called after her.

"Hmmm?" I wasn't sure if those were words or the sound of a mating moose in winter, but I plowed on.

"Keep your mind clear, but concentrate," I repeated, failing to keep the snicker out of my voice. "Next you will be telling me to breathe, but hold my breath. Or fly, while on the ground."

"Don't be ridiculous," Zoe said, peeking around the door frame of the bathroom before disappearing back into the fluorescent tile room.

"I can't be ridiculous Zoe," I yelled after her, holding my hands out like I was meditating. Or something, I mean, I had never really meditated before, so for all I know I looked like a flamingo. "I am busy contemplating the nothing in my mind."

"Ha. Ha. Ha."

"I sound like a yoga master," I continued to prod as Zoe stepped back into the room, her arms full of my equally as disarrayed bathroom things. I guess her organization skills had failed. I didn't move to help her. I remained still, hands out in my flamingo-slash-air traffic controller Zen mode. "But you know, the non-flexible kind who only eats beet juice and talks about how amazing they are. Om"

"You are flexible," Zoe corrected, trying to stuff my bathroom things into the already jammed suitcase.

"I also hate beet juice," I provided, helping to shove and jam and flip around the zipper. "But that's... not... the... point..."

I heaved each word out as we shoved the zipper and buckled the suitcase closed. I waited, watching the tiny plastic teeth in expectation of them popping open, they had before, but thankfully today they appeared to be holding.

I wished I could still cellophane my suitcases shut. It was the only thing that had saved my belongings for years. Let's hope TSA didn't flag my suitcases again. The bright yellow hazard bag I had been given when we landed in L.A. after they couldn't get my bag shut when checking it had been so embarrassing.

"Then what is the point?" Zoe asked, pulling me away from my suitcase vigil.

"That my body keeps trying to hurt people, other people want to kill me, and I can't put two and two together enough so that the body that keeps trying to hurt people will hurt the people that want to kill me."

"You've lost me," Zoe said, quirking and eyebrow at me in confusion.

"I am not sure I followed that either." I sighed and turned away from her, right toward the large mirror the hotel was trying to pass off as artwork, and the burned wallpaper that still smothered the upper corner. The last remnants of the great kissing explosion of Salt Lake City, although in a place with this much religion and angst, there were sure to be a few more of those around.

Although maybe not with fire.

Zoe watched me through the mirror, her long hair pulled in to two braids that were so perfectly messy it might as well have been illegal. Her and Jarron clearly shared more than a few genes. She stood there, watching me, looking so strong, so powerful, so perfectly capable.

My chest tightened, my phoenix perking up in both agitation and what was clearly jealousy.

Of course, the person I would be jealous of was a powerful dragon princess.

It wasn't the first time I envied her strength, but it was the first time I felt even an ounce close to the power that she had.

I needed to know how to control it. And that was all this came down to.

"I need to know how to fight," I said, fists balled at my sides as my skin prickled with goose flesh. "Even if I can't control whatever is going on inside of me, knowing how to beat up or escape a Vampire would be really great."

Okay, not great. Like full on kick-ass. I was filled with beautiful images of me beating up a seductively attractive vampire prince who had come to steal my heart and my blood. I was ready to show this *Parris* who was boss, that was before Zoe snapped me back to reality.

"You can't fight a Vampire."

"Well, damn, so much for badass vampire hunting. A

vampire death was not how I saw myself going out." Way to burst my bubble, Zoe.

Zoe sighed, pinching the bridge of her nose as she always did when I was driving her crazy. I didn't try to restrain the smile.

"Are you sure about that though, I mean I have magic phoenix fire hands. That has got to stand for something." I wiggled my fingers at her menacingly, but she did little more than tweak an eyebrow. Badass dragon princess for the win.

"A Vampire is not going to kill you. Your freaky fire hands will probably do some good," Zoe interrupted. "It takes years to train to take down a vampire without all your special abilities. Fighting them is not something I can teach you in a hotel room overnight."

My soul was screaming at that, the need to burst free and show some amazing vampire slayer skills coming out of nowhere.

Down, girl. I am pretty sure that considering the way everything is going we were going to get our chance.

"So, you can teach me to fight a dragon then."

Was I hopeful? Sure. I mean, they couldn't expect me to go into some battle without being a little prepared. I wasn't going to let the guys do all the work, and my cat-fight staring matches could only take me so far.

In fact, I had already reached that limit, no matter how much Stacia thought I could take her down with a blink.

"Sure," she said, although I was sure she wasn't as *sure* as I was. "For the record, that damn Vampire is right, although I would never admit it. Dragons are slow. And you can escape them if you know their weaknesses."

Wait.

"Escape them?" My face fell, "this is going to be a runaway combat training isn't it?"

"You can't fight a dragon, Elliot."

Her tone was like a battering ram and my already tense and frustrated ego was getting all prickly. The pressure against my skin grew until I was sure I was smoking. Not that I would check, I didn't need to trigger something else.

Of course, I could take a dragon! I could take a vampire. I was so freaking ready, and you are damn sure I was going to prove that to her.

So, I rushed her.

A deep scream ripped at my throat, Zoe's face transforming into pure shock as my shoulder intersected with her gut. I had been hoping to catch her in the boob, but seeing as she was a good foot taller than I was, there was no chance of me reaching that high. I would have to take what I could get.

I had expected her to go tumble down in a rage of shouts and profanity. But no, she stood still, perfectly upright. She didn't even sway.

"Freaking Dragon!" I screeched, trying to hide the laugh from my voice.

I kept running at her to take her down. But like a linebacker against a cement pole, we were going a whole lot of nowhere.

"Move, Dragon," I said with a grunt, slamming into her again.

"Are you sure you want to do this?" Zoe asked, the boredom in her voice only pushing my buttons more.

"You are going down!" I roared, my phoenix screaming and heating in expectation of a beautiful win.

Instead, Zoe's arms wrapped around me and flipped me through the air. Red streaks of my hair flooded my vision, arms and legs flailing as I shrieked and was slammed down to the ground with such force that the wind was knocked out of me.

"Oh god!" I gasped from where I lay on the floor, Zoe straddling me and sitting on my breast plate until I couldn't move, let alone breath.

"Get off me you ugly Dragon!" I teased, using the last of my air like the idiot I was.

"Excuse me?" she asked with a laugh, frustration boiling in my chest as she leaned closer, the fire in her eyes digging into me.

My flesh pricked to life, my blood turning to steam, and I was sure my phoenix was pressing against my eyes.

Not that Zoe would see it.

Except the way she froze over me, her hands clenching around my shoulders made me sure that she did. Awe lined her face, her jaw dropping as she stared at me. I should have been more victorious that she had seen my phoenix. Instead, I used it to my advantage and shoved her off me, right to her back. Flying into cat-fight mode, I pushed and clawed at her with useless frivolity. She laughed once before swinging me around her like a rag doll and wrapped her arm around my neck, shoving me into her armpit.

Well, this was unexpected. I officially had a face of pit and side boob.

"Do you give up?" She hissed, wrapping her legs around me where we laid on the floor, my face still jammed into her boob. I really couldn't move now.

"I can't," I gasped, although all my fight was gone. And so was Zoe's. We didn't move. I froze, a weird buzzing rumbling under my skin where she was touching me.

"Elliot?" Zoe gasped, her tone shifted into some unfamiliar calm, her grip loosening.

But I couldn't find it in me to move.

Drake burst through the door and Zoe scooted back, dropping me from the headlock as she looked away. I fell to the ground gasping for air, and trying to regain that whole empty brain contemplation, but it was proving to be impossible. Zoe's touch was still moving over my skin, like a joint waking up. The intensity ran through me in a weird needy way that I really didn't know how to make heads or tails of.

I mean, she wasn't my mate. So, what the hell was that about, come on Phoenix... make up your mind. The bird screeched defiantly, and Zoe turned making it clear she had heard the noise, Drake however, didn't even flinch.

Okay, did we wrestle our way into an alternate universe? What was happening?

I looked up at her, desperate for some explanation as to what the hell had happened, but she had stepped away, hands on her hips as she greeted her brother.

"What is it, Drake?" She asked, out of breath.

"What are you two doing?" he asked, his eyes looking between us and making me feel even more guilty.

"She's teaching me how to fight," I said with a gasp, pushing myself to my feet and clutching my side. I was already certain I was going to bruise. Not like it would be the first time. "I'm really bad at it."

"I know."

"Wow, thanks Drake," I said, earning myself an impish grin from the boy.

"You'll get better, Ellie, you are probably stronger than Zoe. I mean, if we are going to believe the vampire," Drake said, his face falling as I cringed.

But it wasn't for why I thought. Instead of the hatred for the demon, worry gripped his brow and he stepped closer to me, his protective instinct wrapping around me like a glove.

"Speaking of the vampire," Drake continued, his eyes snapped from mine to Zoe's and my heart nearly fell to my toes.

"What's happened?" I asked, my voice shaking with the expectation of some sort of hidden attack and a dozen vampires ripping at my tasty, tasty flesh.

Ew. I didn't need that image again. I thought the dragon king had been bad enough.

"She's missing."

Wait. That was worse.

I didn't get a chance to find out why though, as my suitcase chose that moment to pop open, sending a shower of hair care products and underwear over the bed, and all of us into attack mode.

Drake grabbed me and held me behind him, while Zoe spit a ribbon of flame right into the now defunct culprit.

"So much for owning clothes," I said longingly, watching the fabric smolder before turning back to Drake. "What do you mean she is missing?"

"I mean Suvi can't find her, and her room was full of a whole lot of blood."

"Vampire's don't bleed," Zoe said, her voice hollow.

"Which is why we have a problem."

13

JARRON

Jarron had walked down these halls more times than he could count. His life had happened in these halls. Killian had taught him to shoot fire without taking out half the marketplace, His father had helped him master his shift. He had dragged many a prisoner, his baby brother included, down these halls to meet their fates.

Now, he followed the long, corded hair of the woman he despised most in this world, toward a room that loomed with the stench of death.

He could only hope that it wasn't his.

They had been hours away from leaving, they were destroying the last of their papers, the last of their life, when Dabria had shown up.

Their father had requested their presence. They had clearly not moved fast enough, and now it was too late.

Killian gave him a sidelong glance before he straightened his jacket, pulling his hair back into a low ponytail. If they were going to meet their death, at least they would look nice doing it.

Killian more than he, but the man looked good in a suit. Of all the things for his dragon to horde, he had to pick the one that made him look like a gorgeous billionaire. Jarron enjoyed nice clothes, and his city-chic look was perfectly manicured day in and day out, but he simply not compete with his brother. The chalk marks on his thighs from the fake billiard game Dabria had walked in on were not helping. Jarron tried to wipe away the marks in his nervous agitation, but he already knew it was pointless.

"So, I never did get to ask you, Killy. How was the circus? Was your mortal... flexible? Did she scream well?" Dabria whispered, carefully prodding as she gave his brother a lustful look before she glanced forward again, leaving them in the silence of her damn clacking shoes and the growl of Killian's dragon.

The look was not even meant for him but Jarron found himself shivering under the sharp glare of the woman anyway. Of course, the tension in both spine and dragon may as well have been from who she was talking about.

He would give anything to make the girl pay for speaking of his mate that way.

Jarron barely managed to restrain the growl that was threatening to break out of his chest and focused forward. Killian's dragon was already making his frustrations known and he would have to let him snarl enough for the both of them.

He didn't like how Dabria was prodding at them. She was seeking a rise, yes, but she always did that. With how she had spoken in Utah, and with how she was tiptoeing around Ellie's existence with all the care of an elephant he was on guard. He would keep his fire burning, hopefully he wouldn't have to use it. Hopefully he would.

He sure hoped Killian was right and that he had been able to keep the information those tourists held from his father. Although, the worry that was gnawing on his gut told him that it wasn't the tourists that had called them here.

Jarron gave his brother one last look as they reached the wide stone doors, the massive things creaking open and revealing the long throne room, his father and Parris standing in the middle.

Parris was dressed head to toe in black leather, which on its own wasn't unusual. But there was something different about the leather, like ostrich hide that had been died with onyx. It looked unnatural. He certainly wished that Parris's odd clothing choice was the oddest thing about them.

Ceres was dressed just as darkly, the dark color wrapping him from head to toe and making him appear even taller, broader. More oppressive.

But worse, it made him look like Parris' little puppet.

"Father!" Killian boomed joyfully as soon as they entered, the false joy perfectly masked by the grind of stone as the doors began to close, locking them in. "I didn't expect to see you so soon! You could have sent a message to Callay, you know. You didn't have to send the whore."

"We didn't know you were still in Rydaim, my son. You seem to be doing a lot of coming and going these days. Besides, my bed mate is always eager to do anything I ask. She's so agreeable. So beautiful." The old man smiled with a lustful grin, but Dabria only scowled, her low growl rumbling with the door, continuing after the groan of its closure rattled the stone cavern.

That time, the thunder of his displeasure pulled Jarron's face into a smile, although the look was short lived. His father was now staring at him, and the man was not happy.

Jarron knew why he had been summoned here, and it

wasn't the tourists. He had disobeyed his father and thrown the auction. He had expected a punishment of some sort. He didn't need the confirmation.

"It isn't you who I have business with, however." He got one anyway.

"Father," Jarron began, his voice quivering in false apology as he slid into the role of subservience and remorseful son, "I have failed you."

"I expected a night of blissful sleep," The King began, ignoring his hasty apology and stepping toward the two men. His gaudy leather shoes were silent against the stone. "I expected a new beautiful Fae for my collection."

"I know father..." Jarron began, bowing his head in apology. "It was Sasin..."

"Stop!" Parris roared, stepping forward and slamming the back of his ice-cold hand against Jarron's jaw.

Jarron howled at the impact, the vampires fist feeling like an icy boulder against the tightness of his jaw. Dragon bones were some of the strongest in the world, it was not shocking that Jarron had heard a crack. Although, the crack did not appear to be in the hand of the demon, judging by the pain that was radiating through his jaw and neck.

How in the world had he managed that? The bastard shouldn't have been able to break him. But Parris' smug smile spread wider, the vampire wasn't surprised. And he certainly wasn't expecting any retaliation from the King.

What twisted dimension had Jarron walked into. Parris couldn't have gained control of the King so easily. Not yet.

The air cooled as Parris leaned toward Jarron, the dragon barely able to keep his fire at bay as he stared at the blood sucker. Stared at the power in his eyes, at the greed that spread his lips.

What he wouldn't give to knock the smile from his face

and crack the cold stone of his head in two. But he was trapped under the grin of the blood sucker, under the chuckle of his father; the man saying nothing of Parris, and the insubordination that had occurred.

"I expect my orders to be followed," Ceres continued, patting Parris on the back as though he had clocked nothing more than a disgruntled servant and not the son of the King.

Things were so much worse than Killian had made it out to be, so much worse than he had assumed after his visit to the market yesterday. Jarron caught his brother's eye a second before Parris turned to Killian and the powerful heir carefully rearranged his features to the disgruntled older brother that he was so good at portraying.

The glance was enough for Jarron to see what he needed, however. Killian was clearly seeing the same thing he was.

"When you defy my orders, you are refuting your place as my son," Ceres said, his voice a low hiss as Dabria came to stand beside him, her hand dragging over his shoulders as she pulled herself into him.

"I know father," Jarron continued, "I should have fought Sasin harder, I have faced him in a bidding war before, but I was distracted..."

"Distracted!" Ceres interrupted with a boisterous chuckle, giving Parris a look as Dabria laughed with such a false note that it could have broken glass. Jarron barely restrained the cringe. "What in the world could distract my great executioner?"

The three of them smiled and laughed as one twisted unit, Killian joining in as he stepped closer to his father, playing the role as he always did. This time, however, his positioning was much more calculated.

Jarron could see his brother now, see the lines of danger

in his eyes, and the bright flare of his dragon behind. Killian was attempting to control his beast, every move slow, every flicker controlled under the tight leash he usually had, but he was struggling. His jaw had never been so tight, his hands so tense. If it had only taken a wooden dowel to his groin to destroy the control on his dragon before, he did not know how long he could hold the beast back now.

Jarron would be lying if he said he didn't want his brother to fail, to lose control. He would be right behind him, and then they could end this.

"It was jealousy," Jarron moaned with some hint of honesty, twisting from his brother to his father, who looked at him with his own furious fire. "I wanted her for myself."

Ceres laugh faded with a snap, a new look taking its place as he stepped closer to him, Parris right on his heels.

"Son," Ceres crooned, placing an overly hot hand on the starched cotton of Jarron's shirt. "Did you for a second think that I wouldn't save some for you as well?"

They all laughed at that, but Jarron couldn't pull the smile to his lips that time.

"It was greedy of me to want her for myself." That one was a lie, it was all a lie, and each word of the lie burned in the fire that Jarron was ready to release.

He was waiting for Killian's sign and he would end it all. He would watch them burn and writhe and die and then they would free Elliot from the dangers that hunted her.

It would be easy, and it would be wonderful to watch Parris melt at last.

"It won't happen again, father," Jarron said, his focus on his father as bowed his head, he hoped the look of servitude would be enough for the old man.

Instead, he punched him in the face.

The old man's punch packed a wicked bite and Jarron

went down to his knees, hitting hard against the stone as Parris laughed, snapping his fingers as three of the hidden exits that had been cut into the stone centuries before swung open, and dozens of feet began to file in, filling the hall with the aroma of ice and blood.

He didn't need to look to see how trapped they were, how thoroughly fucked. He doubted less than twenty vampires were now filing in.

Jarron's head jerked up, his eyes drifting to Killian. Any go ahead for an attack was gone. Any chance of winning was gone. He could survive this if his father's anger didn't extend beyond him losing an auction to Sasin.

As long as Parris hadn't played his final card yet, and with the way the ugly vulture was smiling, he couldn't be sure.

He would have to take this beating. Bitter regret painted his tongue and he dropped his head.

"I will get her back for you," he lied again, curving his back to the man in a low bow, this time in defeat, but not before Dabria's eyes dug into him, her hooded eyes drowning in a detestable evil.

"I don't want her anymore," Ceres snapped, his ugly shoes pacing before Jarron as he began to shift and sway. "I don't want Sasin's used goods. And I have the perfect way to help you remember that. Or rather Parris does."

Jarron didn't have any time to react, to brace, before he felt his father's fire slice over his back, his shirt and flesh pulling apart as the glittering scarlet of his blood began to rain down his side.

Jarron's scream ripped open, echoing over stone and glass as he fell to the ground with the pain. He hadn't screamed, he hadn't shown pain in front of his father in over hundred years, but he couldn't stop this one. The agony that was cleaving apart every nerve ending was insurmountable.

"Vampire's love the smell of blood," Parris crooned over Jarron's scream, his mockery followed by the high tinkling of Dabria's ridiculous laugh.

It dug into his pain, and he jerked, his dragon rumbling to life. He had thought he would be able to take it. He had thought he would be able to keep the beast inside, preserve himself and keep Ellie safe, but these two were really putting him to the test.

Slow breaths. Restrain the fire. He could do this. He had to.

"Do I need to stay here for this," Killian's tense voice barely raised above the strangled breaths that Jarron was trying to force out. Jarron felt as though he was ripping in two as he lifted his head to his brother, the man somehow holding it together.

"No," Ceres said, his eyes not leaving Jarron, the hunger in them more nefarious than he had seen in decades. "But do not forget this either Killian. Do not forget the screams from those who defy me."

There was a pause, a panic that burrowed in his brother's eyes and Jarron forced out a scream, his shout both of pain and distraction pulling everyone's focus as he heaved and locked the agony away.

Ceres smiled, letting his fire unleash over his back again, letting it burn and slice, but this time Jarron didn't even moan. He kept the emotions locked inside, letting only the tears fall.

"I never would, father," Killian said with a growl, his face spread into a smile as he turned, his eyes digging into Jarron as he walked toward him.

Jarron remained still, his body hunched into a cower, his

back sweltering from his father's fire. He could smell the char of his own flesh, smell the blood as he felt it drip over his skin. But he refused to flinch, refused to show any pain. It would only lead to a greater beating anyway.

Killian's face wrinkled in worry, but Jarron locked his jaw together and gave his bulky brother one slight nod, one quiet plea that he would continue with their plan. His eyes fell to the ground, heart twisting painfully as his brother's shoes walked past him and toward the door. He could only hope that Killian knew what to do, that one slight nod had been enough.

They both knew what was coming, they had no way to stop it. Jarron would take the beating, he would heal, but he wouldn't be leaving with Killian anymore.

That was no longer possible.

All he could do was stay here, give Killian the cover he needed to get out of Rydaim, and to get back to Ellie. She needed more than Drake with her to protect her from whatever onslaught was coming.

And it was coming.

Sadness and pain dripped from him as the vampires continued to filter in, and the doors slid shut once again.

"Jarron," Ceres began, and Jarron lifted his head, pushing all his strength into restraining his dragon, and his fire. "You will not disobey me again."

"No father," he said through the clamp in his jaw, the lie biting as painfully as the flames he could not release.

The slinky Vampire stepped forward, stomping all over the King's authority as he raised his fingers, ready to give the order for his clan to attack.

Jarron looked to his father, but the man didn't even question, he only had eyes for the vampire, an odd pride in his eyes as the immortal snapped his fingers and gave the order.

Jarron couldn't even feel the pain, the shock at having lost to the man. He could only lay there feeling each pair of fangs as they dug into his flesh, his silent scream rattling in his head.

14

ELLIOT

"Holy fuck!"

The profane exclamation ripped from me as Drake escorted us into a room I had never hoped to visit, and one I never wished to see again.

Blood dripped from the walls in streaks and ribbons that made it appear as though the ceiling was leaking. There was clearly no one here to bleed, but the blood kept oozing, it kept dripping down the beige wallpaper in crimson streaks that soaked into the industrial carpet, against the chair, against the bed.

My life had officially turned into a horror movie.

I had seen enough in the last few weeks that I was starting to feel trapped in one, but standing here, in the doorway to Stacia's room it had become official.

When she had first come to the circus I had imagined her room being full of pastel hair ribbons surrounded by candles and cat sacrifices. The idea hadn't changed much when I had found out she was a vampire, except for maybe a couple more candles and a blood orgy.

But when I thought of a blood orgy, I didn't think of... well, I wasn't sure what I thought of. But it wasn't this.

This was a goddamn murder scene.

"Holy fuck!" I repeated. I didn't think there were enough holy fucks in the world to really convey what I was seeing.

"This time I agree with you, Elliot," Zoe said, pushing past Drake and I, taking two steps to Suvi, who stood in the middle of the room, staring at the massive pool of blood that filled the queen bed, as if the puddle would reveal something about what had happened.

Like where in the world all this blood came from.

"Vampires can't bleed right?" My voice quivered as I looked around the room, my stomach twisting uncomfortably.

Up until a few nights ago I hadn't seen more than a few drops of blood in a cut or a bloody nose. Since then I had held Drake's bleeding dragon and watched the vampire who had apparently exploded in the middle of her room take a bite from a woman.

I thought that had been bad enough. This was worse. This was like what happens when you open an elevator full of blood and let it drain away.

"No, they can't, and I don't know of any human that possess this much blood," Drake said, winding his arm around my waist. He must have heard the shake of my nerves.

Either that or he could sense my phoenix who was pretty much freaking out. My skin was prickling, heat radiating from my bones as she pressed against them, as they threatened to splinter and break.

My soul was thrashing, pulling me toward the door as if the blood was going to congeal, create a monster, and swallow us whole.

I wasn't going to discount the possibility of anything, especially with how Suvi was staring at the pool of blood, her hand hovering over it. Fingers twisting and fluttering as black liquid dripped from the tips, the magic colliding with the scarlet pond without even a ripple.

"Did she kill those girls?" I asked, the quiver in my voice buzzing out of control as my phoenix began to scream, the sound bouncing off my skull, trapped inside my head as my soul was trapped inside my heart.

Holy hell. Get a handle on yourself. I seriously just made light towers and saved dragons and a room with a little bit of blood was going to be my undoing?

Yeah, right.

Okay, even I knew that it was more than a little bit of blood.

"No. Her feeders are fine, and her glamour is wearing off. They won't remember any of the last few years," Drake whispered, giving me a glance that turned into a double take. "Oh my god, Ellie! Are you okay, your white as a ghost."

"I'm fine," I lied through the clamp in my teeth, sure that he wasn't going to believe me.

He didn't, he instantly began placing his hands on my face, his palms feeling strangely hot against my cheekbones and forehead.

"Yeah, sure you are. You look like you are about to pass out," he said, his eyes burning with worry as his jaw tensed and pulled his prickly beard taunt.

Normally I would want to jump him at that. But not right then. Right then, it felt as though my soul was pulling apart, pressing against bones and muscles and veins until I was coming apart at the seams.

"I'm fine," I lied again, knowing that I sounded even

further from the truth. Hell, I had even started shaking, gaining looks of concern from both Suvi and Zoe.

"What is it, child?" Suvi said, her accent drowning her voice. I had never heard her sound so worried before. She stepped toward me, the black magic or whatever was dripping from her fingers now directed right at me.

Freaky.

"I'm fine," I said again, like I was on autopilot. Forcing my body to hold still from the shivers and pushing my phoenix back against my heart, which took far more control and concentration that I expected it to.

"I don't know what that was," I whispered, my voice strained as I kept pushing at my phoenix. "She must not like all the blood."

Or vampires, or whatever demon was haunting this space.

Good lord, keeping both the nervous energy and the panicky phoenix at bay was taking work.

"You probably shouldn't touch me right now," I whisper warned to Drake as I pulled away. Luckily, I didn't need to tell him twice. He gave me a wide berth, the two dragons staring at the witch, who was still staring right at me.

"What do you feel, child?" She continued, hand still stretched forward as she looked at me with eyes so narrow that I was sure she was using her witch-powered x-ray vision, if that was a thing.

I had no way of knowing, but I was suddenly feeling very silly for running down here in my pajamas, and for never wearing underwear to bed.

Eyes away old lady.

"It's not a feeling. It's a smell."

I was already coiled so tightly that the tiny voice behind me was like releasing a broken spring in a balloon factory. I shrieked, jumped, and launched a streak of fire behind me as I suddenly found myself lodged in between the walls and ceiling of the entry way like a spider.

"Shit!" I shrieked, looking down at Drake who was singed, shocked, and overly worried.

"Please tell me I didn't just fart fire," I pleaded, as I began to shimmy my way back down the wall, glad when Drake was both tall and strong enough to help me down from my predicament.

I didn't even know I could do that.

"Fine, you didn't fart fire. But I would still change your pants." The little voice continued, and I spun from Drake to face a thirteen-year-old that normally had her nose stuck in a book.

Now, however, she stood smiling at me in a room full of blood, wearing what was clearly her pajamas, complete with a fluffy robe.

What was she doing here? A room full of blood was not really a place for any kid. I wanted to pick her up and carry her out, make some excuse about a science experiment gone wrong. But beside Drake, whose discomfort was as clear as mine, no one else was surprised to see her there.

"What do you mean 'It's the smell'?" Suvi asked, giving me a mischievous smile before she returned to the blood-soaked bed, the girl right on her heels.

"There isn't one," Xi said, tucking her book in the pocket of her robe and pulling her stick-straight black hair to the side, the waist length strands still trying to fall toward the scarlet lake. "This blood has no smell. Because it's not blood."

I didn't have to inhale to know she was right. With this much blood the room should be bathed in the scent of iron and salt. But there was nothing, nothing but a faint smell of dust and hairspray maybe?

"This mixture contains powerful hormones and poisons. It drives vampires crazy and disorients them. If they drink it they die, and if they don't it ruins their sense of smell so that they can't track. I haven't seen it in a while. I'm surprised she had this much lying around." Xi continued, swirling her finger through the liquid, letting it drip from her hand like corn syrup. "She put it in here to cover her tracks. So, they won't know she was here."

Her saying it wasn't blood did not help the image of a kid playing in blood. Forget my freaking phoenix, I was sure my stomach was going to turn inside out right there.

Except, she wasn't a kid. And she very clearly wasn't human.

"Wait," I pulled away from Drake, gesturing wildly toward Xi as I stared at Zoe and Suvi. I had hoped they would answer the question, but the two chuckled. Xi shaking her head at me in what was clearly irritation. Awesome. "How many people are you hiding in this circus exactly? And please don't tell me the kid is a vampire or a demon or a dark angel or something else that wants to kill me too, because I don't think I can fight a kid."

"No offense," I added with the look that Xi was giving me, her arms folded over her chest. "I mean, I'll go easy on your or something."

Easy as in, I'll swipe at your face softer. I needed to find some martial arts classes or something. But for supernatural creatures so I wouldn't look like a psycho when I accidentally lit people on fire. That and I would be able to avoid the accidental murdering of mortals.

Yeah, that was the perfect thought to be having in a room full of not-blood.

Xi didn't seem to accept the apology, either way. She rolled her eyes, tapped her foot and sent a shower of sparks from her hand that clung to the walls and bedspreads and everything. The light clung to every inch of the room, spreading wider and wider as it consumed everything.

I gasp-screamed and jumped closer to Drake who was looking as freaked out. This was too close to the whole pillar of fire thing that we had only barely survived. I tensed, waiting for the fire, but there was nothing but Xi's laugh and a tiny pop as the light imploded, revealing a perfectly clean and blood-free room.

"What the hell?" Drake gasped, looking from walls to clothes as if checking his sanity. I would have joined him if Xi wasn't staring at me with a smug little smile.

At least my phoenix wasn't freaking out anymore.

"I'm not a *kid*." Xi said, the disdain dripping from her at the word. "Suvi and I have been friends since before this circus had a tent and we would steal coins from the pockets of the gentry."

"Gentry?" I asked, my confusion dripping from my voice.

"The royals. Rich people in Europe." Suvi said with a chuckle, waving her hand to the side and sending more of those sparks dancing to the stained and worn carpet. "Before your time."

"Are you a Witch?" I asked, truly curious now, Xi however only laughed, the sound deep and strangely out of place for her little body.

The girls smile spread, "I am cooler than you are, trust me. And when you figure it out, I'll help you pick your jaw up off the floor, little phoenix."

My jaw was already on the floor, drooling all over each confusing little morsel Xi kept giving me.

"You know...?" I couldn't get more than two words out

past my shock; my jaw was still wagging, and I was sure the room was getting smaller. But that one may be me, everyone else didn't seem to be having problems breathing.

"I know everything about you. You used to know more about me, but then you chose to wipe your memory."

And my brain exploded.

The room was officially covered with the brain matter of my, Drake, and even Zoe's minds. Suvi, however, stood beside Xi laughing like a mad man ready to take over the world.

I was trapped, staring at the kid, or not-kid, as she smiled, her eyes not deviating more than a millimeter from mine. The dark grey I had seen so many times in our performances full of a sparkling glittering of green and orange.

It should have been a clue to who, or what, she was, but I didn't have enough non-exploded parts of my brain left to think it through.

"I chose to...?"

"Yep. I would suggest you keep it that way. But knowing you, you are stubborn enough you will drink the Kool-Aid anyway."

Xi smiled, revealing bright white teeth, and turned to Suvi, leaving me standing in puddles of my formerly logical thought.

Xi was... something. I couldn't even piece together enough to know

"I will track her," Xi said, holding her still red soaked hand out to the old Witch. "Parris and his bastards won't come here, you know that. That's why she came to you in the first place. Even if they get a scent of her here, now that your spell on her is gone, it will end here. Follow the plan Suvi."

"But what about the dark..." Suvi began, Xi cutting her off with a look.

"I will take Ryn back before it comes." Xi instructed, her voice much to formal for a child. "You will continue to follow the plan as I have laid it out."

"You know I trust you," Suvi said, beginning to bustle toward the door. "Now, Elliot," she stopped right before me, and I jumped pulling myself away from my racing thoughts and to the old woman that I swear looked even older than she had a minute before. "Xi is right, the longer you can wait, the better."

"You mean for my memories?"

"I mean for all of it," Suvi said with a sigh, glancing to Drake who had been hovering beside me the whole time. I had been grateful he had kept his distance, but now I didn't feel quite so much like I was going to explode, and I leaned into him, his arms wrapping around me. "Her power is dangerous. I need you to keep it away from Parris. Stay as far away as you can, for as long as you can."

Suvi didn't wait for an answer, she bustled right past us, Xi on her heels. The fluffy robes and slippers looking strangely out of place given the last few minutes.

"See you in a few years, Elliot," Xi called behind her. "If you can manage to stay alive that long. Enjoy the Kool-Aid, kid!"

She had barely finished speaking when the door slammed shut, ripping through all of us and sending me and Drake jumping. His arms tightened around me, his heart rattling between us, as together, we turned toward Zoe.

"I had no clue," She sputtered out before I could find my words, which was probably better, I was liable to explode.

And we had really had enough of that right now.

"About which part?" I began slowly. "Xi being a some-thing, me knowing her, or me wiping my own mind?"

My hysterics were seeping out anyway.

"All of it," she interrupted, "Well, except that Suvi was hiding Xi, but now I am not even sure about that. Did that seem like Xi was in charge to anyone else?"

Zoe stared at the door, her own shock shaking through her as we stood in the once blood-soaked room.

"What do you think she is?" I asked, wrapping my hand around Drake's, I needed to feel something stable after the rollercoaster I had been stuck on.

I don't think I could take any more ups and downs. Throwing up was still on the table, unfortunately.

"I'm not sure I want to know," Drake whispered, "My dragon was practically bowing down to her. I'm not going to question it, but I am sure as hell keeping you away from Rydaim. Jarron and Killian will get out. And we are going to Denver. They will be there."

I nodded, but I already knew that Xi was right, I was going to drink the Kool-Aid.

I had no idea what that meant. But when I found out, I was going to chug it down.

15

KILLIAN

THE ECHOES OF JARRON'S SCREAMS RAN OVER THE STONE walls in waves that Killian had never heard before. His brother was powerful, his brother was strong, and his brother was pig-headed enough that even from the time he was small he would clamp his jaw and hold the scream inside.

Hearing it now, hearing him plea and yell was a painful slice against Killian's heart, his chest ached in both fear and panic, his dragon rumbling and pushing against his skin in a need to escape. To run back and save him.

He knew he couldn't.

Not with the way Parris had hit his brother, his father laughing as the disgusting vampire fixed him with one look, and Killian knew, he was next.

That should have never happened, he couldn't understand how it had. He didn't know what Parris had done to get his idiotic father to fall for his game, but he couldn't stop to figure it out. Not right now.

Jarron's silent plea may have given him permission to go,

to run, but it did not end the danger. It did not stop the twist of guilt and pain that ran over him.

He never thought he would run from this place, run from this fight. When he had first begun this battle with Jarron he had accepted that it would end with either him claiming his throne, or with his blood streaking the halls.

That was before Ellie. And he knew, as well as Jarron did, that he was not running away from his father, he was not running away from Rydaim. He was running to Elliot, and he could only hope that whatever Jarron needed Callay to unlock could stop this madness before it got too far out of hand.

Before it was Jarron's blood that streaked the halls.

"Callay!" Killian roared the moment the heavy door to his kitchen had snapped shut. The screech of his dragon rode on the back of his words and he heard the girl squeak from the same room they had left her in.

He had never reached the game room so fast. His feet soared over stone and plush carpet before he reached her, huddled around a pool cue he assumed she was planning on using as a weapon. Callay's back was to the table where the schematics of Rydaim had lain unfurled for the last twenty-four hours. Guarding it.

They needed to do more than that now.

"Burn it," Killian instructed, rushing to the wall opposite the still splintered panel and ripped it from the wall. The wood came away easily revealing a door that he had built into the room when he had first constructed the house. In the beginning, it had been meant to store his horde, but it was hard to wear suits that were hidden behind a wall.

Now, it contained only a few relics of his life, and the clippings they had collected as they had tracked the Phoenix. Clippings and letters and everything else that he was sure would lead Parris right to her if it fell into his hands.

They had planned to take it. Now, there was only one option.

"Burn it?" Callay asked, her voice cracking as it echoed through the stone alcove to him.

"Yes, burn it," Killian pulled the two boxes behind him as though the heavy things were full of little more than air.

He dropped the massive things on top of the fragile map, sure the impact would only rip and tear the thing further. Callay screeched like a child staring at the boxes as though they were liable to explode, but Killian could care less. They were going to destroy it all anyway. Her mysterious friend would have to get used to disappointment.

Besides, he had committed the map to memory anyway. Or, at least he hoped he had. Right now, his anger was so high, and his dragon so loud, that his focus was only on escape.

"The guard is sure to be right behind me, and unless you want them finding this and knowing everything we have been doing we need to leave." Killian glared at the face Callay was giving him, turning away to grab the other two boxes that were still in the tiny room. "We don't have time for this, Callay. We need to burn it. We need to leave."

"What happened, Killian?" Callay stuttered, her panic increasing as she tried to keep up. "We can burn it, but where is Jarron..."

The tiny Fae flinched as Killian dropped the boxes onto the pool table besides the others, the wooden legs groaning and creaking as though he had placed a metric ton atop them. In many ways, it felt that way. It had only been three years, but he and Jarron had poured their lives into this. All of this work, all of the searching.

It was a physical ache to have failed so quickly. So easily. They may have found Ellie. But Parris had taken control regardless.

"He's being tortured." Killian tried to push away the failure, push away the regret and the sound of his brothers screams as they echoed through his mind, but they didn't stop, and his dragon pushed against him, pushing him back to Jarron.

He didn't have time for this now, he pushed the beast away and turned to the tiny fae, "He isn't coming. We need to get you out of here, and to Elliot, before they have finished whatever the hell they are doing to him and our window closes."

"But we..."

"We don't have any time!" Killian roared, turning on the tiny Fae who stood there, her jaw tightening as she stared at him. The same look of pain and loss and fear that Jarron had given him staring into him. No, stabbing into him. He took a step back.

"We need to burn this, and we need to leave, and if you won't obey me, then I will do it myself!" Killian's rage flared hotter with each word, his dragon sparking to life as he turned toward the pool table and let the fire in his belly click and flare to life. Smoke twisted between his teeth as ash coated his tongue, the blaze hitting against his teeth as he opened his mouth and --

"Stop!" Callay rushed between him and the table, her hands up in a frantic pause, her silver eyes wide and afraid.

The fear was well deserved, Killian's rage was so hot, his dragon so near the surface that he did not want to calm. He didn't think he could. He needed to destroy the table, and anything that stood between.

"Stop," Callay said again, softer this time, her hands still up even though she cringed as a few drops of flame snaked between his teeth, falling harmlessly to the tile where they sizzled into specks of black soot. He didn't want to see what that would do to her, and neither did she by the way she was shivering.

"Get out of the way, Callay, we don't have time for this," Killian growled, his dragon pouring from his voice in a rumble, but the girl didn't move.

"You do. And you will not continue through this path." Her eyes were boring into his, the silver that had always glowed from inside of her shimmering as though a light had been turned on. The air that surrounded her began to sparkle, her hair whipping through an invisible breeze as she took a step closer, and Killian, without his permission, took a step back.

His dragon was not one to be afraid. Even when it came to Ellie he was not afraid. He was more like the over-worrying boyfriend. But right then, he could have sworn he felt the beast shiver inside of him.

"We cannot burn these." Callay did not look away from him, her eyes dug into his and for the first time his dragon did not glower at the girl. It was just him, staring at a Fae that until now, he thought had been in his service. "We cannot make it look like anything has changed. Unless you want to look guilty and leave your poor brother here to answer for the panic-induced incrimination that you left behind."

"You know I would never do that," he said, the words grinding together through the tension in his jaw. Her incrimination stung, but worse, he knew that she was right.

"And yet, you abandon him here alone?" Callay asked, tweaking an eyebrow. The look was innocent enough, but it was also enough to release the anger that had twisted through him. He did not like being scolded, and even though the situation was dire his pride still burned.

"He knows there is no other way, you know there is no other way. I must leave. Someone needs to be there for her in case this gets worse," he scolded. "Jarron will be fine."

"He will be," Callay agreed, her voice calming down from her own panic, although not enough for his dragon to do more than prickle at the back of his throat. "But not if you do this."

Her voice was heavy, it drained any remaining panic from the room and the dim light began to flicker, reacting to her magic in a spark of black and gold. The bright sparks of light and dark were only adding to the dread of the situation, and he growled at the light with a scowl, as if the thing was doing it on its own.

"Fine, since I no longer seem to be the logical one in this conversation," Killian said, folding his arms over his chest as he stared the fae down. "Why don't you tell me what I should do."

Callay could not have looked more proud of herself, and while the look certainly bristled Killian's pride, it was not enough to break past the fear that had turned the muscles in his back and shoulders to cords of wound-up, and extremely dangerous, energy.

"You are going to leave, alone," she said, her hands slamming together in one clap as boxes, door, and the pane of wood slammed back into place, the entire room looking as if nothing had happened. Even the damage from the pool ball target practice had vanished. "Everything will be as though you simply abandoned it. You went to go find a new woman or something, I dunno," she waved her hand to the side. "I'll figure it out. But the important thing is that everything looks the same, so Parris doesn't suspect that you know what is happening. So, they have no reason to suspect that Jarron is tied to anything. He wants a rise out of you, you know better than to give him that."

He hated admitting it, but she was right. Killian had always pride himself on his calm, of his ability to use his brain over his brawn. But when it had come right down to it, he had been ready to burn the world to the ground.

"I cannot leave alone, Callay," Killian whispered, his voice grinding like sandpaper in the silence. "Elliot needs you."

"Jarron needs me more," Callay interrupted. "This place needs me more. We still have to hold Parris off, Jarron and I can do that. This fight isn't over. Yet. Go back to Ellie, make her feel safe and loved and wanted, because it might be the last chance for anything to feel normal for a while."

"How did you get so wise?" The question was simple, but Callay only smiled, holding her hand up between them and displaying a vial the size of a child's finger.

It was a small tube, like what he had seen tourist puts grains of rice in so many years before. Corked with a red wax stopper, he half expected to find a grain of rice, or even something more nefarious floating inside, But there was nothing. If it wasn't for one tiny air bubble that bounced around near the top, he wouldn't have realized there was anything in there at all.

"Give this to her this when the time is right."

"What is it?" He asked, taking the icy thing in his hands. It felt so useless between his fingers, like he could crush it without thinking. There wasn't even enough water in it to sustain even the smallest of dragons in case of an emergency.

"It is what she needs the most, and will do what she needs most in that time." He quirked an eyebrow at her, but the fae didn't seem to care that the nonsensical logic she had spewed out was quite literally word vomit.

"Could you be a little more specific?"

"I could, but where is the fun in that," She smiled, the light in her eyes sparkling before it began to dim again, a darkness taking over her as quickly as it began to infect his heart. "Besides, you have far more ahead of you, and if you don't leave now, your fun will never reach its beginning."

Dread soaked his soul. So much time had passed since he had raced in here. So much time since he had left Jarron writhing in pain. He didn't know if he had enough time left, or if Jarron's pain would be enough to let him get away. But if he was going to try, he had to leave.

Callay smiled sadly, stretched up on her tiptoes and pressed her lips to his cheek. The action was so informal, so out of place for the girl who had served him for over a century that he froze, eyes blinking into nothing before with a snap of her fingers, that same awful tube that she had sucked him into so many times before wrapped around him. The air was pressed from his chest, his home falling from view until he reemerged, with a tiny pop, just on the other side of the courtyard, tucked into an alley behind a fountain.

He could see the ornate street that led to his house from where he stood in the shadows, he could see the vampires that stood guard, the ugly things not even trying to hide the fact that they were watching the crown prince's home from atop the false roofs and windowsills. And he could see the faint glow of that disgusting mural that he had built around his front door. His heart pinched knowing that it would probably be the last time he saw it.

"Goodbye," he whispered to his home, to the square, and with one glance up to the still illuminated stained glass window: to his brother. Ignoring the thunder of his heart,

Killian pushed the tiny vial into the pocket of his suit and turned on his heels.

He had barely slept the last few days, his focus had only been on the map, and as he plunged himself into the inky black of the alley, it all laid before him. He knew exactly where to go, and exactly how to escape without them knowing.

More importantly, however, he knew how to get back in.

For when the time would come.

16

DRAKE

THE AIRPLANE SHOOK ON TAKEOFF, SEATS AND TRAYS AND luggage rattling as they took to the air.

Drake peered through the window on the other side of Ellie as the plane climbed, as the city, and mountains, and the strangely colored Great Salt Lake began to shrink and morph, replaced by the clouds as the plane began to tilt.

He felt the sway, watched the clouds, and not for the first time he imagined himself out there, wings spread wide, feeling the air get thinner, feeling the burn of the cold in his lungs.

Drake sighed and lay back, pressing his head against the seat as Ellie leaned against him, her hand wrapping around his.

"We will fly together some day," her words were soft, a solemn promise that made his dragon perk up in need, heat radiating over his skin and joining with his.

The vow was one that he wanted above all others, but also one that was an impossibility. The fire that had risen nearly extinguished with a growl, the creature that he held inside of him, suddenly feeling as though he had been ripped in two.

"We are flying together now, Honey," Drake whispered, ignoring the pain and running his free hand down her cheek. The touch spread her smile wider, her eyes sparking brightly in streaks of golden flame.

Oh, how he wanted to kiss her, run his hands over her arms, over her back. His breath caught, even that touch was dangerous. Who knew what would trigger her fire. An explosion in this tiny metal tube was certainly not in anyone's best interest.

He wanted to feel the air, but not as he fell to his death.

"You know what I mean," She sighed, giving him a smirk as she shifted away.

"I do," he said, leaning back into her to whisper in her ear, the long strands of her unkempt hair tickling his nose. "But one shouldn't make promises they can't keep."

"Who's to say I can't keep it?" she teased, the fire back in her eyes as she whipped around to face him. "You don't know what I am capable of."

She smiled at him mischievously, the grin teasing him in more ways than she knew. His stomach twisted and he leaned away, determined to control himself, even as he found himself getting lost in her eyes, in her smile, in the almost hidden constellation of freckles that covered her nose. They were so faint that between the light and all the stage makeup she usually wore he wasn't surprised he had missed them before. Now, however, he wanted to trace each one with the tip of his pinky. Trace the lines of her face and press against her soft lips.

Being this close to her, in public, was already proving to be hard. It was a good thing that his self-restraint was on par, and that this flight was only an hour and a half.

He could last that long. Not like he had another choice.

"Neither do you," he said, but she only smiled and settled into her chair, her hand still wrapped around his as she leaned her head on his shoulder.

Her weight was comfortable, her smell intoxicating, her heat around his hand a warm balm and his eyelids fluttered closed.

He must not have slept long, he had always struggled to sleep on airplanes, even though he was sure he had been on them as often as Ellie.

They were both nomads in a way, no real home. Just running. He wanted to believe the end of that was almost here, not for him, but for her as well. He had a feeling, however, that it was further away than it had ever been.

Someday, he would give her a home. He would build that for her, for both of them.

For all of them.

A baby cried somewhere on the plane, and Drake perked up, looking for the source of the sound, sure that it was that which had woken him up. There was a reason he never slept well on planes, too many people, too many noises.

His dragon was too cautious.

"I woke you up," Zoe said from beside him, his sister strapped into her seat and reading a magazine about the safeties of flying.

No wonder she looked bored.

"And why did you do that?" Drake said through a yawn, careful not to move or speak too loudly and wake up Ellie. Even though that may not have been a bad idea seeing as she was currently drooling on his shoulder.

He hesitated to admit it, but even that wasn't grating on him as much as he would think.

"Because I need your opinion on something," Zoe hissed in return, still not looking up from her magazine.

In fact, everything about her was on high alert. Her body was stiff, her ears perked, he was sure that if she did look at him her dragon would be blazing behind her eyes.

Seeing the straight line of her back and shoulders, each muscle pulled tight, was giving his creature rise. His hackles were lifting even as he leaned back, doing his best to look around him without moving. Something that wasn't working very well.

It didn't matter, however, he sensed what she had immediately.

"Is the *something* the dragon two rows ahead of us?" Drake whispered, eyeing the shaggy blonde hair of the shifter who sat in an aisle seat just ahead. He couldn't tell it was male or female from here, but it didn't matter, they were very clearly a dragon, he could smell the wind on them, his own creature pulling toward it, ready to attack.

Foolish thing. It should know by now that that is not an option.

"Yep, that's the one," Zoe said, her voice a little louder, a little more lighthearted before she dropped it back down again. "Can you smell anything else on them? A vampire perhaps?"

Drake focused, letting his dragon perk up as he tried to get a sense on the beast. A dangerous move, if he could sense them, they could surely sense him. It was better to be aware of the spies sent after you, though. It makes it easier to take them down, especially if that fight was going to happen in a metal tube.

"Nothing," he sighed, knowing it would be easier if the shifter was smothered in the scent of death and blood. But there was only flame and fear. "Why is it here?"

Pressure wrapped around his chest, heat growing as the dragon shifted and turned, diverting their eyes in an attempt to get a look at them. Drake kept his eyes forward, the woman's hazel eyes drifting down the aisle to some nonexistent focus.

So, it was a woman, although he didn't recognize her. Not that that was very surprising, he hadn't been back to Rydaim for a decade, who knows what had changed, and what new hatchlings had grown into adulthood.

"Why is she here," Drake corrected and Zoe smirked.

"No clue. I am, however, surprised that it is a dragon. I half expected a vampire."

"Shhh," Drake responded, furiously looking around him to make sure that no one else was looking. Zoe didn't react, she continued to look through her magazine as calm as could be. Well, appearing as calm as could be.

Drake didn't know how she did it, every one of his muscles was a tightly bound rock, and he was doing a shit job at disguising it.

"It's a movie, Drake. We can't do anything about it here," Zoe said, the code simple, although it did nothing to alleviate the problem.

Drake gave her a look, and she smiled, finally looking at him as she turned the page. Sure enough, her eyes were filled with flame bright enough that even a mortal would be able to tell what it was.

That one glance was enough to make Drake want to shrink away. He may have been powerful, but he was never powerful enough to face Zoe. Even to this day he was surprised they had lost all those years ago.

Except that they had been hiding the girl that was still drooling on his shoulder. It was worth it to lose, worth it to sacrifice his dragon then, as it was now. He carefully, moved some of the bright red hair that had come loose from her bun toward her ear, careful not to touch her, sure the contact would wake her.

"Do something after?" Drake asked, pulling his own magazine out of the pouch in the seat in front of him. It was the same as Zoe's and did nothing to calm the multiplying tension, it was as boring as he expected.

Unless you wanted to learn about parachuting safety or purchase a cat robot. Both of those were options.

"Well, that all depends." Zoe whispered, turning the page again and pointing out a particularly ugly "sock scarf" on the next page. "We are in the dark on whatever is going on back home, while I would love to settle into some good old Family Feud I am also planning on treading very, very carefully."

It took him a moment to follow that accurately.

"Careful as in ask questions before capture?"

"Not that careful," Zoe said, settling back into her seat. "But you will need to keep Ellie away from whatever is about to go down."

"You say that as though you are going into turf war."

Zoe smiled broadly, letting her dragon shine, before putting her magazine away and sitting back, eyes closed.

Zoe maybe the strongest, but she also had the largest conscious, the best sense of right and wrong. That didn't mean that she didn't get into a little fight from time to time. Judging by that smile, she enjoyed it too. She had still been raised by the same man that he had, the same man that Killian had.

And Drake knew exactly how ruthless that upbringing could be. He had barely survived it, and Zoe had come first.

When he was growing up Killian had told stories about how harsh and cruel Zoe had once been. He had never believed it, not until they had started to revolt against the King, the powerful princess capturing Ceres men and throwing them to the wolves.

He saw the same light in her eyes right then, and he would have loved to say that it scared him. But he had a feeling that it meant something much more.

"You feel connected to her, don't you?" He whispered, leaning toward Zoe so that anyone who might be listening couldn't hear. Not that it would matter, this conversation was not incriminating, well not as far as dragons and vampires were concerned.

But there was a weight, a pressure against his chest that he wasn't a hundred percent sure was from the cabin pressure as they prepared for descent.

His heart pounded against his ribs as he waited for the response, his fire boiling aggressively as Zoe turned, the heat in her eyes lessening somewhat.

"Not in the same way you do," she admitted, her voice soft, although not in a whisper, in a calm acceptance that he didn't expect. "But yes, I want to protect her the same. I suppose I love her the same, but not as a bond, as a pair." she shook her head. "I am not sure if that makes any sense."

Drake braced himself, expecting some level of protective jealousy to rise, for his dragon to growl against her, to scream, to rage. But just as the calm in Zoe's voice had surprised him, so did his. That's all there was. Just calm.

He nodded once and leaned back against the chair, tightening his hand around Ellie's, unsurprisingly, she didn't respond. He had shared her room, and at times her bed, enough to know that Ellie slept with the density of a rock. It seemed that the ability extended to the plane.

"Is that bad?" Zoe asked, as the landing announcement

blared through the speakers and Ellie began to fidget on his shoulder.

"Nothing is bad, Zoe," Drake whispered, giving Ellie a smile as she began to rouse, frantically wiping the drool from her lip. "It's only bad if you think it should be. And I don't think it should be. Do you?"

Zoe shook her head as Ellie snapped around, pure horror shaking in her eyes.

"Oh my god, I am so sorry," She said, blush coloring her face. Drake couldn't help but smile at her, at the shock and worry that he wanted nothing more to soothe away.

It didn't help that the blush was darkening those tiny freckles, he thought it had been hard not to reach forward and trace them before.

"Nothing wrong with a little bit of drool," Drake said, forcing a laugh as Ellie pulled away, revealing a large wet spot on his shoulder, nearly the size of a New York bagel.

"She's done that to me before," Zoe said with a laugh from behind him. "That is far more than a little bit of drool."

Drake wanted to agree, but poor Ellie was now so red that Drake was concerned some sort of fire or magic flare up was right around the corner.

"A little bit of drool," he repeated, lifting her hand to his lips.

Gently, he kissed her skin, his dragon heating at the contact, at the waves of fire that followed right behind. One tiny touch and he was lost in her again, her lips parting, her chest heaving.

Before he could stop himself, he was leaning in, needing to be closer.

He could feel the warmth of her lips radiate into his when the plane made touchdown and everyone was jerked back into their seat with a lurch. Drake was plastered to his plastic seat with a gasp, Ellie following suit while Zoe laughed.

None of them said a word as the plane was taxied to the gate. It wasn't that Drake couldn't find anything to say, it was that Zoe was now digging her eyes into the dragon girl ahead of them with such intensity that Drake was surprised she couldn't feel the heat.

Drake certainly could. Even with dragon blood flowing through his veins he was beginning to sweat.

The large drool spot wasn't going to be the only moisture on his shirt if this kept up.

"Zoe," Drake began, ready to issue plea or warning, or who knows what, but right then the steward came over the loudspeaker announcing their arrival, and the blonde dragon was up and racing down the aisle, Zoe right on her heels.

"What in the world?" Ellie jumped up in shock, nearly smacking her head on the overhead compartment.

"Get down," Drake hissed, not that it mattered, everyone else had noticed the chase and were looking from their escape route to them with the speed of a ping pong spectator.

Drake watched their interest, heard the gossip, and knew at once what he had to do. Or rather, what he should do if there had been a dragon, or a burst of flame, but there had been nothing, nothing but two strangers chasing each other down the aisle.

"She needed the bathroom," Drake said a bit too loud, knowing that the excuse was ridiculous but not caring, they would believe it.

Mortals would believe anything if said with enough authority, and it wouldn't take his silver tongue to make it stick.

Well, everyone but Ellie who was raising her eyebrows so high they might as well be flying away.

They walked from the plane quietly, Ellie continually giving him glances until they hit the boarding area, and a very frazzled looking Zoe.

It was clear she hadn't caught her, which only lead to a heavier weight against Drake's heart. It was bad enough that another dragon was on the plane, but now the information that both he and Zoe were alive could be racing to Rydaim at that very moment.

They couldn't do anything to stop it now.

Drake's frustrations released in a shaky exhale, and Ellie went back to looking between the two with a quickly darkening look.

"Will one of you two explain now?"

He really didn't want to withhold anything from her, but the busy gate of an airport was not the place to reveal that there had been a dragon on the plane. Besides, they didn't know anything more than that there had been a dragon on the plane.

Flying, even commercially, to a place with so many mountains was bound to have more of their kind around. Without any true information he wasn't about to jump to conclusions.

"She thought she knew her," Drake finally explained, and Ellie laughed as they walked away toward baggage and past security the security.

"Tell me later then?" She said with a grin, as they left the loading area and wandered toward the wall of people that had come to greet their loved ones.

Drake hadn't expected anyone to greet them, but Killian stood in the middle of the crowd, his height and bulk making him look as out of place as a weed amongst roses.

Except that he was the rose, or rather he held one in his hand. A single long-stemmed beauty that was as red as Ellie's hair, as red as her phoenix.

"Hi Ellie girl," he said, his voice booming over the crowd as Ellie dropped her bags and rushed him, the massive dragon sweeping her up in his arms.

The last time she had seen him Killian had been ready to kill them all, he had left to protect them from Ceres. While Drake should be glad to see him, and to see him alive given the text message and all the worry that had come with it.

Right then, he felt jealous for the first time as their lips crashed together.

17

JARRON

Jarron had never seen the alley so empty. So dark.

The chatter that usually whispered from the makeshift tents of The Forgotten had left, only to be replaced by the scurrying of rats and other tiny beasts as they scuttled through the ripped remains of their tattered homes in search of food left behind.

The Forgotten had gone.

Jarron wasn't sure where they had gone, or even how they had vanished so quickly, but last night he had been here, handing out some food, chatting to the few that he had been able to gain trust with as he tried to get information.

Now there was nothing, nothing but destroyed tents, scattered belongings, and a streak of bright red blood that was sending a chill over his spine. He could feel the creature inside of him rise up, feel the whisper of heat and raw anger against his skin and he clenched the bag of bread he had brought against his chest, squishing the precious loafs as his eyes began to burn.

"Parris," he hissed into the dark alley, turning on his heels and hobbling through the dark, his hip aching as he forced the still healing joint to move. He raced as fast as he could through the twisting alleys and side roads until he plunged through the door and reached the bright white kitchen that Killian pretended he did not care for.

Callay was still there, cleaning flour from the counter-tops after their morning long baking session. She turned in alarm as Jarron banged the door open, shattering the glass pane that Killian had had blown especially for the entry. Callay screamed at his sudden arrival, and the noise, sending a plume of flour into the air and covering her already pale skin in a ghostly sheen.

Jarron didn't feel even a touch of apology. He was fuming too much, both heart and dragon thundering in his chest, attempting to rip their way out. He had kept them restrained to this point, but he couldn't keep it in any longer. Seeing Callay there, alive and safe was only fueling the guilt. He should have been able to save them all by now.

With a roar that rattled broken glass, walls, and every one of Jarron's bones, he let his dragon escape just enough that his pain ripped out of him. His skin bulged and gleamed in glittering gold as the creature pushed against him, desperate to get out. He wished he could, he would shift right here, burn the kitchen to ashen piles. But his hip, his shoulder, the left side of his jaw, they were all still healing from his beating, he wasn't sure what a shift would do to his human body.

He screamed louder. Feeling the bitter failure, feeling the disgust at being trapped here. Unable to do a damn thing.

Callay jumped at the sound, stepping back as Jarron began to rip the loaves apart, throwing bread and paper around like they were party favors.

The roar of his dragon echoed over the marble and

stone until the chunks of fresh bread and the shards of the paper bags settled around him. Only then did he fall to the ground, his knees smacking against the smooth tile with a crack that was closer to a whisper against the roar of his dragon.

"What in the world?" Callay asked, her voice tentative as she remained hidden behind the wide marble island, obviously too scared to come closer.

Jarron didn't care. It was probably better if she stayed away. He felt dangerous right then, even if his dragon couldn't escape, he could still spit fire and consume this pathetic kitchen with the liquid gold that he had been cursed with.

Carefully controlling his anger, he remained hunched on the floor. Echoes of his roar rumbling until he was little more than a feral animal. Maybe he was, everything felt out of control right then. His dragon too close. His anger too hot.

He needed her. He needed his mate, to cry with. To mourn with. But it was only him, trapped in this city. Ellie was a whole ocean away.

The moment he was healed, the moment he could walk without pain and shift without risk, he would be gone, carrying Callay out of here if needs be. But for now, he was here, watching over the Fae, helping The Forgotten, stalking Parris even as the man's minions stalked him. Now, a big piece to that puzzle had vanished.

Jarron attempted to regulate his breathing, to make himself less feral. His massive creature didn't seem interested in that, however, it continued to growl. The sound vibrated through his bones as his skin shimmered like gold, each tear that landed on the tight muscles of his arms looking like magic.

Just breathe, he prompted himself, clamping his eyes shut as he tried to focus on Ellie's face. There was only a river of blood in his mind.

"Jarron?" Callay asked, tentatively stepping around the island as his growl began to subside. Her steps were slow, calculated, his dragon could taste her fear in the air.

"I'm not dangerous," he said, his voice containing too much of a snarl for that to be completely true.

Seeing as her steps didn't change, she clearly didn't believe him either.

"What happened?" She asked, stopping a good ten feet away and dropping to her knees, looking over the floor to where he huddled, hands knotting through his hair.

Jarron lifted his head, his eyes burning with both tears and flame as he looked at her. The girl flinched, but she didn't move back, she stayed still, returning his glance as her hair began to sway, as her own power increased to match his own.

He should have been glad of the support, but he couldn't find it in him to be grateful of anything right then. There was too much death, and it kept growing closer.

"They are gone," he finally said, his voice hard and she flinched. He didn't need to say any more than that, the tiny Fae sagged as though she had been deflated, her own eyes filling with tears.

"Hiding?" Callay ventured, and Jarron looked back to her, although reluctantly. Her eyes were wide, glittering trails of tears falling down her cheeks. There was so much hope in that one word, and Jarron already felt the stab of regret at having dashed it, but he knew he didn't have a choice.

"You know they aren't," he grumbled, pulling himself to

his feet as he wiped the tears away. "I need to know what happened. I need to know what he did."

His voice was hard, his dragon hissing in determination as his throat began to heat and smoke. He knew he should wait until he calmed down, there was too much of a risk that he would give himself away with the level of anger that was pulsing through him. But he had to protect Ellie as he had to protect the thousands of Fae that hid and worked in this city. They were too closely connected now.

"Are you sure that is wise?" Callay asked, coming up behind him as Jarron stepped to the sink, turning the hot water to full blast.

He needed to wash away the golden smears of his tears, wash away his guilt and his weakness and this was the only way he knew how to do it.

"First he and his coven clear out the slave market, and now they are cleaning The Forgotten from the streets," Jarron said, sparks of fire trickling over his face and neck as he began to scrub the top most layer of skin away. He could feel the prickles of growth over his jaw, the beard that he always kept so perfectly shaved, trying to poke itself back into existence.

"I have to find out what they are up to," Jarron finished, slamming the water off with a bit too much force and grabbing one of Killian's bright green towels, streaking it with golden lava.

Too bad that won't wash out. With so much at stake now, he doubted either of them would care, or even if Killian would see the towels again.

"I know," Callay whispered from behind him, her voice filled with all the dejection he felt. "But you don't want to alert them that you know too much."

"I am part of them, Callay. A prince. Hunting for my

father's chance at eternity," Jarron said, leaning against the counter as he turned to her, the poor girl still covered in flour.

He sure gave her a fright, he handed her the towel to clean herself up, and she took it, but the square of fabric fell to her side, as forgotten as the poor souls who had met their end.

The truth of that had never felt so sour.

"Or, at least they think I am," Jarron corrected, shaking his head as he patted away the flour from his knees. "I will play that part and get all the information we need. I may be stuck here, but I won't be idle. If they truly suspect Killian, I am the only one who can."

He attempted to swallow the bitter fear away, but it stayed, lodged in his throat with all the bile and failure that he had been stockpiling for the past few days. He wasn't a fool. He knew it was dangerous, but just being here was.

Being away from Ellie was doing nothing for his health. With a sigh, he palmed the back of his neck, trying to soothe away the muscles that were always in a constant state of ache without her.

"I need to find Dabria," he announced, pushing away from the counter and making a beeline for the now destroyed door. "She always knows what's going on, or has recently slept with someone who does."

He didn't bother to restrain his disgust at that last bit and Callay laughed, waving her hand and putting the glass back into the door with little more than a snap.

Jarron froze as the glass pieced itself back together like a toddler's puzzle, the shards blending together until it looked as though nothing had happened. It was amazing, and even though he had seen it a million times before, it hit him differently this time.

Knowing that that same magic was inside Elliot. Locked away. Exploding out of her.

"She will be okay," Callay said, reading his face like a book. "Go find the little wench. I'll see what I can find out. But I think our time in this city might be at an end."

She gave him a mischievous grin before she vanished with the tiniest of pops, leaving him alone in the kitchen, surrounded by bits of torn bread and fragments of the hope that he had built for so long.

Too bad that didn't go back together as easy as the glass had.

Instead of going outside through the back door, which he preferred, Jarron made his way around to the massive stained glass entry that Killian had had built shortly after they had defeated Zoe and her coup. At the time it had seemed like the perfect monument to their success, a stained glass image of his sister burning at the stake. Now, however, it was little more than a cruel stake in his heart.

Biting his tongue, Jarron hurried past the monstrosity and their neighbors equally as gaudy doors in his race toward the square. He needed to find the woman as quickly as possible, and the easiest way to do that was too make himself noticeable.

Dabria would always find unescorted royalty like a troublesome fly would find honey and she brought all the same diseases along for the ride.

Ignoring the pain that was shooting through his leg and back, Jarron continued his hobble into the square, expecting to see the stands and sellers set up around the fountain as they usually were this time of day, but everything was empty, there wasn't a tent. There wasn't even a straggler from the usually busy market. Just piles of trash and forgotten boxes. Everything was silent.

Even the water from the fountain flowed a little less joyfully than it had that morning. Well, as joyfully as it could considering it represented the blood of the 'mortal scourge' his father had plans to destroy. Jarron forced himself to stay impassive, even though his insides were tightening in disgust, and continued toward the square, toward the last seller who was packing up his belongings.

The man was moving fast, but froze when he saw Jarron racing toward him, a look of horror twisting though his brow. Jarron wasn't used to being the recipient of those looks. That level of hatred was usually reserved for Killian, not for him, and it turned his blood to ice.

His impassive stare fell to a scowl as the man went back to packing up his things, continually looking over to him as though he was expecting Jarron to strike him down at any second.

It didn't make any sense. Only yesterday The Forgotten had been in their homes, the market had been alive. It had all been normal. Well, normal to those who didn't see the cruel underbelly.

Something had happened, and the closer Jarron moved to the truth the more the lies grated against his soul.

The terrified seller glanced up again as he placed the last box on the cart, ready to make a run for it. Jarron almost picked up in a sprint to catch him, until the man looked again. But not at him. At something behind him.

Jarron froze in place, slowly turning on the spot as his mouth began to fill with ash.

He had been hoping to find Dabria, but this was so much worse. Parris was sprinting right toward him, a nefarious smile on his face. Of course, he was here, of course he had followed him. All he needed was to race past the vampires that were perched like little birds around his house.

If Jarron had thought his blood had turned to ice before, it was nothing to the dark chill that overtook him as the vampire came closer, the wicked man's smile stretching. Jarron's skin burned in anticipation of a bite, his muscles tensing. He was ready for a fight, even if he didn't have the full use of his arm quite yet.

He had never trusted the little man, but, the idea of being alone with him was no longer wanted.

"Parris!" He announced joyfully, swallowing all his fear and panic and carefully arranged his features as he clapped the vampire on the back in greeting. "I didn't expect to see you here. The market is not your usual haunt, although the market seems to have disappeared. What's happened, man?"

Parris' smile fell as though someone had slapped it from him, "Didn't you hear?"

Jarron's mind ran through the last few days, the last few hours, searching for anything that he should have heard. He hadn't been present enough around the dragons to hear anything. At least not that he would share with this blood sucker.

"Hear what?" Jarron's voice was hard, the rough edges cutting through the silent square in a growl that was so like his father's that anyone else may has scuttled away in fear.

But Parris only smiled, the same grin stretching his face wickedly. It almost looked as though his face was being sliced in two.

"There was an attack this morning. The Forgotten stormed the throne room, armed with spears and rocks of all things," Parris laughed as though it was the most ridiculous thing he had ever heard, and while Jarron tried to join him, the sound didn't quite come out right. His temper flared as his dragon woke with a spark, the sneer that covered Parris' face doing nothing to calm either him or his creature.

"I ordered the market closed as a security measure as we search for the rest of the insects."

"*You* ordered..." Jarron questioned, his stomach twisting further, his mind moving as fast as he worked to catalogue each lie the revolting man was spewing out.

The Forgotten were more likely to put on a musical number for the king than to attack him, and the amount of blood that was in the alley did not lead him to believe that anything that the man was saying was true.

Except that blood or not, there would be only one reason his father would let Parris make an order like that.

The twisted vampire had finally taken control.

They had seen the beginnings of that the other day. Seen the control, now there appeared to be no going back.

"We still have meat and the blood of the vermin in the tower," Parris said, wrapping his arm around the heating dragon as he began to lead him away. "Inform your brother, I am sure he would like to join us."

Jarron hesitated. Callay hadn't told him how Killian had gotten out yesterday. He had no idea if revealing that the crown prince had left the city would save his brother, or how much it would doom him.

With the smile the vampire was giving him, he was sure he was doomed anyway.

"He isn't in Rydaim," Jarron said, his voice hard as he tried to step away from the vampire's acidic touch, but the man held him tight, leading him toward the staircase that led to the throne room, to a hundred dead bodies and a future that he had clearly failed at preventing.

His stomach twisted with each step, pulling him back even as he was forced forward.

"Shame. Shame." Parris said, the tone darkening so that Jarron was sure it wasn't a shame at all, nor was it a surprise. "I am sure he we will be back soon, there will be more feasts soon. Perhaps even one in his name. I am sure of it."

Jarron jerked toward the vampire, to the vile man that was now smiling at something only he could see. The light of success was brilliant in his eyes, greed the color of his brother's blood was ringing his eyes.

It was then he knew that he should have left, that he should have risked the shift and taken Callay out of here, returned to his mate. He knew it was a risk to his safety, but now it was a promise. He couldn't leave, and Killian could not return with the repulsive hunger that shone from the blood suckers' eyes.

Rydaim was moments away from falling.

Jarron had left his heart in the states, and he was sure his pride somewhere in the middle of the square.

But, as he limped behind Parris, following him to a massacre that would tear him apart even more, he felt his determination grow. He would defeat this man, even if he was alone to do it.

Even if it ended in his death. Even if safety was the only gift he ever gave the girl who had claimed his soul.

18

ELLIOT

I COULD STILL TASTE HIM ON MY LIPS. I COULD TASTE THE warm flavor of mint, coffee, and vanilla Chapstick that somehow meshed together in a perfect combination. Like a morning latte, which was saying something because I preferred my coffee black. But standing next to Killian, his hand wrapped around mine as we walked down the hall of the baggage check, the taste of him on my lips, I was suddenly understanding the obsession.

A Killian latte would taste delicious.

Oh. My. God. I really needed to get control of myself. I was sleepy from the plane, my mind still trapped in first-kiss-bliss, but that woke me the hell right up.

"You okay, Ellie?" Drake asked from the other side of me, flanking me like I was royalty. Or like I was in extreme danger. With both of them so close I was starting to wonder about the girl on the plane, but I wasn't about to bring that up now. Zoe was already in full blown security detail mode as she hovered behind the three of us, looking around as if she was waiting for a tiger to pop out from behind one of the pillars.

Or a vampire. Probably a vampire.

"Yeah," Just thinking about what it would be like to taste Killian. "Just tired from the flight."

It wasn't completely a lie, plus talking about licking people in the middle of an airport can't be something I want TSA to be listening in on.

Drake gave me a smile and ran his finger over my jaw. He didn't touch me more than that, but even that was enough to warm my bones and send a shiver down my spine as the warmth from Killian and the heat from Drake intersected.

I was an Ellie sandwich again, although this time one of the key players had changed, with Killian taking Jarron's place. All the frustrated tension drained from my body like a sieve, my phoenix prickling against my heart and pulling me a million miles away. I may not know where he was, but I was sure I could find him if I needed.

Activate the powers of the tethered string. That sounded was cooler in my head I was sure.

"Where is he?" I asked as quietly as I could, turning to Killian as we exited to the loud loading zone where Killian said he had a car waiting.

Instead of an answer, Killian gave me a tight-lipped stare, his hand tightening around mine as he pulled me closer, guiding me toward a line of sleek black vehicles that I was sure included the battered rental car Suvi usually provided in its midst.

He clearly knew exactly who I was talking about. Which made that tight-lipped stare he was giving to the cars even worse. "That isn't making me feel very confident, Killian."

"I would have to agree with that. We expected both of you, and a third," Drake said, his words carefully coded as he shifted my suitcase that he had insisted on carrying. I still wanted to rip it out of his hands. Not only did

I not need a man to carry my stuff, but I really didn't want to run the risk of everything tumbling out of it and all over the airport floor. It wouldn't be the first time that that had happened, you had to carry it a certain way...

"Let's talk in the car," Killian said, pulling us to a stop beside a black minivan with windows that were tinted so dark it looked like something out of a spy movie.

I even expected the thing to be full of computers and panels with blinking lights. Instead, it was leather seats and the aroma of new car spray. So definitely better than the overly dented car that we normally had to use in the cities, even without the spy equipment. Besides, with Killian tense expression, I had a feeling we were going to turn it into a spy vehicle anyway.

"Nice ride, Kills," Zoe said with a smirk, beginning to load the luggage into the back. "I never took you for the minivan type."

Normally, I would laugh, chuckle, guffaw, something. But my phoenix was now ruffling angrily in my chest, pressing against skin and heart in a million fluttering feathers. I didn't dare make a sound, I wasn't convinced that what would come out would be entirely human.

"What?" Zoe was clearly oblivious. Well, oblivious to us, she was still checking the loading zone for vampires or werewolves or some mugger to pop out and steal our luggage.

I mean, not that I knew anything about how that worked. I was still relying on my internet education of the supernatural, which was still proving to be as unreliable and useless as possible. Like with vampires. According to the interwebs, and nearly every vampire book ever written, Vampires can't stand in the sun. I mean, I wasn't best friends with Stacia or anything, but I was sure she had stood in the sun at some point.

Well, stood in the sunlight in the practice tent. I really hadn't seen her anywhere else. And, who knows, maybe Suvi had given her some special blue body lotion that could stop her from bursting into flames. I was going to go with that, but only because picturing Stacia covered in blue Smurf goo was wonderful.

"Tell us what happened. Where is Jarron? Is he okay?" Drake demanded the second the sliding door to the van had snapped shut and Zoe had thrown the ignition.

The car pulled away, sliding into the traffic as I slammed into the back of the leather seat. It would have been comfortable if every part of me didn't feel like it was covered in nails.

"He is still in Rydaim," Killian said, the tension in the car dripping down my back like ice as everyone waited for him to continue. But he sat, jaw tight as he stared out the window.

"Oddly enough, we figured that part out," Zoe snapped, turning around long enough to give her brother a glare. "Your text was a bit too ominous for us to let you get away with that. If we need to rush in and pull him out, now is your chance to say."

"I'm ready," The words were out before I could stop them, not that I would have. I was so completely, partially ready for this. "I may be an untrained hybrid creature with no memory, but I'll pull out some miracle at the last minute. I have a track record to uphold."

"Like glowy hands?" Zoe teased, shooting me a snickering smile. Her red ringed eyes dug into me the same way they had for so many years, except this time I didn't feel quite so much frozen, as I did determined.

If Jarron really was in trouble, I would find a way to get to him, and then I would conduit explode or spit a javelin or use glowy hands or something.

I was starting to realize I needed better names for all the crazy I was able to do.

"Like anything to keep him safe." I folded my arms over my chest, and sat back, staring out the window and watching the buildings get bigger. The city grew the deeper we moved into it, but it wasn't the city I was watching, it was the mountains.

They were even bigger than those that towered over Salt Lake City. These hovered over us though they were a guardian, looming over the towns and forests as though to keep the humans safe. They were just mountains, but I had a feeling they were more dangerous than I wanted to believe.

Zoe had told me once that mountains were a great hiding place for dragons. Even without the caves, I was sure there were some here, watching us.

"I will keep him safe," I said more to the mountains than to anyone in the car, as if the phantom mountain-dragons had anything to do with our current situation.

"He's fine," Killian said, his voice tight. "At least, as well as I know. Callay stayed with him and will get us a message if something happens and we need to act. But they have ways out. And as far as I can tell, are safe. Although, if something does happen, I am fairly certain that Callay will be able to get him out on her own."

"Get him out? So, he is trapped." Drake's voice was hard, his panic fueling the tension in the car as the engine roared to life and Zoe floored it. The car sped over the freeway, weaving through cars as she plunged us closer to the city.

Closer to the mountains. Or farther away from whatever is behind us.

My heart pulled harder, the damn thing turning to a rock that was making it impossible to breathe.

"Not trapped. There are ways out. Callay seems to have been hiding a fair bit of information from me. We don't need to go in guns blazing. Yet," Killian clarified, his voice rumbling as his dragon peaked through his eyes and my stomach dropped even further. Everything was a rock of nerves and boiling fire. I didn't know if I was going to explode, cry, or a combination of both. And it better not be both, I didn't need to add fire tears to my weirdly named arsenal.

That seemed painful.

"Yet?"

Killian nodded once, "Something happened. I have never seen Parris more in control over the old man. I don't know why, or how, but something has changed."

"You are being far too ambiguous to make me feel calm about the situation," Zoe snarled, her eyes forward.

"Well, hopefully Jarron has been able to get more information," Killian said, giving me a look that as strong as he tried to appear was screaming behind his eyes. "We will see him soon."

I swallowed, but my mouth was so dry it barely did anything. I knew he was lying. I knew the truth was hidden somewhere in his eyes.

But damn it all, I was too scared to ask. I was too scared to see.

Right then, it was easier to hope.

"How much time do you think we have?" Drake turned around in his seat to face us, and the engine roared again,

Zoe speeding around a tiny yellow car, and taking the first exit toward the city.

"If we need to rush in and rip the bastards head off, we can," Zoe said, her voice hard as she stared down the street.

Or I can. I had been wanting to rip heads off for a while, who says that Zoe should have all the fun? She looked like she was ready to ram all the cars that stood between us and our destination, anyway. She could clear the way, I could rip the heads.

Thank god it was just a minivan. I would hate to see Zoe behind the wheel of a tank.

That tense rock from before mutated into a screaming ball of heat, my skin prickling and pulling as the goose flesh made a return.

I felt dangerous. I felt ready, I just had to hold off a little longer. If the minivan couldn't survive Zoe's road rage, it really wasn't going to survive a tiny contortionist shifting into a Phoenix.

"Not yet," Killian's voice was approaching a growl now. "But we should build a plan in case something goes south. With everything Parris is doing... I think it's time we build our rebellion."

Zoe and Drake exchanged a look from where they sat up front, their eyes quivering in a stare that was equal parts fear and exhilaration. This was doing nothing for my current impending shifter predicament.

"What does that mean?" I was seriously scared to ask.

"It means we should have kept some of Stacia's fake blood." Zoe's voice was dripping with a villainy that I don't think I had heard before. It ripped into me as she pulled the car into a large hotel parking lot.

"I don't like the sound of that. Is there a vampire fight I should be preparing for?"

Zoe only smirked and opened the door. "Not yet."

I really didn't like the sound of that. Once again, I was hit with the imagery of me fighting a handsome vampire prince, only this time it didn't end so well. Cue overdramatic swallow.

If Zoe thought that was the end of that conversation, she was mistaken. I had no problem with cornering her in a dark alley to get my answers.

That sounded wrong.

The hotel was large and looked a bit nicer than Suvi's usual. But right then I could care less, all I needed right then was a shower, and maybe a few minutes to figure out how to get to Jarron. They were talking about battle plans and escape routes like it was a game of tag. Part of me wished it was, but I couldn't get that room out of my mind, the walls dripping with blood when Stacia ran away, taking her warning and burning wrist with her.

If I could stop the vampires, then I could save Jarron when the time came. I needed to figure out how. Because I was sure they didn't want me coming on that adventure, not that they could stop me.

Maybe I could go invisible or something. I wouldn't put anything past my latent mutant abilities right now.

My mind was buzzing when Killian stepped around the car. I barely registered anything passed some grand breakout plan that I was going to lead, just his broad shoulders holding the door open for me.

"Will you go on a date with me, Elliot?" Killian asked as he held the door open, and I promptly fell out of it.

"You tell us that Jarron is trapped, and ask me on a date?"

"We aren't running in guns blazing yet," Killian's hand wrapped over my arm, helping me to my feet as he pulled me to him. "I want to be with you, I want you to smile, before everything falls apart."

Damn him and his husky voice. All logical thought had left my brain, and I stumbled away in search of air.

"Of course, I would be the first to ask her out, and you would be the first to take her," Drake chuckled as he caught my elbow, his fingers trailing down my arm as he stepped back to the hatch, and to the array of suitcases and duffle bags that had seen Zoe and I through far too many cities, and far too many countries. She was already there, pulling out the rolling cases. Thankfully my stuff wasn't in a yellow hazard bag this time, but one of my roller cases had been taped shut with TSA tape. So, a slight improvement.

"Well, I would invite you along, little bro. But, I don't think we are to that stage in our relationship yet." Killian said, earning himself a look from Drake and a hysterical choking noise from me.

The fog horn had made a return. At least I didn't hiccup fire that time.

"Or ever." I managed to splutter out. At least Drake had the sense to look as uncomfortable as I felt.

Kilian smiled, giving me a wink that swooped through my already dancing stomach. I guess those butterflies had built themselves a theme park.

I hated roller coasters.

19

JARRON

EACH STEP TOWARD THE THRONE ROOM HIT AGAINST JARRON'S already tight muscles with waves of dread, and it wasn't all from the chill that had taken over the air. The lingering chill of a few vampires he could handle, this was different. His heart was thundering in his chest, pushing against bones and lungs until he was having trouble keeping each breath as just air, and not the smoke and flame it wanted to be. Parris was watching him too closely for that, his eyes shifting constantly as the vampire walked the dragon toward the door that stood open.

Stood silent.

With all Parris's talk about The Forgotten that had charged the throne room, Jarron had expected there to be screams. He had expected the aroma of blood to linger in the air like perfume. But there was only the icy chill of a vampire, only the dread of the silence that pressed against his chest with nearly as much weight as his anxiety.

"This may be the quietest party you have thrown yet, Parris," Jarron said, forcing a laugh into his voice as he quick stepped to the slithery vampire. Keeping up with him was proving difficult with the radiating pain in his hip. His dragon needed to hurry up and heal the thing already.

Yes, he was walking into a trap. Jarron wasn't fool enough to assume otherwise, but that didn't mean he had to walk into the room like a sheep to the slaughter, besides if he was going to fight his way through this, he needed the best possible positioning, and that meant being able to take Parris down first.

Looks like he was going to get his wish and watch the little man writhe in his fire after all.

"Well, you are joining us late, young prince," Parris said, fixing him with a shit eating grin. He wasn't even trying to disguise it anymore. The little man knew exactly what he was doing. "You have missed out on all the fun, now you get to pick at the scraps."

"Much like you!" Jarron bellowed with a laugh that wiped the smug grin right off the vampires' face. "Always the scavenger right?"

He prodded the irritating blood sucker perfectly, letting his grin spread as Parris's faded to scowl.

"Always," Parris's words ground alongside the door, the stone slowly swinging open to reveal his father sitting in the throne at the other end of the hall, Dabria perched on the armrest as she always was, hovering over the old man like a vulture.

Despite the cold, there didn't appear to be anyone else in the room, just the three of them. No bodies. Not even a smear of blood.

Parris had promised a feast. No, he had promised a massacre, but there wasn't any sign of anything having happened here. In fact, the cave didn't even bear the residual smell of blood and bone. It was almost as though it had been cleaned.

"Where's the feast? Jarron hissed to the vampire, but the icy man smiled widely and pushed the door closed.

This was a trap, yes, he just hadn't assumed it to be so obviously so. Either way, he shouldn't complain, the lack of showmanship was certainly giving him an advantage.

Two dragons and a vampire. Even with his injuries, Jarron was knew he could take them, or at the very least maim them enough that he could soar out of the stained glass window and through the large hidden alcove that Callay had pointed out on the schematics.

Callay.

Damn it. He couldn't leave her. So much for his bash and smash escape plan. He was sure the girl could take care of herself, but he respected her more than to leave her to rot.

Pushing his dragon down enough that the creature didn't burst from his skin as he usually preferred, Jarron stepped further into the throne room, his mind moving over escape plans and attack options. Just in case. Trap or not, he wasn't about to go in spitting fire on anything that moved.

That's what had gotten Zoe killed.

Well, fake-killed.

He only hoped that these two didn't know that.

"Jarron, my boy!" The king boomed, his voice echoing over the scrubbed stone, even though he didn't move from his roost, in fact, he barely turned to face him. "I'm so glad you could join us."

"As am I. Although, I was told there would be a party. Instead I arrive to find that you have scrubbed the place clean." Jarron stepped toward the old man, although not as quickly or as far as he had hoped, keeping Parris in his sights was vital, this time he let the icy man pass him, the three of the them predictably standing together.

Well, if he was going to kill them, he might as well do it as cleanly as possible.

Three little vipers, for one line of fire. He liked those odds.

"It was time for a good scrubbing," Ceres said, rising from the throne, running his finger over the armrest as though he was inspecting a polish job. "There was so much blood it was driving the vampires crazy."

Jarron couldn't help but laugh at that, "And since when do we care about the comfort of the blood suckers. They love the blood, they'd lick it off the walls if you'd let them."

Parris' own laugh joined in at that, the chuckle rippling through the cold as he smacked the king on the back, the old man wobbling where he stood. Great, the king was clearly drunk. It usually happened after Parris brought him far too many mortal women, and far too many bottles of Spanish Vermouth.

It seems it was the same result after a few too many Fae. The thought made his stomach twist, and Jarron straightened his shoulders, refusing to let the guilt and disgust that was now assaulting him show on his face.

"So, where are these usurpers then?" Jarron looked around him the exaggerated motions seeking for any sign of the so-called battle. It was the doors and windows he was interested in, however. It was any sign that Parris's cover was about to bolt their way through the door, it was plotting his escape if he needed it. Between an actually drunk father, and a power drunk Parris he was going to need it.

He wasn't interested in a repeat of last time.

He had always wanted to destroy the morbid stained glass masterpiece. He would stick with that, if only to see the thing shatter and fall over the center of Rydaim like multicolored stars.

"There never were any," Jarron spun to the old man, he hadn't expected that, and this time he couldn't stop the shock from shining in his eyes. "We captured the last of The Forgotten and Parris has been given full control of their souls, and their blood."

Slime slithered down Jarron's spine, it snaked through his stomach as Parris's smile spread, as Dabria laughed and ran her finger over Ceres' neck, the old man staring at her appreciatively, his eyes nearly closed in what he could only assumed was pleasure, or he was simply too drunk to keep his eyes open.

It could swing in either direction, and with how the man was swaying on his feet, leaning on the giggling ice dragon he had to wonder exactly how drunk his father was.

Or rather, what exactly Parris had done.

"It seems Parris has been given control of quite a few things lately," Jarron said, his voice a snarl of warning as he glared at the vampire, his dragon heating in preparation.

The man's icy smile spread, the red veins in his eyes popping as they always did when one of his kind was angry, when they were hungry.

He detested the look. The memory of all those bites still too fresh. Jarron could still feel the disgusting fangs pierce his flesh.

"I trust him," Ceres mumbled into Dabria's neck, his hand twisting over her hair, pulling against her skin in a monochrome contrast that Jarron did not wish to witness. He had seen the woman weasel her way into enough people beds and minds over the years. Thankfully he didn't feel her poking around, but that didn't mean she wasn't there.

"I trust him with my people," Ceres continued, still focused on the curvature of Dabria's partially exposed breast.

"Our people," Jarron corrected, but the old man didn't seem to notice.

He didn't seem to notice anything other than the dragon in his arms, which didn't put Jarron in a good situation. As much as he despised Dabria he had no interest in fighting her. Fighting someone who could peak into your mind and predict every move never ended well. He was however, approaching that line.

"Tell me father," Jarron continued, refusing to look away from the vampire, his eyes glowing gold just as the vampires was soaked in blood. "Why do you trust him?"

"Because he gave me Dabria," The man said his voice slurred with lust and booze. "Because he showed me what my sons truly are."

The second half of that answer didn't seem quite so boozy. It was almost as if someone had flipped a switch and turned off the lush and replaced him with the king, the man's displeasure rushing right to the surface. Trap or not, there was something different here.

"And what is that?" He asked the question to Parris, the undead demon the only one who was looking at him. Staring into him. Every nerve ending was twisting with ice and fire at that point, Jarron's dragon pressing against his skin until he could feel the spines of the beast attempt to rip their way through.

One breath and they would all be gone. It would only take a second. He could make them burn, make them writhe, even without a shift. No one was here to see what would have happened. It would all be over so fast. Perhaps he could still leave this battle victorious.

"Little bastards that wet the bed at the sight of a breast, have low self-esteem, and aren't suited to rule over mortals. They would rather sleep with the ugly vermin and keep them a secret. They have no taste, because Dabria is better."

Ceres voice was hard, it growled and grumbled the way it always had, his grey eyes digging into Jarron with all the force and disappointment he had seen in his life. He was used to that look, used to the glare of an impending punishment. But he was also used to the reasoning behind his punishments making cognitive sense.

And everything that man had said was little more than drivel spouted by an impulsive child.

"I'm sorry?" Jarron questioned, Dabria giggling as Ceres stumbled into her as though he could no longer hold his weight.

"Enough Dabria," Parris grumbled, folding his arms over his waist as he stared at Jarron. His dead eyes pierced the Dragon, as, with a thump, his father fell to the ground, limbs tangling end over end as he collapsed like a rag doll.

"What the fuck?" Jarron shrieked, jumping back in expectation of blood or some other body fluid to seep from the man. Not that he would have minded either, he had been ready to end the bastard seconds before. He still was.

Except now it appeared someone had reached the man first. Damn it.

His golden eyes flashed to the pair as his fire flared, puffs of smoke drifting between his teeth. His warning, or rather his fear, was clear.

"Oh, settle down, Jarron," Parris growled, kicking the kings hand out of the way as he stepped around him. "He's not dead, and even if he was we all know you have no interest in avenging him. You're upset we got to him first."

Parris's eyes were so veined with blood they were nearly completely red, but Jarron didn't look away, he looked into the man as he controlled the fire, controlled the fear, and let his anger take control. He didn't even have to look at his skin to know the gold of his dragon was shimmering through. The creature was that close, his eyes melting with the fire that was ready to escape.

Let them burn, The growl roared through Jarron's mind, a rumble of sound escaping his chest as the creature pressed against his heart. He took one slow calculated step toward Parris, the man didn't even flinch.

"Do I want to know what you have done?" Jarron growled, his dragon so near the surface he was amazed the words were distinguishable. "Or should I burn you now."

"You can try, but it won't do you any good," Parris said with a shrug, smiling as Dabria came up beside him her fingers twisting through the shaggy blonde of the vampire's hair. "Besides! You should be glad we ended his rule. A common enemy! Gone! Of course, it also means your inevitable defeat."

"Oh, let's not get ahead of ourselves," Jarron warned, letting his dragon press against his skin, bulging at his shoulders.

Parris' laughed, the sound, loud, obnoxious, and grinding. "I'm ahead of nothing, I have won! I have the king..."

"You have a shell. That is not a man, and no one will believe he is the king."

"Are you quite sure about that?" Parris stepped closer, away from Dabria whose smile stretched as wide as the sadistic bottom feeder. "Are you that blind that you couldn't tell? Did you really think for a second that your father would allow my coven to feed from you? That he would allow them to taste the blood of a prince."

No, no he didn't. He had assumed that Parris had gained his trust somehow. That Parris had won. He may not have been wrong, but his reasoning for it appeared to be very far off.

Burn, the growl in his head intensified, his dragon rumbling as drops of golden fire coated his tongue.

He didn't care what Parris said, he was going to burn the bastard, he had to wait for the right time. Like any good villain Parris was already monologuing, he had to keep him going. Get all the information he could before he let the little man taste his end.

"How long have you been controlling him?"

"Since he brought Killian back from killing your baby brother," Parris scoffed, kicking the arm of the king who was twisted on the ground. "Of course, Dabria gained access far before that. I didn't know that, however, until I found poor Dabria mourning the loss of the prince she hopes to marry."

"Killian can bed his mortal. I will make him pay in the end," Dabria snarled, pressing herself against the vampire the same as she had every other male in a position of power in this room.

Unlike the King, Parris wasn't fooled by the act. He wasn't going to push her away either.

"I could have never gotten this far without this beauty," Parris said, the lust dripping from his voice as his skin faded, the black veins popping around his ears until Jarron was sure he was wanting to feed.

Jarron had no interest in witnessing the exchange. It was disgusting enough watching Stacia take a bite out of her feeders.

"You needed Dabria to succeed," Jarron said, forcing a laugh into his voice and thankfully pulling the two apart.

"No," Parris snarled, the dark lines in his skin increasing. "She just sped up the process. I no longer needed to gain that idiot's trust. I already convinced him to hand over The

Forgotten to me, and I tricked you and your brother into finding the Phoenix. I hope you've found her, and killed the one who is guarding her. That woman has caused more problems for me over the last few years than she has since I first destroyed her, nearly as much as that blasted donkey. It would be nice to be free of them both. But I will settle for the return of my Phoenix. She was my best creation and I would love to sink my teeth into her again."

Jarron's anger doused as though it had been drenched in ice water, the flame rolling back into his belly as shock and confusion ran through his veins, tensed in his muscles like springs ready for release.

"The Phoenix..." he began, his mind and dragon still trying to roll over everything that the blood sucker had said.

"Yes," Parris sneered, his smile stretching as he clearly missed the point. "I created the brat, and then Elliot and one of my blood slaves stole her and three others from my farm. It was a bane to lose them. With your help, and Killian's stubborn pride I am closer to finding the girl than I ever have been before. Dabria has been tracking the mortal whore and Killian. We know the circus burned, and we will find the beast before you end her. She's a scorned woman, did you really think she wouldn't figure it out?"

He smiled, his fangs peeking beneath his lip as the things protruded, ready for a bite, for an attack. Jarron didn't know, he didn't care, his anger was too high, he didn't hold back anymore. He took the risk.

With a bomb-like roar he released his dragon, letting the creature scream to life as his bones twisted, as his body pulled, as flame shot from his throat. He didn't even try to save his clothes, he let his dragon rip through them, ribbons of golden fire streaming from his jaws as his wings unfurled.

His fire looked like molten lava, the heavy spire dripping

through the air and landing right on Parris and Ceres. Gold covered them, the toxic ribbons cutting into his father's body and eating it away, the same way it had for every other dragon he had executed.

Thousands. He had watched his fire burn and condemn thousands, including his baby brother. Watching it do the same for his father, for Parris, somehow made up for every single creature he had cursed.

As much as he had tried to change the title he was the golden executioner, and he would enjoy this one.

Ceres screamed as his mind released from Dabria's hold, the man scuttling away from the ribbons of fire, his face and torso sliced apart with lines of gold. Screaming as his dragon tried to combat the burns, Dabria ran to his aid, her ice dripping around her in a pathetic shield.

Parris, however, didn't so much as scream, he didn't move, he stood still, his arms out as Jarron's fire continued to cover him, the last of it dripping away as Jarron roared, his dragon rearing up, ready to run for the mural.

His leg slid, the broken bones having snapped more in the shift. Screw it, he could fly through the cave. He would have, if Parris hadn't stepped forward, his red eyes digging into the golden scales of Jarron's dragon, smiling at the shimmering thing, completely unharmed.

Jarron had drowned him in his fire, but there didn't even seem to be a scratch on him.

Just a smile as the now naked man took one slow calculated step closer.

"Dragon fire can't hurt us," Parris said, his voice barely rumbling over the screams of his father. "Well, all but yours. And thanks to the feast you provided the other day..."

Parris licked his lips, Jarron's dragon screamed at the action, at the depravity of the creatures that were now streaming through the side doors, surrounding his dragon with shining blue swords in their hands.

Both Jarron and his dragon recognized them at once. Dragon scale swords. The only thing strong enough to pierce his hide. Wielded by the only creatures fast enough to make use of it.

Jarron roared as Dabria laughed, the tinkling sound making it clear where they had gotten the scales from, and how deeply the girl's treachery had reached.

Jarron was surrounded, he was trapped. There was only one way out. He would make it, or die trying.

For you, Elliot. To protect you. Always.

With a swipe of his tail, and one line of fire, Jarron took to the air ready to soar through the window, and fly back to his mate, back to the woman he needed to reach before they did.

His feet had barely left the ground when a shout surrounded him, and more than a hundred sharp points pierced his hide, ropes swinging around him and attempting to pull him down. His dragon screamed, but he did not stop moving. Thrashing against swords and ropes he rampaged toward the window, toward freedom, toward her.

With every broken step more knives sliced into him, cutting at his wings, at his legs, slicing tendons and muscles until he collapsed to the ground feet from his destination.

His dragon screamed, he screamed, his heart breaking as he stared at the faces of the mortals painted into the glass, at the golden blood that dripped down smooth surface. He couldn't have failed. He couldn't have. He tried to move, to pull himself forward by his claws, to throw himself out of the mural if needs be. But his torn tendons screamed, ropes wrapping around him as they tethered him down.

"Now, now," Parris said, his frozen hand hitting painfully

against the snout of Jarron's dragon. He tried to wiggle away from the touch, but with so many swords piercing his sides he could do little more than lay still, drowning in his golden blood as it dripped over his sides.

"You aren't going anywhere Jarron. You are going to help me bring the crown prince and his little phoenix to me. And then, then I will really take my crown."

20

ELLIOT

IT WOULD FIGURE THAT THE DAY AFTER HALF OF MY WARDROBE
went up in flames that Killian would insist that we go out to
dinner.

"What kind of dinner are we talking about?" I asked,
refusing to look away from the massively ornate dresser that
occupied my new hotel room, and would soon contain the
tangles of clothes and everything else that I owned.

Well, everything that was left, anyway.

Suvi had put everyone from the circus up in a moderate
hotel room near the campsite, and Killian had promptly
moved me over to the massive suite he had rented at a
neighboring hotel. I had been traveling for most of my life,
and I don't think I had ever seen anything as luxurious as
this before. There were fish, actual fish, swimming underneath the glass floor in the lobby.

Rich people did weird things.

It was clearly too much, and I did try to say no, but
Killian and Drake were insistent and I since I got my own
room and bathroom with a door. The whole thing was like

staying in a house, like the Golden Girls, if they all dated each other.

And were magical Shifters.

The idea of Blanche turning into a sexy mermaid was almost too much and I turned toward Killian, barely restraining the grin, and instead found myself struggling to breathe.

He still wore the same suit from the airport, but two subtle changes were making the already dashing, yes dashing, suit that much more of a twisting, needy, sex appeal. He leaned against my door frame with the jacket thrown over his shoulder, like the cool guy from some bad boy flick. The stubbly growth on his chin and his long hair was adding to the look in obnoxious ways. My real problem, and what was making it hard to breathe, was that the top few buttons on his shirt were popped, revealing a bit more of that tattoo that I had seen poking around his neck on that first day.

I couldn't see much, but what I did see resembled flames. You know, like the kinds that were now boiling under my skin. I swallowed, and he grinned, pulling his fingers through his unbound hair as he looked, dare I say it, embarrassed. I had never seen his hair down before, but looking at those shaggy curls that pulled past his shoulders and I knew I never wanted to see it up again.

"Is it a fancy dinner?" I managed to croak out, my voice resembling a frog after an all night rave as I tried to pull my hormones back together. "Because I don't have anything for a fancy dinner."

To be fair, I didn't have anything for any kind of dinner. Well, unless the dinner was at a gym. I wasn't about to tell him that, however. Not with that wicked little grin pulling his dimples back into existence. I didn't want to risk the suggestion of not wearing clothes to dinner at all.

Killian and I hadn't exactly got off on the right foot, and I could tell he was trying to make it up to me.

I didn't need my hormones getting in the way of that, because right now they were practically tangoing over to undo one or two more buttons on his shirt.

Cha-cha-cha.

"I think I can take care of that," he said, his smile tweaking mischievously as he looked around the corner and Zoe popped into existence, a bag from a store I have never heard of in her hand.

"Killian said you need clothes," she said, giving her brother a glare that I was sure was meant to melt the flesh right off his face. "And seeing as I owe you clothes anyway."

She shrugged, and I stepped toward the massive bed that I had thrown the contents of my suitcases onto, the tiny bag looking far too organized amongst the chaos.

"Be nice to him," she whispered as I fumbled with the bag, filled with equal parts curiosity and dread. It wasn't often that I was given clothes. Hell, it was never, especially when a hunky dragon was involved.

"I am being nice to him," I hissed in return, quirking an overly dramatic eyebrow in her direction. Zoe, the girl who practically warned me to stay away from the oldest of her brothers was now telling me to be nice to him.

"Are you sure everything is aligned straight in that mind of yours? Think mindlessly, be nice to the scary brother?" I grumbled, but she only fixed me with a look and strolled out of the room, waving her hand behind her.

"You'll see what I mean."

And I did.

I hadn't even pulled the first article of clothing out all the way before it fell right back into the bag.

Article. One. Singular. Well, one dress to be exact. One black, slink, obviously form-fitting dress.

Judging by the lacy bits that were under it, Zoe had clearly bought me some under things as well, that while needed were not something I wanted Killian to see. No now, not ever.

And certainly not under the dress. Or out of it.

Out of it. Just like I wanted to see him out of the shirt. I might be in denial.

Flame and embarrassment wrapped over me. I wasn't sure if it was because I was blushing, or because I was close to exploding. I wasn't going to take a chance either way, and I ducked my head.

Not that it helped, Killian was already walking toward me, and my feet were completely frozen to the floor.

"Beautiful, Ellie," He whispered, throwing the jacket on the bed, his hands wrapping around mine as he gently pulled me into him, and I stumbled like a newborn calf.

Heat swirled around me at his touch, and not just on my hands. The heat radiated over my arms, my back, and stretched through my bones until everything felt warm. The gentle hum of my phoenix filled the air as my soul began to purr, my skin pricking as I lifted my head to look at him. I almost wished I hadn't.

Good god. I had forgotten how perfect he was. Perfect scruff, perfect emerald green eyes. Perfect teeth as he smiled down on me. Perfect dimples. And now, curse it all, perfect hair.

I wanted to so badly to touch it, to run my fingers through it and pull it closer to me. Pull him closer to me.

Settle. I warned myself, but the single word wasn't nearly enough for me, or for the bird inside of me. Her wants for him was as strong as they had been when I was naked and behind a dumpster.

"Killian," I whispered in reply, failing miserably at keeping my voice strong. Which did nothing to stop his mischievous grin. The damn thing spread, and I am sure he could hear my heartbeat with how much it was pounding.

I am not sure how my legs were keeping me upright and not collapsing into his arms at this point.

"Beautiful," he repeated, his free hand tracing over my jaw, and turning all the heat into a damn inferno.

Screw it all, well not all. And not him.

Well, not yet.

Shit.

I dropped my focus as his eyes began to sparkle in greens and yellows and I knew I was hitting the Russian Roulette of self-control.

I was going to lose, especially with the way his finger was tracing my jaw, gently lifting my chin to look at him again.

Good god, where had all the oxygen in this room gone?

"I know we have had a rough start, but I would like to take you to dinner. I would like to know you and I would like you to know me. Will you join me?"

His voice ran over me with that husky rumble that my phoenix loved, and the damn thing erupted, singing one hollow note that echoed through the air. Killian's face wrinkled into a smile and those two perfect dimples dug deeper into his coarse facial hair. Holy mama.

My stomach flipped, the heat on my skin flaring like a freaking warning light. I needed to step away, to find space and air and not explode. It was either look away or fall into and jump aboard the Killian express.

Bobbing my head down, I was graced with the perfect view into his partially opened shirt and the perfect pectoral lines and that damn shadow of a tattoo peeking out from behind the neatly pressed white shirt.

Oh my god. This was a mistake. Look away!

Too late, I was trapped, and my phoenix was pulling me forward, my skin heating, flame threatening.

Snapping my eyes shut, I forced myself to take a step away, even though my legs had turned into little stems of jelly. Killian, however, didn't take the hint and kept his hand wrapped around mine, his thumb tracing the bones and tendons along the back.

Damn it all. Could he stop now? I really liked this hotel room.

"Are you going to let me get dressed, then?" I forced the question out, my nerves making the question sound like the song of a deep-sea fisherman. "I should probably take a shower too."

"I'll see you in an hour, Elliot," He whispered, thankfully dropping my hand as he backed out of the door, closing it with the faintest of snaps.

It was then I fell to my knees.

"Oh. My. God." I gasped to the floral designs in the carpet, every muscle in my body shaking as I worked to relieve the pressure, to extinguish even some of the flames that were invading my muscles.

I thought our almost kiss from before had been hot, well, up until the point when I kicked him in the balls. And the kiss at the airport had been unexpected. But the last few minutes had been like fire on a stick. I could barely breathe and the fiery need to run after him and tackle him to the ground was not calming down.

Perhaps agreeing to this dinner, alone, with him, had not been a good idea. I mean, if standing beside him, smelling the musk that always drifted from him was giving me heart palpitations than I obviously had no hope of not turning into a nuclear warhead at dinner.

The city of Denver would have no idea what hit it.

Okay, I had an hour to get myself under control. I could do this.

A shower to burn off the rest of the heat, and a whole kettle of blue tea later and I stood in the lacy underwear that fit a bit too well, holding the dress in front of me.

I could already tell it would fit like a glove. Like a perfect show every curve and every muscle glove. I was used to that. I mean, I lived in leotards with low cat backs and mesh that was cut dangerously close to a nip slip.

But this, this slinky dress with the low front, and no back, and no zipper to speak of was making it hard to breathe. My hair was pulled up, the light dusting of makeup that I opted for outside of performing already in place. It was just the dress.

"Ellie," Killian called from the door, a gentle knock following behind.

"Shit!" I screeched as I jumped, the dress falling to the ground.

So much for building myself up to this.

"Just a second!" I called as I slipped into my strappy heels and pulled the dress over my head, carefully smoothing it as much as I could before opening the door. I hadn't even paused to look at myself in the mirror. Knowing what I looked like would not be any help to controlling my 'mating instinct' tonight, so I wasn't going to risk it.

I was already boiling over with blue tea, which I instantly knew wasn't enough the moment I opened the door.

The suit was gone.

I mean, he wasn't naked, but for the first time since I had

met him he wasn't wearing a suit, well at least a three-piece number. The jacket was leather, the pants casual and the button up shirt below had more color in it than I had ever seen him wear, the teal striped with green of course.

His hair was down again, and I instantly knew I was fucked.

Royally no bars held, fucked.

Who cared what I looked like when I was going out with Dr. Danger here. It would all be coming off soon anyway.

What the fuck? Why did I think that?

Obviously because I was screwed.

Could you overdose on blue tea? Maybe I was delusional. I had no clue, but I also had a feeling I was about to find out.

"Hi," I said lamely, still ogling both hair and dimple.

"Hi beautiful," he responded, pulling his hand through his long hair before he offered me his arm and led me into the sitting room where both Zoe and Drake were sitting, their heads bowed over what looked like tiny plastic building blocks on the coffee table.

"Elliot," Drake gasped as he caught sight of me, sending whatever multicolored creature he had been creating tumbling in pieces over the carpet when he rushed over, his eyes practically dancing with joy.

Oh god, he was reaching toward me. My entire body was still too warm, everything was still too dangerous.

Breathe. I could do this. I just needed to limit my touch to one at a time.

Ignoring Killian's growl of frustration, I stepped away from him, reaching toward Drake who instantly swept me up in his arms. Thank god it was only his hands against my skin, only the burning of his palms as they ran over the exposed flesh on my back, adding to the already tornado-like force that was eating away that last of my self-control.

"You look beautiful," he whispered in my ear as he held me against him, the hot breath of his words sending a shiver down my spine, and my skin into a prickling heat.

Okay, so maybe one touch at a time wasn't helping. I was beginning to think I wasn't going to be doing any breathing tonight. The faster I could get to the car, and separate seats, and breathing room, the better.

Maybe I could convince Killian to drive the van and I could sit in the very back.

"Have a great time," Drake said, his voice low as the corner of his mouth tweaked into a smile that I didn't quite accept. I had been so used to Jarron prodding his brothers on that Drakes honest hope and support was like a breath of fresh air.

You know, if I could breathe.

"I know Killian will take great care of you." He said honestly, dropping my hand as he shot his brother a look, the two exchanging a grin that I really hadn't expected.

I mean, the last time I had talked to Drake about Killian there had very clearly been some tension there. But all of that had seeped away. I was sure that Jarron still being in Rydaim had something to do with it.

"Only the best for my girl," Killian whispered, pulling me back into him before leading us toward the door.

"Be back by midnight," Zoe called from behind us, fixing me with an all to knowing wink as the door snapped shut.

First the lacy underwear, and now this. I was going to have a very serious talk with her. The threat of exploding was still way too real, which made anything beyond a gentle hand hold a national emergency.

And even that was pushing it.

It didn't matter. I would make it through tonight, and then we would talk. Right now, however, I needed air.

Which was going to be hard seeing as Killian had ditched the van and sent for some chauffeured thing.

Thank God Killian let me roll the windows down on our way to this place. The Lincoln Town Car smelled way too much like leather to begin with, and that mixed with Killian's minty musk was making my head swim. The driver didn't seem very happy about my request, but if he knew the alternative I was sure he would be thanking me for saving his life.

The suite. The car. The dress. It all made me wonder exactly who was funding this little escapade, but one step into the restaurant and I was sure Killian was either a millionaire, or had taken out a second mortgage on his cave thing.

I wasn't going to guess, part of me really didn't want to know anyway.

Until, like a slam to the side of the head I remembered one very big piece to the puzzle. He was a freakin' prince. The crown prince. It's not that I had forgotten per se - more that I hadn't seen anything that showed me exactly what that meant. Until now, as he wound his arm around mine and walked me into a building that I was sure was like dining inside a castle in France.

The chilled air was filled with the aroma of wine, bread and what I was sure was cheese. Each table was lit by candlelight and smothered by a million twinkling fairy lights overhead, not real ones, I had to remind myself.

I mean, I guess faeries sparkle. But none of these mortals know that. In fact, it looked like a fairy tale, and in my shock all that threatening fire had thankfully vanished, extinguished in one tiny puff of 'what the hell have I gotten myself into'.

"Killian," I began, the second the awe of the place had worn off and my nerves set in.

Every one of these people were beautiful, they were put together, they were a mirror of everything I was not.

I swung on silks and entertained these people. I didn't eat with them.

"I'm not sure I should be here," I began, my focus still pulling around the room, as though I was desperate to find a familiar face.

Killian's hand tightened around mine, his thumb warm as it began to caress my skin, his dragon's fire trailing behind the touch. I could see the beautiful creature in his eyes, The glistening jewel bright color sparking with a different kind of flame. His hand trailed from my hand, up my arm, and over my back as he pulled me into him, every scrap of skin he touched igniting under him.

There was nothing safe about this, but I couldn't pull myself away either, I let myself fall into him, even though my head was swimming even though my bones were on fire.

"You belong with me, Elliot," He whispered, lowering his eyes until they met with mine, until those bright spots of color dug into me, and reflected the fire that was streaming through my own.

"My heart belongs to you," he continued, pressing his forehead against mine. "You are a part of my soul, Ellie girl. And tonight, I want to treat you like the princess you are."

Shock wrapped around me, seizing any possible comprehensible speech from existence as he pulled away, only to lean back in and press his lips to my forehead in a shower of liquid heat that moved down my skin as though I had been blessed by my fairy godmother's wand or some shit.

It sure felt like it with how the world was glittering. Either that or I was high on some unknown drug. I was going to go with the magic wand, if only because it made me seem a bit saner. Albeit the margin was slim.

"I want you to feel like my princess," he whispered against the skin of my forehead, his breath igniting the lingering heat of the kiss into an inferno. "Because you are my princess."

And there went my breath. Again. He better be careful or he would have to be conducting mouth-to-mouth resuscitation before the night was over, and that was a truly terrible idea.

Our lips together in any form right now, would end in more than your usual disaster.

Killian didn't wait for an answer before he led me away, which was good because I couldn't give him one anyway. I was still consumed by the shadow of his lips against me, my heart filling my mind with images of those same lips against my neck, my lips...

"Reservation for Cuelebre," He said in that husky voice and I perked up, thankfully right out of my delusions and to the maître d'.

The man turned up his nose at me before looking down the list and grabbing two of the equally as frilly and pompous menus.

"I don't think I have ever heard your last name before," I whispered as we began to follow the snooty man through the dining room, the twinkling lights drifting in and out of focus as we stepped around pillars and hanging sheaths of white gauze.

In a way, it reminded me of Suvi's office. If Suvi had been a princess in the 17th century.

Killian was right, being here, escorted through the sea of silverware and drifting eyes, I kind of did feel like a princess.

And the dress was sure helping with that.

"I don't have a last name," he said as we reached the table, stepping in front of me to grab the chair before I did, and pulling it out for me. "It's a pseudonym, although it's not much of one."

He guided me toward the table with ease, his hands lifting to my shoulders as he leaned down from behind, the scratchy scruff from his face rubbing against my cheek and sending shivers down my spine.

"It's an old medieval word," He whispered in my ear before he pulled away, stepping to the other side of the table. "It means Dragon."

"Still better than nothing."

He smiled at that, his scruff pulling into his dimples as he sat, his shaggy curls dancing around his shoulders.

"Two glasses of your featured wine, and no bread," he said to the maître d' before the arrogant man sat the menus down and scuffled away, giving us a sideways glance as he did so.

I was suddenly worried that we had said too much, either that or the unnaturally red color of my hair had offended him. I had spent so much of my time in hiding that I had never spoken about anything supernatural in public. Well, anything more than Zoe would allow, which meant hushed whispers and overly worried stares, usually right after I had thrown myself off some structure or another.

"Don't worry," Killian said with a smile, casually grabbing the menu and pulling it open. "For all he knows we are talking about a video game."

It was the second time I had heard that excuse, and I suddenly wondered if it was the go-to. I mean, did video games have a lot of dragons in them? I hadn't played enough to know for sure. Zombies, sure...

Oh my god.

"Are Zombies real?" I asked without thinking, my voice a bit too loud as I leaned over the table, my palms hitting the surface with a bang that if my sudden tirade about Zombies hadn't pulled focus, that had.

Great.

A few eyes drifted our way, upturned noses looking down on us before they went back to their wine. One woman, a bottle blonde with an obviously bad nose job, sipped her glass of white with open disdain that rattled me in all the wrong ways.

Yeah, I may not fit in here, but I was realizing it was only because I wasn't a snooty prick. I gave her a look that said as much and grabbed my delivered wine glass and downed the thing before she could look away, chugging it all before the poor maître had had a chance to give his spiel about when and where the grapes had been grown.

I slammed the glass down, gesturing him to fill the thing again, only realizing too late what I had done.

American booze might be weak, but I hadn't had a drop of any alcohol since we landed in the US. I was too young here, well I was before Zoe had officially declared me an adult.

Four months without alcohol and I chugged a glass of wine. That was going to hit me, hard.

Killian broke out in a loud boisterous laugh as both the maître and the woman stared at us with unabashed shock.

Yeah, lady, I drink better than you on your best day. I gave her another smile, already regretting my choice and she hmphed so loud I was sure her wig toppled a bit on her strangely shaped head.

Killian's laugh faded as he too downed his glass, gesturing for the still-shocked matron to fill them up again.

He did, giving us both a scowl before scuttling off and thankfully taking the bottle with him.

"That was a mistake," I mumbled to myself, taking a few sips of water and opening my menu, desperate to get both food and water in me before the repercussions of that hit.

Killian's request to forgo bread was the worst thing that could have happened right then.

Of course, now I had other problems. The menu seemed to be made for princes and other wealthy French men.

Carabineros Prawn Tartare - 72 USD

Coconut Crusted Légine - 84 USD

A Tasting of Vegetables and Meats - 68 USD

"What the hell?" I gasped, my profanity only adding to the shock that Mrs. Hairpiece was locked in. "Killian. This can't be right."

I gestured to the menu, but the rugged prince only smiled brighter, both of those damn dimples pulling his cheeks in before he leaned over the table, his hand stretching over the table for me.

I looked at the hand, at the needy fingers, and felt my heart catch, although not as much as it did when I put my hand in his and the bright light of his eyes sparked in the candlelight.

"You are my princess," he whispered again, before leaning back, his fingertips trailing over my palm and leaving glittering lines of heat behind.

Thankfully, it didn't leave a trail of actual light. It wouldn't be the first time that had happened, but I didn't need Ms. Hairpiece seeing that.

"Princess or not, this place is ridiculous," I said, not really wanting to look any further. "Can we please go get a hamburger?"

"You can get a hamburger here," he said, the mischief clear in his eyes, even though he wasn't even looking at me.

"Yeah, you're right," I didn't try to disguise the sass that time. "I can get a Norwegian Souffle Patty, filled with pickled radish and what I am sure is a fish?" I shook my head. "I'm not even going to try to pronounce that."

Killian chuckled, his eyes dancing as he met my eyes.

"You shouldn't. I am sure it's as disgusting as it sounds."

"Then why are we here?"

He smirked and leaned over the table again, drawing me closer with his eyes. I gladly obliged, although I stubbornly kept my hands under the table, I was already starting to feel a bit spinny and I didn't want to see what would happen if I added a heat touch of doom to the booze equation.

"I'll tell you a secret," Killian said, his voice leaving pleasurable rough patches down my spine. "Places like this have the best steaks. Easy, familiar slabs of meat that are cooked to utter perfection."

Hunger gleamed in his eyes as he sat back, leaving the menu closed. He clearly didn't need to see more. No wonder he had said no to the bread, he didn't need that expanding in his stomach and taking up all the room for his precious steak.

I actually found my mouth watering thinking about it. They often didn't serve steak at hotels or in the staff kitchen. I was going to take full advantage of this.

"Fine. I'll have the steak, but can we please bring back the bread? I am liable to get very drunk, very fast, if we don't." I said, folding my arms over my chest as I leaned against my chair in the most undignified way, earning yet another look for Mrs. Hairpiece. I was really hoped the thing would fall off before the night was over.

"What's wrong with that?" He asked mischievously, shooting me a wink before he lifted his wine glass up in a bizarre toast.

"Well, first, I am having enough trouble keeping my hands off you without being inebriated." Oh my god, why did I say that? His smirk was so not helping that, and now that I have said it, the need to run and jump into his lap was feeling like a very near possibility.

I guess the wine was hitting me harder, and faster, then I thought.

"And second," I continued, before I used the table as a hurdle and landed in his lap.

I pulled my hand out from where I had been hiding it, wiggling my fingers as little streams of smoke drifted from behind my nails. I didn't think I needed any more explanation than that, and with the way his face fell, it was clear I didn't.

"Okay," Killian said as he took a sip of wine and placed the glass back on the table, toast forgotten. "Bread. Now. And possibly less touching?"

"That would be for the best," I said with a smile, tucking my hands back onto my lap and went back to focusing on my breath.

"At least until later," his smirk was clear, his voice full of raspy need as he leaned closer, the smell of mint and musk whispering over to me. I waited, bones tensing at whatever snide of flirtatious remark was coming.

I never found out.

"Why, hello Killy," Someone said from directly behind me, a ribbon of cold snaking over my skin as the smell of ash consumed the air. I froze in place, my hand hovering over the menu.

I knew that voice, and I didn't need to turn around to see her, not that I would recognize her anyway. I had never laid eyes on the woman.

"Hello, Dabria," Killian responded with a growl.

I promptly lit the tablecloth on fire.

21

ELLIOT

FIRE SPREAD OVER THE TABLE IN A WAVE OF VIOLET THAT WAS so unnatural that even with all my mysterious magic, I couldn't figure out how I had caused it. But as waiters and waitresses rushed over with rags and glasses of water, Dabria's violet eyes boring into mine, I realized that I hadn't.

"What are you doing here?" Killian asked, his voice a snap as he jumped up, throwing his wine over the table and sending the already violent waves into a storm. The flames stretched toward the ceiling, catching the hanging gauze on fire as more patrons began to scatter, more staff running to the rescue with buckets of water, yelling at us and everyone around them in a panic.

Water hit against the flames as Dabria laughed, but instead of the water extinguishing the flames, they grew taller. They spread faster.

It was only a second later that the sprinklers turned on, and all hell broke loose. Water streamed over us in sheets, dripping from the ceiling as the flames spread. Screams rippled alongside the flames, everyone rushing toward the single exit in a mob of fear.

So much for a fancy steak.

Killian swept me up from where I stood, staring at the flames and pulled me against him. Dabria laughed, the twisted sound echoing with the sparks of fire and drenching my already sprinkler cooled skin in waves of ice. I shivered, both water and evil dragon glare rattling my bones.

The crowd pressed around us in their mad escape, Killian standing like a boulder in the flow as he held me against him. Fire reflected in the frightened mortals' eyes, their fear clear.

And also, terribly misdirected.

They ran from the fire, when they should be running from the girl who stood before me and Killian. At least they were going in the right direction.

Away from the dragon who stood looking like the villain in a superhero movie in high boots and a leather jacket, her long hair braided with strips of purple and blue. The ice water fell over her skin, streaking over the already beautifully smooth brown until she looked like she was sparkling.

She was beautiful, in that supermodel you've lusted after your entire life, way. The look she was giving me was only helping to accentuate that. Evil. Deadly. Lust.

It was all there, and not all of it was directed at me.

"Look away," Killian hissed, his arm tightening around me and breaking my focus. "She can see into your mind. Eye contact makes that easier. Fear makes it easiest. She can consume it. She's a viper."

The warning was not unfamiliar, but it could not come at a worse time.

I really didn't need Ceres' little minion to find out I what I was. Hopefully, my luck from last time would hold out and she wouldn't think me anything more than a mortal. Now to block out everything else, just in case.

If Zoe thought I packed my suitcases badly, she didn't want to see the frantic mind packing I was trying to accomplish right then.

I was nothing but a boring, old, mortal.

Yeah, this was going to work.

"Killian," I whispered, looking up to him as tiny drops of freezing water fell over my face, his eyes hard and dangerous when they met mine.

I wasn't scared, I didn't have to be, even with a dragon I was sure I could take care of myself, well, not without blowing my cover. Looking at Killian, however, and the dark determination that now lined his eyes, any residual fear melted away.

"Mine," I whispered, wrapping my hand around his, the hot eruption of heat from his touch melting away the ice from the sprinklers.

Killian's eyes darkened with the flame I had only seen a few times before, his skin pricking as he leaned down to me, the tip of his nose pressing against mine.

His long hair fell around us like a wavy brown curtain, blocking out the cries and the screams for one moment, and it was just us, standing in the rain.

You know, if the rain was in the middle of an apocalypse.

"Mine," he repeated, kissing my nose gently and the heat in me grew, it pressed against my heart as my phoenix pressed against my skin and I was sure the blinding flame was clear in my eyes.

This time, however, it didn't bring a smile to Killian's lips.

"Stay behind me," he said, his voice a firm order that I wanted to fight, probably would have too if I didn't need to stay hidden from the king, and that meant I needed to stay hidden from Dabria.

Even thinking her name twisted my lips into a sneer. Ugh.

Killian's hand clung to mine as he turned from the slowly depleting restaurant goers, to the woman who stood in the middle of the flames.

Or, at least, I assume she did. I could only see Killian's back after all. That and the unnatural purple flames we were now surrounded by. I had seen enough of her, and enough of the restaurant however, that I could easily piece two and two together.

"Aren't you cute with your little mortal appetizer," Dabria said with a harsh laugh. "Are you ready for your main course?"

Clinging to Killian's slick jacket, I snapped my eyes shut and focused on blocking my mind. I didn't need another visit from the demon horror hall. Or to burst into random flames. It was really too bad I couldn't control my glowy hand or time freezes...

Or maybe I could. Maybe I could try.

"What are you doing here?" Killian asked again, his voice hard as it lifted over the flames, over the last of the screams. Most of the people had escaped now, it was probably seconds before the firefighters got here.

And who knows what would happen when they saw the three of us chilling in the fire. We didn't have a Suvi here this time to keep the mortal fire brigade away.

"Checking up on you," Dabria said, her sour voice snaking over my spine. "Your daddy is worried, you keep disappearing. And now I find you hiding mortals you told your father were dead. Have you been lying to the king, Killian? What are we going to do with you?"

"Not hiding. Not lying," Killian answered with a snap, his arm snaking around his back to hold me closer to him.

It wasn't needed, I didn't think I could hold myself any closer to him. I was glued to him like peanut butter to a dog's mouth. All my effort was focused on keeping my phoenix hidden, well, as hidden as I could be while trying to summon a time freeze.

Because I knew how to do that. I didn't. It's probably good neither Killian or Dabria could see me, I was sure I looked constipated again.

"I didn't want to share. Least of all with you."

"I don't see why not?" She crooned, the flickering flames growing closer as she did, the taps of her shoes sounding like a battering ram in my head. "We could have had a lot of fun with that."

She was clearly referencing me, the harsh tone a whip against my spine and I jerked, the air pressing against my chest as my self-control slipped and I opened my eyes, sure I had frozen time.

But the fire flickered the same, the disgusting taps of Dabria's shoes grew louder. Closer. I had no less stopped time than, I was going to be best friends with Dabria.

Which I wasn't. Although, I would love to show her what *that* could do.

"We could have made her writhe. And scream. And bleed." She stepped closer with each word, my mind twisting as my anger began to pulse under my skin.

The emotion started to boil, and not because I was surrounded by spires of violet flame, but because my rage was very clearly getting out of hand. I needed to rage and burn and stop time, but hiding all of that from Dabria was more important right now.

You are nothing but a boring, every day, human, I reminded myself, focusing on the drops of cold water that were hitting against my neck, dripping over the side of my face, on the way the purple fire flickered in sparks of color.

"This one is mine." Killian said, his voice hard as it scratched through the air. Dabria didn't even seem to flinch, she only laughed. If there was a sound that was more irritating and fake than her voice, this was it.

I wanted to slap her. At least I wasn't ripping her head off. Because I really, really wanted to.

Man, I seriously needed to work on my self-restraint.

"Well, put me down for sloppy seconds." She was eager. I was disgusted.

I'll show you sloppy seconds you...

Killian's growl vibrates through his chest at that, his skin rippling through his jacket, as though something was trying to get out.

Freaky, holy mother!

I could feel his dragon, I could feel the spines push against his flesh, press against his jacket from the inside.

I tried to pull away, but he held me there as the little drops of ice water landed against his leather jacket and evaporated into puffs of smoke.

I wasn't the only one who was struggling with the whole self-restraint thing, it seemed.

"Well," Killian boomed. "You've seen me. I'm well. You can tell Father that I will be back in Rydaim soon."

"I think, if you were wise, you would make it sooner. We are planning a party for you tomorrow. It would be a shame if you were to miss it," she said with a laugh that was so hysterical that for a moment I thought she might have been losing it, that was until it lowered to a growl, and her hand twisted around his bicep, her long perfectly manicured fingernails pressing into his leather jacket.

Holly Hannah! Leave it to a maniacal dragon to have

talons like that, I hadn't realized she was so close. My phoenix rippled inside me and I jerked, ready to grab that hand and throw her across the room. I wasn't sure if I could, I mean Zoe's training from the other day had taught me absolutely nothing. But I sure as shit wasn't going to let her touch him either.

I barely lifted my hand to snatch and karate chop hers away before her ugly talons vanished, yanked away with a soft gasp that hissed over the flames as Killian roughly removed her.

"I will return home when my job here is done. You need nothing more from me."

"Well, I wouldn't make it too long. Jarron is waiting for you, he's so eager for what's coming," she taunted. Even I didn't miss the warning that was lined there. The threat.

It buzzed in my mind and pressed against my heart so powerfully that I knew my phoenix was entering the danger zone. Everything was too warm, the tiny pricks of energy that were flicking at my skin suddenly feeling as though they were attempting to rip through it, my fear and anger coming right with it.

Jarron.

Something was wrong, she had done something. My heart felt ready to burst as I shifted my weight, my heart, mind, and soul pulling me in three different directions. Although, all of them to the same place, I could already feel the tightrope that connected us pulling me toward him.

"And what is Jarron eager for?" Killian asked, his words as carefully chosen as hers were, which fanned my flame more.

I resisted the urge to rattle him. He needed to demand answers, to make sure that Jarron was okay. Swear and rage and throw her around or something. I realized, with the sharp sound of her laugh that he was not going to get them from her, even if he decided to turn her into a rag doll.

This was simply a game of cat and mouse that I did not understand.

"Come home and you will see, you can bring your little pet if you would like," She said, stepping around Killian to reach me. Killian tried to shift, to keep himself between me and the beast, but she kept moving, she kept coming.

Damn she was stubborn. But stubborn in that sick and twisted way that I wasn't. I really did not like the idea of having anything in common with her.

Ice and fire whispered over my skin as she reached me, her breath drifting over my face, and pooling against my fear. I clamped everything shut as tight as I could. Even if that was the last thing I wanted.

Oh, how I wanted to glare at her with all the fire in my eyes. To bare my teeth and show her all that I was hiding. She would deserve it, and it would be glorious.

But not yet.

I would not let even a single flame of my fire escape. Not this time anyway. Not until I could guarantee she would see it. That she would burn in it.

I didn't have the control yet. So, a boring mortal I would remain.

"I am sure everyone would love to see the little hooker squirm as you burn her." Her chilled breath tickled over my skin and I shivered. The words, the cool, it was all fueling the internal battle that might as well be the next world war with how it was threatening to rip me apart.

Not yet, I chanted, knowing full well I was losing that battle. I may not like hiding, but my soul was dead set against it.

"I want to see what happens when you do."

I flinched again, her voice slamming into me. But not because of the chill, but because this time it was in my head, it buzzed through the dark corners and pushed and prodded.

Prodded at my phoenix. Prodded at me. I wanted to twist, I wanted to move away from the pressure that was beginning to pound against my skull. I wanted to scream.

But I refused to move, my eyes and soul twisted up tight as I locked everything away and let her dig around, desperately praying that I hadn't left anything lying around.

"I am starting to see the appeal. You are too brave for your own good. It will get you killed soon enough," she hissed into my mind, the ice in her voice threatening to rip me apart. "Thank you for helping me find him."

It was then my eyes snapped open, and I looked right at her. She was beautiful, even with the disgust and hatred that twisted her lip, furrowed in her brow. The vile emotions somehow only heightened it.

A beautiful villain.

I wanted to twist her into pieces all the more. I was sure my phoenix was screaming in waves of flame.

But Dabria didn't even flinch. She clearly didn't see it.

"What makes you think you can take me, little mortal?" she scoffed, as the building began to creak, the flames having eaten away the tables, and licked up the sides of the massive pillars that held up the ceiling like the claws of a demon.

It was terrifying and did nothing but help enhance the wicked scowl of the woman who was glaring at me.

"Do you still think he is yours?"

I know he is.

"See, that bravery will get you killed."

The heat in my chest reached a boiling point, my mouth

filling with ash as my hands heated. I was sure they were on fire, ready to melt the skin from her disgustingly beautiful face.

"Fucking Bitch!" I screamed, throwing myself at her.

I didn't get more than a step before Killian's already twisted arm swung me around him, he and I switching places so fast that my hands and my hair formed one long streak of red.

"Move Killian," I shrieked, pushing against his back to reach Dabria, who was now laughing as though we were putting on a show.

My bubbly rage was officially uncontrollable, if Killian didn't move soon my hands were going to melt away his leather jacket into nothing. The thing was already bubbling which was freaky enough as it is. I didn't even know leather could do that!

"No, Ellio--" He raged, stopping himself half way through my name.

I knew why, but at that point I really didn't care.

I would burn the shit out of her pretty little face and then she would have nothing to go home to tell daddy.

"I think you've done enough damage here don't you think?" Killian growled, shooting me a stony glare, his eyes smothered by a black flame before he turned back to her.

The look was horrifying and should have been enough to stop my rage. But it wasn't. She, however, was.

"Perhaps," she said with a laugh. "That's a nice little girl you've found Killian. I would hate to think you have hidden something. I would hate for Jarron to have to pay the price for your foolish arrogance."

I stopped fighting. I could have sworn my heart stopped fucking beating. Her words hit me like a battering ram topped with knives, that were coated with poison and wielded by a clown. Every single stabby point sliced through my skin until I couldn't even find it in me to breathe.

So much for vague and irritating threats. Dabria was clearly going in for the kill. No wonder she was laughing like a clown, she was holding all the cards and she knew it.

Oh God.

Had I given her that? So much for wrapping things up in an iron clad box. My need to melt her skin off had clearly given me away. She laughed harder, until she sounded like one of those knife wielding clowns.

Psycho.

"Thanks for the road map, kid," she buzzed inside my skull.

I peeked around Killian's frame, my still smoldering hand wrapping around his equally as hot one and met the violet stare of the girl who I realized had used me, tricked me.

Who was ready to hurt us all.

I will rip you apart limb by limb.

She smiled wider. Okay, so it may not seem like much of a threat right now, but wait until I make it happen.

"What are you planning?" I don't think I had heard Killian's voice grind so darkly before.

He stepped toward Dabria, his massive bulk towering over her. She smiled, twisting her hair over her long, manicured claws.

"Come home soon, Killy," She crooned, the roof rumbling dangerously overhead. "We miss you."

The crack of the roof escalated, the sound of her laugh twisting right alongside it as her body began to twist and expand.

I had seen a dragon before, but I had not seen a person

become a dragon before, and watching it now I had no idea how someone could fit such a massive beast inside of them.

Her limbs began to stretch, her neck elongating as her laugh twisted into a growl, a low screechy howl that played up my spine like a xylophone from a haunted house. Dark twisted fear accompanied each note, the emotion digging deeper as wings unfurled from her back, as the roof came down on top of us. Burning pieces of wood, stone, and who knows what else collapsed as the now screeching beast took off into the air, a line of purple and blue fire ripping from her jaw.

Killian grabbed me, trying to pull me down and away from the restaurant that was now nothing but a smoldering ruin, but I was frozen in place, watching the dragon soar back to where Jarron was.

Where I could not reach.

Not yet.

22

ELLIOT

I HAD BEEN COVERED IN ASH ENOUGH THANKS TO MY PHOENIX that you would think I would be used to it by now. Used to dirt, and feeling the grit in every freaking crevice, even the not-so-good ones.

Trust me when I say that butt-crack ash is the worst. Even more so with this ash. There was something about this ash that made butt-crack ash feel like the worst kind of wedgie with the world's biggest thong.

This ash smelled like oil and felt like a gritty sand against my skin. It was full of flecks of wood, fabric, and everything else that had fallen over us as the restaurant had collapsed.

It made me feel dirty. I would have given anything to head right to the shower, and wash both the ash and the memory of this night from body and mind.

That sure as hell wasn't going to happen. And not because I was having a hard time calming my soul down enough that I wouldn't boil the water and melt the tub. But because Dabria had been there and her threat was still ringing in my head.

Or more like hitting against my chest like a toddler with a jackhammer.

I knew what she was talking about, and I knew that it was all my fault.

Not in the pouty angsty teenager way, either. There was no moping and running off to my room and slamming the door. This whole thing was legitimately all my fault. I had missed it.

Kilian's arm felt like a jacket around my shoulders as he led me to the hotel room, not that I needed it. I wasn't lost, and I sure as hell wasn't cold. I was already boiling hot, and he just as much so, so we were pretty much a furnace walking down the hall of the hotel.

A walking, talking furnace. Well, not so much talking as scowling and growling. Between Killian's dragon and the grumbling call of my soul I was sure we sounded like a broken-down furnace.

I'm surprised the wallpaper wasn't peeling behind us.

Not that I checked. The freaking hallway could have caught fire, I still would have kept scuttling down the halls of the hotel with all the intensity of a steam roller, ready to bust down the door to the suite.

We almost did anyway.

Wood cracked and splintered under Killian's fist as he pressed the door open, barely waiting for the lock to unlatch. I flinched, the sound was familiar and I half expected another roof to fall on top of us, and more ash to drown my hair and skin, but it was only an overly beige hotel room, and two dragons in their pajamas, hunched over a board game.

"I'm proud of you, Killian. You're back on time," Zoe said, moving her piece over the board without looking at us. "I honestly didn't expect you two back before dawn."

She laughed at her own joke, the hollow sound falling flat as it plunged into the stunned silence. I wasn't even sure anyone had heard her. Drake jumped to his feet the moment he caught sight of us, any laugh, smile, or blood that was in his face instantly draining. He looked like a ghost, and moved like one too, stumbling toward us as if he thought he could move through the table, chairs, and everything else.

"Ellie, what in the world?" he gasped, trying to gather me into him. Killian wasn't going to give up his hold on me that easily though, his hand was clinging to my waist even as Drake held me against him.

I was sandwiched between them, heat and smoke and ash everywhere. Heat rolled off our skin in waves, combining and growing until I was sure the air was melting in the mirage air thing. All the liquid fire was doing nothing to help me calm the internal furnace that was still emanating what could possibly be considered unhealthy levels of radiation.

Killian's warm heat spread over my bare back, radiating through his fingers in warm bubbles that blended with the sparks of Drake's fire, twisting down my spine from where his breath rolled over my skin in a freaking title wave.

I tried to restrain the gasp, but it came anyway, the sharp inhale screaming with one sharp note of my soul, my phoenix pressing against my heart to reach them.

No, to reach him.

Jarron.

The electric shock of Jarron's touch was missing. His smile, his laugh.

Oh god.

Jarron's loss was an iron bar in my chest, made so much worse by Dabria's visit. Echoes of her threats were knives against my soul, the ragged edges of my heart beginning to tear apart.

Or rather, it had been fucking torn from my chest, ripped out, stomped on and thrown from a cliff. I had seen it in a movie once, so I knew it was possible. Just not here in a hotel room.

Not that my magic couldn't figure out a way to make that happen.

Everything seized, and my eyes started to burn, ugly tears boiling over and streaking down my face in what I was sure was all too noticeable rivers. This time, I didn't care.

This time I let it hurt.

Or rather, I let it boil, my anger swelling right alongside.

"Are you okay?" Drake whispered, pressing me against him, his fingers running over my ash coated hair as Zoe rushed over to us, any drop of humor gone now.

"What the hell, happened?" She shrieked, her panic slamming against my pain and I stumbled back. That ragged whole was getting worse. "You didn't burn down someone else's livelihood, did you?"

"Well, we didn't," Killian said with a growl, his fingers gently caressing my skin as he stepped away, rushing past us to a large roll top desk that was nestled between the two high windows.

I half expected him to tear it from the floor and throw it out the window with how he was fuming.

Hell, *I* wanted to tear it off the floor and throw it out the window. Fucking Dabria.

"Dabria did." I choked, the words were practically screaming with my rage.

I swallowed back bile, or flame, or whatever was threatening to explode out of me. Zoe's face fell, any mischievous prodding instantly extinguished by the bright red flames that swallowed her eyes, the heat burrowing right into me as my own swelled to match it. We were a little bubble of hostility, well except for Drake.

His calm was unrequited. Solid as a fucking rock, as usual. I probably wouldn't have been able to sense his fury if I couldn't taste it in the heat that was radiating off him, feel it in the long cords of his muscle that tensed around my waist and pulled me into him.

"Dabria?" Zoe said, irate as she looked from me to Killian, who emerged from his scavenging with a notebook emblazoned with the hotel's logo, and a thick black marker. He looked victorious, although I had no idea why, every hotel had those.

That and a Bible, but I had already had enough of an apocalypse for one night.

"How did she find you?" I was surprised Zoe wasn't breathing fire.

"I don't know!" Killian raged his anger twisting my guilt as he upended the coffee table and sent the remains of their board game scattering over the plush carpet. Tiny people and cars rolled away like the survivors of an avalanche. They tumbled under the couch to be forgotten, well, until an unfortunate vacuum cleaner would pick them up and toss them in the trash.

I wish they would just come now, suck up this mess that I had accidentally made and make it all disappear.

"She was there, dressed like everyone else, she obviously knew we were going to be there." I wasn't even sure he was talking to anyone anymore. He set the coffee table back down, staring at the now empty surface as if it had wronged him, placing sheets of paper all over the flat surface in weird patterns.

For a moment I thought he had lost it. He was staring at

the papers as though they were about to reveal some secret message.

Maybe they were. For all I knew Dabria had infected his brain too.

"So, she's following us?" Zoe snarled, the rage in her eyes growing as they flicked from me to Drake, some secret message passing between them. I would have called them out, I would have demanded answers, but right then I was too busy trying to stop my stomach from upending itself. My snarling phoenix was sure not helping, she was as irate as I was over my fault in this.

No, over my failure in this.

She's wasn't following *us*. She was following me. Which, I mean, meant she was following us, but still, this one was all on me and my stubborn head. I hadn't realized it. I hadn't known enough to know that all those stupid threats actually meant something.

"The woman on the plane?" Drake asked very quickly, his hands running over my spine. Soft, tender, comforting. Well, it would have been if every single spark of fire wasn't digging against my already raging guilt.

"No," I said, pulling away from Drake as my stomach threatened to invert itself, the heavy words weighing as much as an elephant in my gut. "This one is my fault. She's done something to my head. She's following me."

The words felt as heavy coming out as they did locked in my chest. Too bad the weight didn't leave, not with the three sets of eyes that turned on me, digging into my already boiling conscious with looks that ranged from confusion, worry, and in Zoe's case betrayal.

"That's not possible, Ellie." Drake was clearly trying to comfort me, but I didn't need that. Not then. Not with Zoe staring at me like she was going to eat me or something.

I stepped back, wiggling myself away from his supportive reach. Yes, being right next to Drake was probably the safest place to be given the look that Zoe was giving me. Oh, she was pissed, but I had seen that look before and I really didn't need Drake to play middleman.

"What do you mean 'she's following you'? What did you do?"

"You say that like I went and asked her to follow us." There was no point in trying not to sound snotty. It would have come out anyway. My phoenix was already snarling.

"You said she didn't see what you were?"

"She didn't." I stepped closer to her, despite Drake trying to pull me back into him. I wasn't about to let that happen. "When she was in my head, she said she was going to take Killian down, and that I was going to help her. I didn't know what it meant. But she said it again tonight. She thanked me for helping her, so I guess she wasn't being a bully. She's tracking me somehow."

The words tumbled out like so much rage induced vomit. Foul-smelling refuse that stunk up the room and twisted all their faces into tangles of fear and pain.

"A tracker. She put one on me years ago. I knocked that bitch right out of my head in a few days." Killian shot me a glance before returning to his papers, now pulling a marker over the textured white sheets, leaving a black line behind it.

"A tracker?" I mumbled to myself. That word sounded familiar, like a beat-up car your grandfather would drive, or the name of the hot guy in high school.

Whatever, my mind was too occupied with freaking Dabria and whatever she was doing to Jarron to think clearly.

"Yeah, well, I guess she likes to poke around in my head

and leave little treasures behind to fuck us over. She's like a little rat." Wasn't going to lie, the imagery fit.

"Then set a trap and kick the little vermin out next time. Clean up her shit so you don't doom us all." He wasn't even looking at me, he was still focused on the papers, his voice as dark as his scowl.

I understood why, but the others didn't.

"You say that like I know anything about how the mind-reading-psycho dragon operates," I said, taking a step toward him and his bubbling rage, only to be pulled back by Drake whose eyes had turned an angry shade of fiery-brown.

"What the hell has gotten into you, Kills?" Zoe snapped, slamming her hands on the back of one of the chairs and sending a crack through the room that shivered both walls and gaudy mass-produced portraits. Hell, even I jumped. With that much strength, I was surprised the chair was still standing. "I thought you were going to box up all your temper after you destroyed a very angry witch's livelihood. But you, what? Destroy a restaurant and are being a bitch to Ellie."

"I'm not being a bitch." His voice was a snarl, I would agree with Zoe if I didn't understand where the rage was coming from.

"You are being a bitch."

"They have Jarron. We thought he was trapped. But I think he might be captured." His voice choked in the air as he continued to draw line after line, the thick black striped intersecting until I recognized what it was.

Well, recognized what it could be through the squiggles.

A map of Rydaim.

I stared at it, everything buzzing around me as their conversation continued. The map, and the fact that Jarron was lost somewhere in the squiggles was continuing to buzz in an angry rock, pressing against my soul.

Down, girl, I scolded, taking a step forward. *We will get him back.*

"Have Jarron, how?"

"Tortured. Shackled. They would clearly have to do something to keep him there. I don't know, Zo," Killian said, finally looking away from the map to me the black in his eyes was gone, there was only the green, only the drowning worry that matched my own. "But Dabria said enough. If I had to guess, I would say they were planning a public execution."

"No!" The word burst out, and I jerked forward right to Killian and those eyes I thought had perfectly understood me.

Screw that. I understood nothing. I jerked away, the fire burning and pulling as I stepped toward the map, as if I could reach through the air and pull Jarron to me.

Safe. Sound. And away from Dabria, Ceres and anyone else with blood on their claws.

I would take them all down, and I would take them down now. My phoenix was nearly screaming in preparation.

"I did this."

"Dabria did this, and that bitch deserves what is coming for her. We will deal with you and whatever mess is in your head in a minute," Zoe said, her finger wagging in my face like a stern grandmother. I didn't even care, I didn't even turn.

She could have been charging at me on the back of a rhino and I don't think I would have flinched. I was too focused on trying to make sense on this damned map, find some secret in the lines and circles that Killian kept adding, as if they would tell me what in the world was going on.

Just because I had figured out it was a map didn't mean I could read it. I had never been there. I could have been looking at a perfect artists representation for all I knew.

But I hoped not, otherwise Rydaim was an ugly toddler's drawing.

"You know Dabria. She's all talk, Killian," Drake's voice was hollow, it rattled in my head echoing through the tunnel as I stared at the map, my soul buzzing with what I could have sworn was Jarron's electricity.

Sharp little pricks of his touch rippled through my muscles, stronger. So strong I was sure he was right there...

This damn map. I had thought Killian was losing it making the thing, I was now imagining my kidnapped mate right beside me. No, not behind me, stuck in a mess of papers. Which was clearly worse.

Crazed panic was an understatement. It didn't get better when Drake came up behind me, either, his warm hand pressed against my back. I jumped high enough I could have touched the ceiling. Okay, maybe not that much, but still.

"It could be a trap," Drake continued, his fingers tracing the muscles on my back that the sinful dress revealed. "To get you back. To get us all back there."

"She doesn't know what I am," I said with a shake of my head, taking one last look at the map before I pulled away. "But she does want Killian."

"No," Killian corrected with a snap, throwing the marker across the room as he stood from the now completed map. "She wants the crown and right now she thinks I am the quickest route to that. Well, she did. She could care less if it's me, or Jarron, or even you as long as the result is her as some deranged queen of the Dragons."

So, she really was just another villain in this twisted fairy tale. Fitting.

"We have to stop her. We have to go to Rydaim and get Jarron out." I was firm, determined, and full over all the growly frustration that my phoenix felt. I was ready to go right then, and not because I needed to prove myself or go kill Dabria with guns, or beaks, blazing. Although I would be lying if I said that wouldn't be super cool. But because Jarron was my mate and I would do anything to save him.

"No, Elliot," Drake whispered from behind me, even though his voice was as hard as mine. "We can't take you there. I won't let you go there."

"You won't *let* me?" I asked with a hard laugh, turning on the guy as my phoenix ruffled angrily in my chest. "I won't stay here! I'm done hiding. We need to get him. I will if you won't."

I would have zoomed out the window right then, if Killian hadn't blocked my path, his frame towering over me, his warm hands pressing against my shoulders and filling me with waves of warmth. But it wasn't the usual warm bubbles I had come to expect from him.

It was boiling.

It was mad.

I could see the emotion clearly in the green of his eyes, the bright emeralds digging into me and fueling my own.

"I know you want him, Ellie girl. I won't let him die, I promise you. But Drake is right, it's too dangerous for you. I will go get him," Killian's voice ground on me that same way it always had, his hands trailing up my shoulders, past my neck, to wrap over my jaw.

The touch was calm, comforting, and I could feel that deep part of me pull into him. Wanting him, but I wouldn't let it. Not right then. I would have been proud of myself for finally having control of my damn emotions, if, you know, I didn't feel ready to explode in other ways.

"Zoe and I can get in and out of Rydaim," he continued, his voice breathless. I guess he was having trouble breathing too. "We know it. It's familiar. You can stay with Drake--"

"NO!" I pulled away, all my anger and frustration boiling over. "I won't let you two go off and leave. Don't be a fool, Killian, she is waiting for you. She's expecting it--"

"And if she is tracking you, then she will see you coming. She will see us all, and saving Jarron will be impossible," he interrupted, leaning over me so that I couldn't look anywhere but at him, at the dark smoke that had once again overtaken his eyes.

There was only darkness there. A darkness that I hadn't seen since the alley, since that night with the whole ball busting incident.

It was different here; the danger was different. The hunger behind it didn't scream quite so loud. It wasn't ownership, it wasn't his dragon. There was something electric in his touch, the fire that pressed into my skin

"And if you show up, she will know I am alone." I really wasn't going to let this go down without a fight, or make it happen either way, but they didn't need to know that yet.

"She thinks you are a mortal Elliot. She has no reason to come here. But even if she does come here, I will stop her," Drake said, and as much as I hated it, I turned from Killian's touch and gave him a look that said everything that I couldn't. Everything that I didn't want to.

How?

"I won't let you risk that," I phrased it all the best I could, it didn't appear to decrease the emotional stabbing, however. He still cringed, his eyes darkening to a brown that was as hard as stone.

"You know I will do anything to protect you, Ellie," He whispered, but the half-truth in the words cut him as much as they cut me.

"And I will do anything to protect you," I whispered, turning to each of them in turn. "All of you. That includes Jarron."

"You aren't ready, Elliot." Zoe said, cutting through what could have been a tender moment. "You don't know enough, you can't control enough..."

"Yes," I scowled, letting all the daggers of my frustration cut through the air and right into her. "And that is going to get so much better the more I hide in the shadows and learn to perfect my glare."

"We are..." Zoe began, but I cut her off with a wave of my hand.

"Don't say protecting me, because I will definitely lose it. We want my memories back. Kaley or whatever isn't here. So, we go there. We get Jarron, get my memories. Then, I will know how to control all the things and I will kill the king and end this thing. Easy."

Okay, not so much easy as nearly impossible, but I still wasn't planning on giving up that easy.

"I already have something for the first part of that," Killian began, stepping forward and pulling a small glass vial out of his pocket. "I meant this to be a gift for the end of our date. The return of your memories, your life. It doesn't seem like a gift anymore."

He held it out to me, the thing smaller than his pinky and corked with what my brain was screaming was blood. The red wax making the whole thing look that much more ominous.

"Or Something?" I asked, looking from Killian to Drake.

The down-turned shock on both his and Zoe's faces however made it clear that this was all news to them.

"Callay wasn't very clear. But she hasn't been clear about anything lately," Killian said, holding out the vial to me.

I took it reluctantly, half of me expecting the world to rewind and all my memories to be returned with one touch. It was nothing but glass, however, strangely warm glass. Although, that was more likely because it had been in Killian's pocket, in the middle of a fire, while his dragon was threatening to rip through his skin.

All that heat and the vial could have exploded.

Holding it up like one does in a wine tasting, a teeny tiny wine tasting, I peered into the transparent fluid. Okay, maybe not so much transparent as full of glitter. There appeared to be a weird opaque shimmer through it, like someone had crushed up a pearl and pushed it in there. It was strangely beautiful, the shimmer, the light that refracted through it in waves of glitter.

I wanted to touch it, okay maybe more like inhale it and wrap myself up in it.

"What is it?" I wasn't sure if Zoe said it, or if I did. I couldn't tell the difference, and it was hard to think beyond the vial right then.

The shimmer was familiar, just like the heat that was emanating from it, just like the heat that was rising from inside of me to meet it. Warm, comfortable, waves spread over my skin and all the fear, all the anger. It vanished.

Everything vanished.

Everything but the liquid smoke in the glass, the shimmering pearl dancing over the sides, swirling faster, shifting through the water as though it was alive.

Alive as it danced in time with the heat that pulsed through my veins. The heat in my chest swelled as one clear note rang from my soul as my phoenix burst with life. My song exploded louder than I had heard before, but I didn't jump, not at that, not at the trailing ribbons of red smoke that began to stream from my hands, pouring from me as the song grew, swirling through us all.

"It's beautiful," I whispered, knowing I wasn't talking to anything but the pulse of my soul that was aching inside of me.

I couldn't wait anymore, I popped the cork and chugged it down, Zoe's screech of alarm barely breaking above my song.

The liquid was as warm in my throat as it was in my hands, just as soothing. I could feel it move through me, but not just in my stomach, in my veins, in my skin. The vial was now a chilled vessel, empty and dead. All the glittering magic was now inside of me. Swelling. Burning.

It was everywhere, it swirled through me, my pulse boiling as my phoenix's song began to fade, leaving us standing in a silent, beige room. Everything looked as though nothing had happened. If it wasn't for Zoe's panic I would say I had imagined the last few minutes.

"What the holy hell was that?" I shrieked, the vial falling to the ground as I jumped from it, suddenly worried it would grow legs and walk away.

"Fae magic," Killian said, his voice hard as he dropped his barricade from a still fuming Zoe and rushed to me. "Are you okay, Ellie girl? I'm going to kill her if she hurt you. That was some trick."

"I'm fine," I said, letting myself melt into him, even though I was still watching my hands waiting for them to start glowing, or some influx of horror stories to occupy my brain.

There was nothing. Not even a shadow of the weird hair

smoke thing I had seen. I was starting to think I had hallu-cinated.

That's a parlor trick I didn't want.

"Anything?" Drake asked, his hand wrapping around my own and pulling my focus.

I shook my head. It was hard to ignore the weird disap-pointment there. I mean, I wanted to know my past, but now that I was faced with it I was kind of scared what it would hold.

I really wasn't ready to add vampire to my supernatural repertoire.

"I'm actually okay with this." I said, pulling away from Killian to kick the empty vial under the couch with all the other forgotten Life pieces. "If my life was going to turn into Alice in Wonderland I was seriously going to start ques-tioning my sanity."

"Great, so that was a bust," Zoe said not a hint of a laugh in her voice. "I say that Killian and I go to Rydaim in the morning. I do not think it's wise to wait any longer than that."

"I believe you are right," Killian's voice was calm as he stepped over to the map, pulling me along with him. Zoe and Drake followed as though they were on a string, everyone standing around the squiggles as though they would make any sense.

Although, somehow, this time they did. Standing here with Drake and Killian on either side of me, everything began to fit together. A building, a road, what I was sure was a fountain.

I stared at the circle, the thick black lines simple and nondescript. Nothing about it said fountain. Nothing about it said that it should be anything, except that those thick black lines were pulling me right into it. Just as tight as when I had called for Drake.

Thick coils, wrapping around my heart, pulling me right to him. He was right there.

"Jarron," I whispered, my fingers fluttering above the lines as though I could pull myself through the paper and to him. He was just on the other side. I knew right where he was, and I knew how to save him. After all, I could stop time. You can do anything when you can stop time.

I mean, I wasn't consistent. But I would force that out of me for this. For him.

"I have to go." I was firm. Killian wasn't having it.

"We can't risk it," Killian said, his hand reaching toward me. "Zoe and I will bring him back to you."

The skin of his hand was rough, comforting. At least it was supposed to be, but it was going to pull me away from where I needed to go. Away from Jarron.

I needed them with me, together. We needed to be together, not a million miles apart. There was only death when we were apart.

"Then you will die, too," I spat, stepping back in horror.

But not from him. From me. I don't know why I had said that, I don't know why I was thinking that. *There was only death when we are apart*. It all sounded like crazy talk that Suvi would say when she looks at her bones. I must be losing it. Smoke inhalation or some shit.

Except that I knew that it wasn't a lack of brain cells, and that every word was true.

"I have to go to, we all do," I said, turning to Drake, needing him to trust me. Needing him to believe me.

"It's not safe," Drake whispered, reaching toward me with the same hopeful comfort that Killian had. I jerked away. I didn't need his comfort. I didn't need their pacification. I needed Jarron.

I needed them all in one place. I needed them together with me.

I didn't know why, I didn't know how. I just knew.

"I have to be the one to save him," I said, the words blending together as my head continued to spin. As the room began to shift. I needed to get out of here. I needed to get away from here.

I needed to get to Jarron.

My phoenix screamed as I turned, my skin heating as she pressed against me, ready to escape, ready to soar.

I was ready to run.

I didn't get further than one step before black swallowed the world and I tumbled head first into the coffee table.

23

ELLIOT

WARM, WET AIR TICKLED MY NOSE, IT PRESSED AGAINST MY skin until everything was slick and hot and strangely uncomfortable. Like I had decided to go for a swim in a vat of spaghetti.

Because that seemed normal. Last thing I knew I was running for Jarron, and now I was in spaghetti. No, not spaghetti.

Steam. Hot, sticky steam that stuck to my skin and pressed against my heart, the tense things feeling as though it was beating from a million miles away. The steam was everywhere, pressing against everything until it was all I could see, all I could feel.

"Sorry, I didn't see you there."

My own voice echoed through my head, it pulsed through the steam as though it was coming from it, although I knew it was mine.

"I noticed, but it's really fine." Smooth, sweet, just a hint of a laugh. I knew the words and I recognized them at once.

Jarron.

His name came in time with my heart beat, pressing

against my soul as my phoenix screamed, and the steam began to part revealing the tile room from that first day I had met him, and there sitting on the top step was the blonde super model.

His hair sagged over his face, dripping over his skin. Sweat trailed down his bare chest in lines of wet that made my lips throb. I bit the lower one, pulling the flesh between my teeth with as much strength as I could, needing to check that I was still alive, or wake me up from this dream.

This beautiful, torturous dream.

"Yeah." I felt the lie roll of my lips, the agonizing false-hood screaming even more painfully in the replay. No, everything is not okay. You are not okay Jarron, can't you see that?

"My friends just challenged me to skinny dip and then took my clothes and ran."

He smiled, that same heart-breaking grin I loved so much was truly breaking my mother fucking heart. His dark eyes sparked as steam drifted in front of him, the gold in his eyes that I had come to recognized as dragon reflecting through the dark depths.

I didn't remember that. I think I would have remembered the streaks of gold when I met him the first time.

It was beautiful. He was beautiful.

"Figured it was something like that. You here on a school trip?"

"Something like that." The words seemed dead.

"I'm Jarron," his voice was full of a smile, his hand eager as it extended toward me, as the white steam snaked through his fingers, dancing like the red smoke from the vile.

So familiar.

"I know," My words deviated from the memory as I

placed my hand in his, and the live wire of his electric touch slammed into me.

If I wasn't stuck in a dream, I would have been certain I had been electrocuted. My whole body shook, my veins igniting as the memory shifted. The steam room didn't change, nothing changed. Nothing but Jarron, whose eyes were now sparking gold as his smile spread, as he began to stand, the towel sagging down his waist until it clung to his hips. Barely staying on.

"Jarron?" I whispered, steam rolling between us he stepped right to me, his hands trailing over the bare skin of my side, pressing my body against his. Every naked bit pressing against him.

I was suddenly very glad for the towel. Dream or not, I didn't need to wake up hot and bothered.

I was already angry. Adding horny to the list was not on my to do list for the week.

"Elliot," Jarron whispered, his nose running over my jaw as he prompted me up, my focus drifting into the now pure gold of his eyes. "Darling."

My heart clenched painfully at the name, and his hold increased, pressing against me, pressing me against him. All I saw was his eyes, the golden flame swallowing everything.

Forget breathing, not that that wasn't hard enough in the steam that was glittering and dancing around us. I tried to move away, the steam pulling me into it, but Jarron held on, his eyes consuming me, until the gold was everywhere. Golden flame.

Flames that were drowned in the sound of screams. The smell of burning flesh.

I jerked away, my own scream joining the others as, before I could get a good look at the golden fire that was surrounding me, it all fell away. The dream faded to nothing, taking that terrifying fire with it.

"Elliot!" Killian's panic ripped through the last of the dream, cutting it to shreds, and leaving me gasping in the steam.

It swirled over us, the slapping of water against stone rumbling behind where he held me in his lap him, his hands soft against my back as I lay against his chest. My legs straddling him like I was a rag doll.

It took me a second to realize everything was bare. Well, almost bare.

I could kill Zoe for her frilly underwear contribution right about now, it was the only thing that was between Killian and me. I groaned and tried to move away, which really meant I flopped around, I could not get my body to respond to save my life. Everything was still spinning, everything was aching. My bones felt like they were splintering apart, desperate for his touch. For Jarron's touch.

I was starting to realize why steam rooms don't have a merry-go-rounds. Because that's a thing in the first place.

"Killian!" Drake's voice boomed through the fog and I flinched, the heavy pounding of what I was sure was a fist against a door acting like a battering ram against my heart. "Is she okay?"

"Yeah, she's awake," Killian called over me, the volume of his voice in my ear sending the already spinning room into overdrive.

I really needed to get off this ride. I moaned and tried to step out of the car. I fell sideways into Killian.

"Is she okay?" Drake's voice came again, farther away this time. He must not be on the ride.

"Yeah, give us a minute."

Or twenty. I was seriously having trouble focusing, or

even thinking straight considering I seriously thought I was on a carnival ride. I needed to breathe, and all this steam and heat and skin was making that impossible.

"Ellie girl," he said again, his hand soft against my back as he coaxed me awake, pressing me against him. Probably a good idea seeing as I had nearly crashed into the tile floor trying to get off a phantom carnival ride. "Can you talk to me, baby? God, I was so worried."

"Where am I?" I managed to stutter out, my words as blurred as the steam filled room.

"In the bathroom, we turned the steam on," The normally rough grind of Killian's voice was soft as his fingers trailed over my back, tip toeing over my bra strap as he traced my spine, his fingers pressing against the back of my neck as though he was checking for injuries. "You passed out. You were so cold. We needed to get your temperature up."

"Is that why I'm naked?" I asked, letting my hands drift up to his equally as bare, and equally as muscular back. "Is that why you're naked."

"Nearly naked," he corrected, flicking at my bra strap. "And yes, we needed to get you as hot as we could, as fast as we could."

It shouldn't bother me. I mean, the first time I had seen him I had been wearing significantly less. Less as in nothing.

I had been wearing nothing.

Jarron had seen the same.

My heart pulsed, the dream, the memory pulling in my mind and triggering that same tether in my chest. I pushed it away, I may be able to think clearer, but I wasn't ready to lead a search party.

Not yet.

"And you?" I asked as I tried to pull myself upright, something that proved impossible without Killian's help.

His hands curled around my shoulders, supporting me as I sat upright, my legs pushing into his waist as everything kept rocking and rolling around me. Killian's hands drifted to my back, pressing against my spine as he held me still, his dark green eyes pulling into me.

His hair was still down, the curls sagging around his face as sweat dripped over his face, rinsing some of the ash away. Or at least trying to. He was still covered in it, I was sure I was as well, although the sweat that had begun dripping over my skin was doing its best to wipe it all away.

Ash had built up in the rough growth of his beard like glitter, it stuck to his hairline like the worst kind of dandruff and streaked over his face in ribbons of dark that made it look like he had been crying.

He *had* been crying, I realized with a start. The lazy sludge of my soul shifted and swayed as the tiny caw of my phoenix burst to life in my mind, the creature pushing me toward him. I'm surprised I didn't fall over when I lifted my hand from his waist, the appendage feeling like a dead weight as my fingers pressed against his cheeks, wiping away the ash, the tears.

"My suits are dry clean only." He whispered, his voice nearly swallowed by rushing water that was pouring through a faucet somewhere in the steam. I was sure that wasn't the only reason he had elected to strip down to his boxers. His tight, boxer-briefs that I was sure left nothing to the imagination. "Are you feeling better?"

I nodded, the movement thankfully not making everything rock.

"Good." He murmured. "Because I need to ask you something."

My focus drifted from the streaks that covered his face, to the ever-brightening green in his eyes, the light growing bright and dark as ribbons of steam drifted between us.

"You're beautiful," I had never heard his voice so soft before.

"That's not a question." I was having so much trouble breathing I was amazed I could get the words out, they were nearly swallowed by the heat the was rocking through me.

My fingers drifted down the trail of his tears, pulling over his jaw, his neck, and to his collar bone, where the twists of the tattoos that had been haunting me since that first day poked out from behind the depleting ash. Beautiful black lines, right below my fingers.

Heavy streaks that made it look like the smudged marker of his map were painted over his skin, stretching from his shoulder, all the way over the other collarbone. The tips of black poked out from the shadow of ash that was concealing the design, taunting me. I couldn't resist any longer. His breath shuddered underneath my touch as traced the lines with the tips of my fingers, wiping away the ash to reveal what looked like flame.

A long streak of fire cut into his skin.

It would make sense that it would be fire, considering he was a dragon and all, but that wasn't all of it. There was something else here, something that was very much not a dragon.

Steam condensed on his skin in drops of ash filled water, the wet streaking under my fingers as I wiped it away, as his heat moved into me, radiating through my muscles until everything was on fire. The lines on his chest rippled as he shivered underneath my touch, making the fire move as though it was alive.

Pressing my palm against his chest, I wiped away the last

of it, revealing the body of what I had assumed to be a dragon drawn into his strong pectoral.

It wasn't a dragon.

"It's me." The word choked as my fingertips traced over what was clearly a phoenix. What I had thought was a line of fire was actually the long burning wing.

"When did you get this," I asked, my hand flat against his chest as I jerked my head up, his eyes soft, and somehow sad.

"When we started looking for the Phoenix," he shook his head. "When we started looking for you. I had no idea what it would mean..."

His voice choked as my focus fell back to the tattoo, his hand leaving my back to trace over my shoulder, tugging at my bra strap before drifting to my hand, covering mine with his and pressing my palm against his skin, against the phoenix tattoo, against the throbbing pulse of his heart.

"I always carry you near my heart now," he whispered, his thumb drifting over the back of my hand while the others pressed into my back, pressed me closer to him. "My heart is yours, Elliot."

I leaned into him, sweat and condensation covering our bodies as I slid against his skin, as I slid so close I could feel him against me, feel his chest, his pulse, his breath. The heat of his exhale rattled over my jaw as he held me against him, letting his nose sketch the line of my jaw, the scratchy growth on his chin rubbing over the skin until everything shivered.

My phoenix pressed me closer, needing to feel him, to be with him. His hand left mine, his palm a rough ripple of pleasure as it pulled over my shoulder, down my back and toward my hip. My breath shook at the touch, and I was sure that if I wasn't on fire already I would be soon.

"May I kiss you?" he whispered, his cheek against mine as he whispered in my ear, the warm husk of his voice rattling over my spine.

"Is that... the question?" I gasped out, tilting my neck as he pressed against me, his lips so close I could feel their heat.

"Yes." I shivered under the breath of the single word, the heat adding to the firestorm that was already threatening to break from me.

Fire. Explosions. It was all on the table, and I could care less.

There was no stopping it now anyway.

"Please," I breathed, the word barely out before his lips pressed against my neck, the rough growth of his beard adding to the sensation, adding to the burning fire that was trying to rip me apart. I let it. I let it grow.

I was not afraid to play with fire if this is what it meant.

I moaned, the low sound rippling with my phoenix's call as I twisted, turning toward the kiss, toward him, and shifted my weight until our hips pressed together, his lips moving over my neck and to my jaw. Toward my lips.

I made contact first.

Crashing my lips into his, I let my fingers trail over his shoulders, twisting in his hair and against his skin bring him closer. To feel every part of him.

To let his heat fill every part of me.

His lips followed mine, my hips leaning against his. The heat turning into an inferno as he began to swell beneath me, his teeth nipping at my bottom lip, at my neck. And then everything exploded in a flash of white.

Steam rushed past me as I was thrown across the room, a scream of metal, phoenix, and death ringing in my ears as the world broke apart in a million sparks of red and gold that fell around me. My fingers reaching for the sparks of gold as if they could stop me. They didn't, and I slammed into the tile wall with a sharp crack of tile or bone or both echoing in my head. As if I didn't already hurt enough, the lingering aches burned brighter as I slid down the wall my eyes fluttering open in expectation of flame, sure a bomb had gone off with the force of the impact.

The world drifted in and out of focus as my head throbbed and burned, drifting from black to white as the bathroom mutated and burned.

"Killian!" Drake's muffle voice broke through the buzz of steam that was ringing in my ears, the panic adding to the ache as my head throbbed.

"Killian!" I joined in his yell, my voice hollow as I tried to yell through the noise, to see through the white that my brain couldn't quite pull into focus.

Ignoring the ache, I pulled myself around, crawling on all fours toward where I was sure Killian had been.

"Killian," I said again, my voice less of a yell and more of a fruitless gasp.

Everything ached. Every slow motion as I dragged myself across the floor was agony and I collapsed with a sigh, expecting Killian or Drake or even Zoe to scrape me off the bathroom floor like roadkill.

Instead, I came face to face with Jarron.

The entire world was drowned in a white light. But this wasn't the steam room, and it certainly wasn't the bathroom. I didn't recognize his place, but with the heavy grey stone and the stench of blood, I didn't really want to. Jarron sat against the wall, looking through the lone window with a look of defeat that stabbed all that burning rage back to life.

"Jarron?" I gasped, grateful when the word exploded

from me and didn't sound like a buzzing, slurred mess, which it could have with how my head was hurting.

Jarron jerked at his name, twisting toward the sound with wide, frantic eyes. His hair fell over his dark eyes, not a ribbon of his dragon present as he searched for me, looking right past the exact spot I was spread out on the floor. Even with the buzz in my head it was clear that he couldn't see me.

Great. Hallucinating for the win.

"Darling?" Jarron hissed, leaning toward where I was, still searching. "If you can hear me, stay with Killian. He will protect you. Drake too. Don't be stubborn, darling."

Okay, so maybe not hallucinating.

"We are coming to get you," I said, my voice growing firmer as the buzzing in my head began to fade, as the white light that was swaddling everything began to dim.

"Killian! Ellie!" Drake yelled from somewhere in the distance, the sound of his voice buzzing as though it was part of the light.

I batted it away, trying to move closer to Jarron, a slightly unreasonable part of me thinking that he would see me that way, that I could pull him out of the dungeon or whatever that he was in.

"No, Ellie," Jarron pleaded, shifting his weight as his eyes continually searched for mine, the sounds of a chain dragging against metal echoing against the buzz in my mine. "You have to stay away. Stay there. It will be okay. Whatever happens, you will be okay."

I didn't miss that he didn't say he would.

"No," I gasped dragging myself over the tile floor. Everything was getting darker, I needed to get to him before it was too late.

"I love you, darling."

He was gone before I could respond, the white light fading to nothing, and I was left in the steam filled bathroom, little fires sparking all around us, each one lit by what I clearly recognized as my feathers. So, not sparks. Feathers.

There were hundreds of them, all shimmering in red and golds and purples, and every single one of them on fire.

Killian sat on the now cracked and broken toilet seat, his eyes wide as he stared at me, to the place where Jarron had been. He had clearly seen, and he obviously didn't know what the hell was going on either.

"I'm going to save him," I said from where I lay on the floor, aware I looked ridiculous making a promise like that when I lay on the floor of the bathroom like slug in lacy black underwear.

Luckily, he had the good sense not to fight me on that, because nothing could keep me from Jarron. Not anymore.

24

CALLAY

"Fuck"

Stubborn ass princes. All I was supposed to do was keep them from getting killed. That's it. How freaking hard was it to keep four royal brats out of the clutches of a vampire for a couple hundred years?

This task was supposed to be a walk in the park. A small price to pay, even with my restrained magic. But no, one by one I've had to sneak them out, convince them to leave, bring them back to life, and now he has one, and of course it's Jarron.

The guy is so self-sacrificing he probably tried to figure out how to send a message to the Phoenix. Or end himself like some kind of Martyr.

If Parris created some little hybrids with that guys' fire, we were all fucked.

"Fuck."

I let the word echo over the kitchen that had become a bit more of a home than I would like to admit and pulled my hand into the endless abyss of my magic, pulling out one long rainbow striped hair from the dark corner where I stored my most treasured possessions.

Although, I wouldn't count this as treasured so much as an irritating necessity.

I had four of these left, she better not be upset at me for using two so close together. First the map and now an 'I'm sorry, I failed' visit.

I hated these, and she was always so bitchy.

"Fuck." I snapped again and pulsed my magic once through the long strand of hair. The strand ignited in a rainbow of light that spread from end to end, glowing like a beacon before it began to glitter. The light was beautiful, the strings of color that fell over me and the kitchen were mesmerizing.

Every damn time I did this I found myself getting lost in her magic. Well, until her magic tried to kill me.

I hated this part.

Pain rippled up my spine and I clamped my eyes shut. I had taken this trip enough that I didn't need the scenic version. Especially when the scenic version tried to burn the retinas out of my eyeballs.

It may be the pure light of magic, but it burned enough with my eyes snapped shut. I heaved a sigh of relief when the light left, replaced by darkness and damp.

"I didn't expect to see you again so soon," the little voice called, pulling me out of my travel-induced tension and right into a rainforest. South America if I had to guess.

Everything smelled of dirt, wet, and smoke. But the smoke wasn't the dragon fire I had become used to, but instead a tiny smoldering campfire that two beautiful people sat beside. The girl sat with her long hair draped around her face, her large grey almond eyes focused on a book with a half-naked man on the cover. The man who sat beside her however, while wearing a shirt was just as attractive. I would say he was Japanese if I had to guess, his shaggy black hair perfectly framing his strong jaw and kind eyes that were looking at me as if I had appeared out of nowhere.

Which I had.

I was sure I looked like a phantom bursting out of the wall of trees they were surrounded by. The dense forest was already making the night even dark, but between my pale hair and skin I was lightly colored enough I probably looked like a ghost too.

"If you are coming to tell me about Jarron, I already know," the girl said, not even looking up to me. Meanwhile the guy shook his shaggy black hair, fixing me with a smirk as his blue eyes flashed.

I couldn't help but smile. The guy was seriously built, and while he may not be Fae his magic was pulling on my own. I had never felt a pull quite as strong as that before. Not even with Jarron, and I was the first to admit that Jarron was smoking hot. But this guy?

Damn. Jarron who?

"This is Ryn," the girl said, gesturing to the guy, and still not looking up from her book. "He's a crown prince I am taking home so he can choose his bride. Finally." The guys face fell. "He's not very happy about it."

I wasn't very happy about it either. Wait -

"How do you know about Jarron, Xi?"

The girl looked up then, her silver eyes shining as she folded the corner of her book and put it down.

"The same as I know about everything else," Xi said, as cryptic as always. "Did you give her the vial I made for her? I have high hopes she will drink it immediately."

"I did. But dammit, Xi, if you knew this was going to happen why didn't you warn me?" I snapped as the fire sparked high into the trees. I was sure my magic had caused the spike, not that I cared enough to apologize. "I was here two days ago for the map. And you seem to have picked up a super model since then."

"If I had told you, I am sure your inappropriate crush would have caused you to prevent it from happening," Xi fixed me with a look and it took all my power not to scowl at her. Damn it, of course she was right, but did she had to be so right in front of Ryn?

"If I knew this guy existed I am sure we wouldn't have had a problem." I winked at him, truly unabashed flirting.

I didn't get to stretch my flirting skills often, so you better bet I was taking the opportunity.

Xi's eyes hardened, her lips tightening into a line. Ryn, however, chuckled at the outburst, and a smile spread over my lips. Jeeze, his smile only helped the whole super-hot thing he had going on.

A blush was already coating my skin, my smile spreading as I giggled.

Damn it. I giggled.

Xi didn't seem too amused. She stood slowly, walking around the fire with slow, calculated steps. Her eyes not so much as leaving mine.

Talk about an evil glare. I stepped back, and I didn't feel a bit bad about it. Xi could be fucking scary for a fourteen-year-old.

"A word to the wise, Callay," Xi said, leaning into me with a smile. She was one of the few people that were close enough to my height to meet me eye to eye. She swore it was the Fae blood, but I wasn't convinced, she was ancient and looks like a pre-teen. I was a good couple hundred years old, but at least I just looked short.

Fae blood didn't do that. Whatever made her was deeper than that.

"Don't go after Ryn. All Fae magic wants him, they are drawn to the ancient spell of his species. You want to jump him if I had to guess, and he isn't even singing." She smiled, and I backed away, instantly vowing to wipe the guy from my mind. She really didn't need to tell me more than that.

Mermen were trouble, I had no interest in mixing with him.

"I think I've had enough of princes, anyway," I said honestly, although, if he was the crown prince, it was no wonder the kid was traveling with Xi. His older sister was notorious for luring mortals under sea.

The fact that he had the balls to return to that said a good deal about his character.

"Good luck, handsome," I said with a wink that sent him blushing.

"Don't get too excited, you aren't done with princes yet."

"Shit, Xi, don't do this to me." I was a tad bit whiny, but I was sure it was justified. "It's been almost two hundred years..."

"You wanted to be an eternal, Callay," Xi interrupted her eyes flashing dangerously. "You hunted me, you found me. But everything comes with a price--"

"I didn't think it would be a two-hundred-year price!" I shrieked, interrupting her, and regretting it immediately.

As old as I was, there were still shreds of the foolhardy girl with her head full of fairy stories remaining, and the look Xi was giving me was humbling me right down to the bottom of that

I had clearly gone too far.

Child or not, the look she was fixing me with was pure ice. She smirked, looked back at Ryn who had wisely decided to stare at the fire as if it was a new lover, and stepped slowly, calculated, right up to me.

"If you want me to put you back where you came from, I can," Xi whispered, taking one last glance at her book before throwing it in the fire. "Middle of Prussia, early 1800s wasn't it. I believe there was a war going on?"

"There was a few." I grumbled, her warning was met, and I really didn't need to hear more.

My family had been starving. I had left with a fool hardy notion of finding some tiny mystic to make everything better. Instead I found her, and in my awe wished for the one thing I had wanted most.

If I knew the price, if I knew what really lied inside the creature I had found, I would have run the other way.

Well, maybe not, we had been starving. Everyone had been.

"What do you need me to do?" I whispered, knowing she had won. Again.

"Go back to Rydaim," Xi said, a smile stretching over her face before she stepped back to the fire, and Ryn, who was now fully engrossed in our conversation. "If the top of Killian's house doesn't explode in the next few days, take Jarron and use the last of the hairs to reach me."

"If the house doesn't explode?" I gasped, my voice a squeak. "Should I be concerned?"

"You survived one war, Callay," Xi said. "You are tricky and knowledgeable. I am sure you can handle this. Now say goodbye to Ryn."

"Goodbye Ryn." I guess this conversation was over.

Xi snapped her fingers, sending the lights from the fire to her skin, clinging against her as she prepared to send me back.

"The next time I see you, Callay, I will have recovered the child."

"The child?" The words choked out in a gasp, my heart feeling like it was going to explode. "My child?"

"Trust me, Callay. All of this is close to an end." She smiled, but my stomach was officially ice.

"You aren't going to tell me any more are you?" She only shook her head now, her eyes glittering.

"Fucking Unicorn," I snarled as her magic flared pressing against me, Ryn still smiling by the fire as Xi produced another book and settled in beside him.

"I heard that." Xi said as her magic pulled me back to Rydaim.

This time, I was sure I saw a smile on her face.

Fucking Unicorn, indeed.

ALSO BY REBECCA ETHINGTON

THE WORLD OF IMDALIND

THE CIRCUS OF SHIFTERS

ABOUT THE AUTHOR

Rebecca Ethington is an internationally bestselling author with almost 700,000 books sold. Her breakout debut, The Imdalind Series was cited as "Interesting and Intense" by *USA Today's Happily Ever After Blog.*

From writing horror to romance and creating every sort of magical creature in between, Rebecca's imagination weaves vibrant worlds that transport readers into the pages of her books. Her writing has been described as fresh, original, and groundbreaking, with stories that bend genres and create fantastical worlds.

Born and raised under the lights of a stage, Rebecca has written stories by the ghost light, told them in whispers in dark corridors, and never stopped creating within the pages of a notebook.

Find me online
www.rebeccaethington.com
contact@rebeccaethington.com